# The Exiles Return

# The Exiles Return

*a novel*

Elisabeth de Waal

*with a foreword by*

*Edmund de Waal*

PICADOR

New York

THE EXILES RETURN. Copyright © 2013 by The Estate of Elisabeth de Waal. Foreword copyright © 2012, 2013 by Edmund de Waal. All rights reserved. Printed in the United States of America. For information, address Picador, 175 Fifth Avenue, New York, N.Y. 10010.

www.picadorusa.com
www.twitter.com/picadorusa • www.facebook.com/picadorusa
picadorbookroom.tumblr.com

Picador® is a U.S. registered trademark and is used by St. Martin's Press under license from Pan Books Limited.

For book club information, please visit www.facebook.com/picadorbookclub or e-mail marketing@picadorusa.com.

Design by Steven Seighman

Library of Congress Cataloging-in-Publication Data is available upon request.

ISBN 978-1-250-04578-2 (hardcover)
ISBN 978-1-250-04579-9 (e-book)

Picador books may be purchased for educational, business, or promotional use. For information on bulk purchases, please contact Macmillan Corporate and Premium Sales Department at 1-800-221-7945, extension 5442, or write specialmarkets @macmillan.com.

Originally published in Great Britain by Persephone Books

First U.S. Edition: January 2014

10 9 8 7 6 5 4 3 2 1

# Foreword

*by Edmund de Waal*

I have read and re-read this novel by my grandmother Elisabeth. The yellowing typescript with some tippexed corrections was handed over to me by my father, along with a clutch of Elisabeth's school-reports from the Schottengymansium in Vienna, and a manila envelope stuffed with essays on economics from her studies at the University. There were a few lambent pages of autobiography describing her childhood at the turn of the century in the Palais Ephrussi on the Ringstrasse – the carriage-horses, the interminable teas with great-aunts – and a clutch of letters between her and a favourite uncle. But there was very little else. My father had joked in the liminal moment as the files were passed across that I was now the keeper of the archive. In the many, many months that followed in archives and libraries, tramping streets in Vienna, Paris and Odessa, in search of the

family story that had become so compulsive for me, I realised that this archival penury made complete sense. My
grandmother had spent her life in transit between countries:
she kept only the things that mattered to her. And these
pages did.

This untitled novel, now called *The Exiles Return*, was not
published in her lifetime. In conversation with her about why
writing matters, she never revealed what this fact meant to
her, and it was only recently that I found this single and extraordinary page:

> Why am I making such a great effort and taxing my
> own endurance and energy to write this book that
> no one will read? Why do I have to write? Because I
> have always written, all my life, and have always striven
> to do so, and have always faltered on the way and hardly
> ever succeeded in getting published . . . What is lack-
> ing? I have a feeling for language. . . . But I think I
> write in a rarified atmosphere, I lack the common
> touch, it is all too finely distilled. I deal in essences, the
> taste of which is too subtle to register on the tongue. It
> is the quintessence of experiences, not the experiences
> themselves . . . I distill too much.

This is Elisabeth's voice, tough and self-examining, inca-
pable of self-pity; but there is also a sense of her deeply-felt
need to write, something she kept close to her throughout
the succession of disappointments as the manuscripts of her
novels (five altogether, three in English and two in German)

were rejected. What she wanted was to create novels of ideas: in her writing she tried to bring into balance a heady combination of intellectual and emotional influences, the adamantine rigour of her academic life and the lyric imperative of her life as a writer of poetry and fiction. In *The Exiles Return* the two principal protagonists, Resi, the young and beautiful girl, and Professor Adler, the exiled academic, dramatise both these parts of her life. And it was a life of great drama.

Elisabeth de Waal was Viennese and this is a novel about being Viennese. As such, it is a novel about exile and about return, about the push and pull of love, anger and despair, about a place which is part of your identity, but which has also rejected you. *The Exiles Return* is alive to this complexity and it stands, in part, as a kind of autobiography in its mapping of these emotions.

She was born Elisabeth von Ephrussi in 1899, into a dynastic Jewish family that had adopted Vienna as its home thirty years before. It was an extraordinary moment in an extraordinary place. Her home was the Palais Ephrussi, a vast slab of neo-classicism adorned with caryatids, on the newly constructed Ringstrasse, the arc of civic buildings and Imperial monuments erected to reflect glory on the Habsburg Empire. The house, marble and gilded, was a calling-card built by a rich and aspirational family of financiers, one of many on the street known derisively in the city as Zionstrasse: the street of Jews. Elisabeth's mother, a beautiful and appropriately-titled Jewish baroness, had been born in the Palais Schey a few hundred yards away. Cousins lived next door. It was a comfortable – if complex – world in which to be born.

This fissile combination of money and status, the question of where you come from and where you belong, was part of the make-up of Vienna. As the capital city of the Empire, the streets were full of every nation and every ethnic group. From her bedroom window, looking through the branches of the lime trees across to the University, Elisabeth could see and hear the marching bands of Imperial regiments from across a swathe of Europe. As one of the protagonists of her novel, Professor Adler, reflects, in the sleepless hours before his return, '. . . from all directions of the compass they had come, seeking their fortune – Czech and Pole and Croat, Magyar and Italian, and Jew of course, to mix and feed and enrich this German city, which through them became unique and truly imperial.' Elisabeth's memories were of a polyglot upbringing in a polyglot city. And her writing was born from an unselfconscious ease with different languages. She could choose which language to write in, as much as to read in:

I was born and lived in Vienna, so German was the language which surrounded me, the Austrian kind of German with its soft and sometimes raucous vowels and muted consonants, a speech that could be coarse but never cutting, but the literate language nevertheless. It was for me, as I grew up, the language of Goethe and Schiller, later of Rilke and Thomas Mann, of Kant and Schopenhauer and the language in which Reinhardt's plays were produced. But it was not the language of my small, immediate and intimate world as a child. That was English.

Elisabeth's childhood in this exceptionally privileged household, surrounded by servants, was also one of fearsome social conventionality. Her parents – a scholarly father with a wonderful library, and socialite mother with an unparalleled dressing-room – disagreed passionately about her education. Elisabeth prevailed and was allowed to study with teachers from the Schottengymnasium, the well-regarded boys' school across the street from the family house. At the end of the First World War, just as the Empire was crumbling in unrest and desertions, Elisabeth graduated. Her certificate reads as a long list of *sehr gut*. This allowed her to enter the University to study philosophy, law and economics. It was, in one sense, a very Jewish choice: all three disciplines had strong Jewish presences in the faculty. But it was also a deeply personal decision. She loved the way in which ideas work, and through this rigorous academic training she felt completely at home within philosophical discourse. This can be seen in her lifetime correspondence with the formidable Viennese economist and political scientist, Ludwig von Mises and with the political philosopher, Eric Voegelin.

But Elisabeth also had another writing life. She was a poet. Like many of her generation she was captivated by the lyric poetry of Rainer Maria Rilke, the great and radical poet of the day. In his poetry Rilke combined directness of expression with intense sensuousness. His poems are full of epiphanies, moments when things come alive. Elisabeth was introduced to Rilke by an uncle and started a correspondence of great significance to her, sending poems to be critiqued and receiving long and thoughtful replies, often accompanied by copies of the poems he was writing. When you look at the collected letters of Rilke, you realise that many of his correspondents were young, poetic and titled: Elisabeth was one of many. But the cache of letters, taken with her on all her lifetime of travels from Vienna to Paris to Switzerland, and then into her new life in England, was intensely symbolic for her. It was a benediction for her as a writer from a writer.

Elisabeth's languages gave her an expansiveness across literature that was breathtaking. After she met and married my grandfather, Hendrik de Waal, she learnt Dutch and they wrote poetry for each other in that language. When living in Paris in the 1930s, she wrote for *Le Figaro*. She wrote reviews of French novels for *The Times Literary Supplement* in the 1950s. Her first two novels were written in German, and her last three in English. No wonder I found her bookshelves so bewildering. When I was visiting her, as a student of English literature, conversation would swerve across genres and countries – a haphazard reference to Goethe would invoke the final scene from *Faust*, learnt eighty years before. We talked of Rilke and Hugo von Hofmannsthal. And then of Joyce – and she produced her edition of *Ulysses*, bought from Shakespeare and Co, with its shimmering azure paper covers. I find it is uncut from page 563. And Proust. She re-

read Proust constantly. When I found her single page describing her 'quintessence of experiences', I felt this could be someone describing Proust.

*The Exiles Return* is profoundly autobiographical. In the figure of Resi, the beautiful girl lost in the social milieu, there is the glimmer of projection. And in Professor Adler, the academic whose need to return to Vienna is at the heart of the book, and who has to evaluate where he belongs amongst those who stayed, I think there is a strong sense of an alternative life being lived out. There are compelling moments of Elisabeth's experiences too in the encounter between the character of Kanakis and an estate agent he consults about a property purchase. You can hear the memory of her encounters with Austrian lawyers, when she tried to find and restitute the looted family art collections and property, seized at the Anschluss in 1938. And you can feel it in the estate agent's tremor of anxiety when he's asked about two recently acquired paintings hanging on his office wall:

> 'I just thought they furnished the room, gave it a certain cachet, within the limits of what I could afford. Yet they did in fact belong to a gentleman who must have been an acquaintance of your family, Baron E—. You might possibly have seen them at his house. Baron E— died abroad unfortunately, in England, I believe. After they had recovered what could be traced of his property, his heirs had it all sold at auction; I suppose they had no use for this old-fashioned stuff in their

modern homes. I acquired the pictures in the auction rooms, as well as most of the things you see here: all quite openly, publicly and legally, you understand . . .'

But above all the book is about the heartbreak of returning:

Finally there he was, on the Ring: the massive pile of the Natural History Museum on his right, the ramp of the Parliament building on his left, beyond it the spire of the Town Hall, and in front of him the railings of the Volksgarten and the Burgplatz. There he was, and there it all was; though the once tree-bordered footpaths across the roadway were stripped, treeless, only a few naked trunks still standing. Otherwise it was all there. And suddenly the dislocation of time which had been dizzying him with illusions and delusions snapped into focus, and he was real, everything was real, incontrovertible fact. He was *there*. Only the trees were not there, and this comparatively trivial sign of destruction, for which he had not been prepared, caused him incommensurate grief. Hurriedly he crossed the road, entered the park gates, sat down on a bench in a deserted avenue, and wept.

*The Exiles Return* is a novel of great vividness and great tenderness, which at its heart depicts what it might mean to return from exile. Within its pages it reflects a truly ambitious writer and a woman of considerable courage. Elisabeth returned to Vienna weeks after the Anschluss in 1938 in order to save her parents in their moment of greatest need. She managed to get her father to England in 1939. And she returned immediately after the war to find out what had happened to her family. She fought for a decade to get justice for the wrongs that had been done, battling the intransigence, hostility and derision of the authorities in Vienna. Yet she did this without losing her ability to live fully in the present and not be held hostage by the experience of being a refugee.

*The Exiles Return* was finally published in London in the week of the seventy-fifth anniversary of the Anschluss, the cataclysmic, convulsive act when Austria allowed Hitler to enter unopposed into Vienna. The poignancy of this anniversary, when there are so few people left of the generation that remember it at firsthand, is unmistakable. But to be able to stand by the book at the Austrian Cultural Institute in London and talk of it – with both of Elisabeth's sons present, her grandchildren and her great-grandchildren – was extraordinary. For it was not a melancholic occasion. It was a powerful affirmation of how stories can survive and find audiences. The following day I was in Vienna to give a lecture at the Palais Epstein on the meaning of memory. Standing in a courtyard similar to that of Elisabeth's old childhood home, I reflected that exile refers not only to people, but also to stories. And that in the work of restituting stolen property, which Austria is slowly undertaking, at last there is another dimension: that of the return from exile of the stories of the dispossessed families of Vienna. This novel is part of this.

Edmund de Waal, 2013

# Part One

# Prelude

It was in the middle fifties, a short while before the conclusion of the so-called State Treaty which led to the withdrawal of the Allied Occupation forces and finally restored Austria's independence, that a small item appeared in the local news columns of the newspapers. It concerned a fatal accident which had occurred in the country house of an American millionaire. A young American society girl who had been on a visit to her Austrian relations had died of gunshot wounds while inexpertly handling a gun. The gun had gone off and killed her. There had been one eyewitness of this unfortunate event and one only, the Jesuit Father Ignatius Jahoda, who had been able to testify that no other person had been implicated in the shooting, which had been purely accidental. Since it had happened in the American zone of occupation, in a house belonging to an American citizen, and

the victim had also been American, no Austrian being involved, it had been deemed wise by all the authorities concerned to treat the occurrence, perhaps rather irregularly,
on a quasi-extraterritorial basis – so as to put no strain on
Austro-American relations in this last period of the occupation which would soon be coming to an end. Therefore
the incident was officially considered closed.

This did not prevent the tabloid newspapers from sending their young reporters into the district, the Forest District of Lower Austria, to find out what they could of the
surrounding circumstances. For the mere mention of a millionaire and a 'society girl' gave the incident a succulent flavour bound to be relished by the bulk of their readers more
interested in the 'human angle' of such a story than in the
legal niceties which had been applied to it. Millionaires
are glamorous, always interesting to hear about, as if the
mere fact of reading about them cast a glint of their gold
over the drab mediocrity of the reader's circumstances,
and especially if there is a pinch of sly satisfaction when
something unpleasant or scandalous happens to them. And
'society girl' has somewhat similar connotations. Typists
and young lady shop assistants enviously absorb the aura of
expensive clothes, long manicured fingernails and total
freedom from routine, crowded tramcars and cheap meals,
but death from gunshot wounds is equally unlikely to come
their way.

What the young reporters did find out was the name of
the owner of the house, a Mr Kanakis, and of the girl victim

of the accident, a Miss Larsen; also that several young men had been staying in the house at the time, and that another young man, not a guest, had been seen in the park in the early morning, although they had not been able to track him down; anyway, he had probably had nothing to do with the affair. But they did find out that the girl was supposed to have been engaged to be married to Mr Kanakis. The names, both foreign ones, did not mean much to the Viennese public, with the exception of one elderly taxi driver whose cab was regularly stationed near the Opera. Having chewed over the information for a while, he turned to his young neighbour and said, 'Kanakis? Of course I know who he is. He must be the son – no, the grandson – of the Kanakis for whom my father was coachman. They lived over there, in that house on the corner of the Ring, opposite the Hotel Bristol. They had a huge flat, the whole of the first floor, my father said. Greeks they were, very rich. They kept their horses and carriage in the courtyard. I remember sitting on the box as a small boy with my grandfather when the horses had to be taken out for exercise while the family were away. That was much more exciting than this thing.' He jerked his head over his shoulder at the taxicab. 'Kanakis, of course I know who Kanakis is.'

His young colleague was only mildly interested in these reminiscences. 'In any case, he seems to have landed himself in a proper mess,' he commented, 'shooting his fiancée. But the Americans have quashed the whole affair, luckily for him.'

'But he didn't shoot her. It was an accident. They say.'

'How do *you* know? I bet he did. She was probably carrying on with one of the other young men in the house, and he was jealous. Very temperamental, these Greeks. Anyway, who cares?'

# One

When the train pulled out of the great echoing hall of Zurich
Central Station, gathering speed as it travelled eastwards
along the shore of the lake, Professor Adler knew that he had
passed the point of no return. He was committed, he was
going back. As long as the train had been standing in Zurich
he could, he told himself, have got out. There was the platform, just under the window of his sleeping compartment,
there was even a porter, looking up expectantly at the two
large suitcases and the coat and hat hanging on the brass
hook opposite the long, narrow red plush seat. It would have
needed only a tiny gesture, or just a smile, and the man
would have been with him, hauling down his luggage, speaking to him in the guttural intonation and sing-song inflexion
of Swiss-German, which he had not heard for so many years.
Adler kept his eyes fixed on his suitcases, and the urge to

stretch out his arm was very great. For a few concentrated seconds he was deeply conscious of his freedom of choice. Then, at the instant when the mounting tension became almost unbearable, the train gave a jolt and began to move. He sat down again. He was alone in his compartment, a second-class one designed for two, but the train was not full, and he had had it to himself ever since he had boarded in Paris. It was only a short time ago that long-distance rail services into Central Europe had been re-established and not many people were travelling.

Adler sat by the window and looked out at the flat shore of the Zurichsee and then, as this receded, at the meadows dotted with apple trees and the neat farmhouses with gabled roofs, sliding past with increasing speed. The suitcases were still in the rack above his head. His sense of freedom to do as he wished, and the accompanying tightness in his chest, had left him. Instead he felt like an automaton, like a piece of machinery that, a long time ago, had been conditioned to behave in a definite way, to carry out certain instructions, and was now doing so, mechanically, according to plan. At the same time his mind was quite clear and able to reason about it, to maintain that he had all along been, and still was, a free agent.

He could, of course, have got out in Zurich. It would have been perfectly plausible for him to have undertaken the long journey from America in order to go there. He could have gone to call on an eminent colleague with whom he had corresponded about their different methods of studying the structure of certain molecules in a type of hormone cell. It would have been quite obvious to everyone concerned that he wished to have a live discussion with Professor Schmidt and to observe his laboratory work at first hand. If his wife happened to have told anyone that he was on his way back to Vienna, it would be clear that she had misunderstood his intentions, or wilfully distorted them. Their closest acquaintances knew that he and Melanie were barely on speaking terms and that she had been bitterly opposed to his going. So, if she had denounced him to her friends for having deserted her – crazy, irresponsible, sentimental she had called him – and for having set out to go back to that 'little hole of a country that had turned them out', well, he could say that he had never meant to go there. He had come to Switzerland to see Professor Schmidt.

But now Zurich was left behind. He had not got out, so this explanation of his movements had become untenable. Or had it? The Arlberg Express in which he was sitting would not stop again until it reached Buchs, at the frontier. But Buchs was in Switzerland, on this side of the Rhine; here only a little river that formed the actual boundary between Switzerland and Austria. He could get out in Buchs if he wished and wait for the next train back to Zurich. No one would know. And even if they did – why would it matter? He had been deep in thought about the chemical structure of certain secretions and had not noticed when they got to Zurich, and all of a sudden he found himself in Buchs. That's what he would say. He was an absent-minded professor, the kind that hunted for his spectacles while they were still on his nose. Then he smiled at himself. He was really being ridiculous! Who was he arguing with, who was he trying to convince? He was not accountable for his actions to anyone, to anyone in the world. Not even to Melanie. Or least of all to Melanie. She had never understood him or made the slightest effort to do so. She had no insight into his feelings, and would not take any notice of them if she had.

Since they had been in America, Melanie had made a life of her own, setting herself up as a *corsetière* and making a tremendous success of it. Suddenly the rather nondescript, meek-looking little woman who had been his wife had discovered in herself a stupendous ability for business. She had started making foundations to measure, to special order, and women had flocked to her; first to the tiny living room of their little flat in a shabby Upper West Side street, now to her elegant salon in uptown Madison Avenue. He had been very grateful to her at first, she had made it possible for them to make a start in New York; for it had taken a long time before he was earning even a modest salary and had secured an appointment as assistant pathologist in a hospital sponsored by a Jewish foundation.

That was a thing that had taken him completely by surprise – this virulent anti-Semitism rampant in so many walks of American life, even in academic, even in medical, circles. He had scarcely known it in Vienna. Of course, it had always been endemic there, but in such a mild form that one had almost been able to forget about it, until the threat of Hitler made it loom huge and terrifying. He had not been prepared for it in America, where, although there was no danger of physical extermination, there was an ever-present insidious consciousness of it, like a suppressed toothache which one could never quite forget. But it had no place in politics or in business, and Melanie flourished entirely un-inhibited. Gradually she drew her clientele from the more fashionable and, in the end, from the most exclusive society, and treated women whose names were stars in the social register with blatant familiarity. They did not, of course, in-vite her to dinner, but she got her satisfaction out of them by unashamedly humiliating them in her salon, especially the not-so-young and the not-so-slim who were the majority of her customers.

'Take off all your clothes, please, Mrs Waterhouse. I can't make you a foundation unless I can see what I've got to build on. Yes, everything please, the slip and the bra – what a dreadful bra! No wonder you look as if you had a bolster on your chest. There! That's better. It's the body itself I have to study.' And the poor woman would stand up in her naked-ness, shivering in spite of the temperature of the room, which was tropical even in winter, while Melanie walked round her appraisingly, making derogatory comments. 'Not quite a Venus, are we, Mrs W? But there, we can't all be bathing beauties, not when we're getting on a bit. And we all do, it comes to all of us. Well, that's why you come to me, isn't it? You wouldn't need me if you were trim and slim. You're my bread-and-butter with all your little disfigura-tions, so it's not for me to find fault with them is it? It's my job to remedy them, that's what is expected of *me*. And Mr W isn't Adonis either, I don't suppose, so who is *he* to complain? The left hip is rather thicker than the right, isn't it? And the left breast. But we'll even that out, and smooth away the bulk just above the waist. Now, I'll take the measurements myself, here we are. We don't want any unnecessary prying eyes, do we? And I do all the fitting, my assistants only work on the garment itself. Very well. First fitting a week from today.' And then she would quote some astronomical price, and her client would remonstrate: 'Really, Mrs Adler, I was told you were expensive, but I was given to understand –'

'I'm sorry, Mrs Waterhouse, but yours is a very difficult case. Of course, if you prefer to abandon the project – I never force myself on anyone, even if I have studied my subject.'

Then, having submitted to the ordeal, the order is given, and three weeks later Mrs Waterhouse is beaming with delight. She feels so comfortable, her couturier congratulates her on her figure, her clothes simply glide onto her and she moves with undreamed-of ease. So the next half-dozen clients are advised to go and see 'that awful woman' who makes such heavenly foundations that it's worth submitting to the worst indignities in order to possess one.

This was what Professor Adler was remembering – and not the structure of hormone cells – when the train began to slow down as it approached Buchs. One day, when she was in a playful mood, Melanie herself had given him this description of a typical interview with one of her most stiff-necked clients. At the time she had told him about it, it had nauseated him: it was not, perhaps, the situation itself, which he might have found comical, but the relish he saw in his wife's face as she described it, which had sickened him. Melanie was making a lot of money and good luck to her – if she could command such high prices for the excellence of her products. But in her gloating over the humiliation of her customers she was humiliating him too. A nerve of moral fastidiousness in him revolted against this behaviour, against her very person. He had become aware that the increasing luxury of their surroundings, their furniture, their food, his wife's and his daughters' clothes, was being paid for with money thus come by. Certainly, his own contribution to their way of life must have become proportionately ever smaller.

For a long time he had hardly noticed anything, wrapped up as he was in his work, unchanging in his personal habits. It was when Melanie had suggested buying an apartment in one of the new luxurious blocks of flats under construction – when he, taken by surprise, had in all innocence protested that they surely couldn't afford it – that his eyes had been decisively, brutally, opened. His mind flinched from the scene. Melanie had rounded on him with real venom. Of course they could afford it, no thanks to him. She didn't believe he hadn't known how much she was earning. Did he think they had been living these last years on his derisory salary? Had he ever made the slightest effort to get it increased? Perhaps he had, and been ashamed to admit that he had been refused? She must assume that he wasn't worth more. In this country, she had said, a failure is a failure and a success is a success and there's a good reason for both. You've only yourself to thank or to blame. He could thank his lucky stars that he was her husband and the father of her daughters, or he might still be poring over his notebooks in that evil-smelling tenement where they had started off.

That was not true. When he had got his appointment at the hospital, they had moved into a perfectly respectable apartment, small but adequate. In an unfashionable district of course. He didn't care about that, and hadn't thought that she did. Then she had begun to expand her business and her contribution to their income had been very welcome, especially as it helped to educate the little girls. But now? The girls were grown up and sided entirely with their mother. They were smart, business-like, in love with money, and intent on having a good time. They had jobs, they had boyfriends. One worked in a department store, the other for a travel agent. They no longer spoke any German, although he was sure they understood it – they could not fail to do so, since he and Melanie still used it at home. He himself, he suspected, had never got rid of his Viennese accent when speaking English, but Melanie had deliberately cultivated an American voice and intonation. By sheer exaggeration she had succeeded in obliterating all vocal trace of her origin, except to the most discerning ear. To this day, he hardly recognised her speaking voice if he heard her on the telephone or in the next room.

And yet, when he had told her that he was going back to Austria, she had denounced him as if she were being threatened with the loss of her sole support and protection. There had been scene after scene. Why was he deserting her? Had she not been a good wife to him – faithful, loyal and hardworking? What did he reproach her with that he wanted to leave her, to break up their marriage after more than twenty years?

At first he had argued that he had no desire to desert her, all he wanted was to go home. Would she not come with him? Or promise to follow him as soon as he had reestablished himself? This suggestion had infuriated her even more. That did not surprise him.

Remembering it all as he sat looking out of the window at the meadows and the apple trees and the cows, the neat villages and scattered farmsteads, he admitted that the proposal had been disingenuous. She would never give up the life she had embraced with so much zest, her financial success and her independence. He had not really wanted her to come. She would be miserable if she had to live in Vienna again. He was not sure if he wasn't going to be miserable himself. He couldn't know what it was going to be like, how he was going to fit in. Melanie was sure that he was going to be totally disillusioned. Perhaps she was right. Yet the urge to go had been irresistible, and he had then suggested that she divorce him, and had made this proposal in good faith. But it had made her even more angry, if that were possible, than his offer to take her with him. She had a horror of divorce, the very idea incensed her. It appeared that under all the veneer of her emancipation, in spite of all the examples she saw around her, the old atavistic principles of her faith and tradition remained deeply ingrained. She was his wife. She was not going to be cast off – as she felt she would be – even if it was she herself who did the casting. And then she had indulged herself in ludicrous accusations. Go then, go if you must, she had shouted at him, and find yourself some silly smirking hussy, younger than I am, prettier than me, the woman who has slaved for years to keep the home together and to bring up your children – some soft, sensuous creature to rekindle your waning appetite – but I'll make sure you never marry her, not while I'm alive you won't, the slut!

Well, that was that. It had all been very undignified, sordid, and perfectly ridiculous. The thought of renewing his love life had never entered his mind.

The train was slowing down. Professor Adler shook himself out of his obsessive reminiscing and saw once more what was actually before his eyes. Buchs. He went into the corridor and pulled down the window to look out. In the old days the train used to stand here endlessly for customs formalities. He remembered a holiday he had spent with his parents in Lucerne as a small boy. What a long journey it had been, and how bored and impatient he had felt standing in this dull little station, with nothing to look at except the boxes of red geraniums in the stationmaster's windows. He leaned out and craned his neck to see whether there were any there now, but his carriage was standing rather far down the line and dusk was falling. He couldn't make out anything. It did not occur to him that only a short while ago he had been hesitating whether or not to leave the train here before it crossed the frontier. Then, suddenly, before he had had time to remember this, the train moved on. It had stopped for barely five minutes.

In a few moments they had crossed the little river and were approaching the mountains. And just as suddenly and unaccountably a wave of some unidentifiable emotion swept through Kuno Adler. Apprehension? But of what? It felt like a physical sickness, a mental darkness. He was not an automaton now: he was an animal, tense, wary, charged with feeling, stripped of reason. He heard steps coming down the narrow passage, and a voice next door: 'Austrian passport control!' The words were repeated a minute later at the entrance to his own compartment.

While putting his hand in his breast-pocket to extract his passport, he looked at the man in the doorway. A young man, smooth face under the round peaked uniform cap, a small straight nose, a rather delicate mouth with red lips under a thin pencil moustache. Grey eyes, smiling. A good-looking fellow. But it was the voice, the intonation that hit a nerve somewhere in Kuno Adler's throat; no, below the throat, where breath and nourishment plunge into the depths of the body, a non-conscious, ungovernable nerve, in the solar plexus probably. It was the quality of that voice, of that accent, soft and yet rough, ingratiating and slightly vulgar, sensible to the ear as a certain kind of stone is to the touch – the soap-stone that is coarse-grained and spongy and slightly oily on the surface – an Austrian voice. 'Austrian passport control!'

Kuno Adler handed over his passport, his American passport, with a sense of defiance, as if challenging him to question its authenticity. The man leafed through it, looked at the photograph and at Adler himself for what seemed an intolerably long time, probably twenty seconds, cocking his head to look at him from all angles. All right, all right! Adler thought, of course he can see that I am a Jew, a refugee. What of it?

'Coming back?' the man asked, closing the passport and handing it to him.

Adler had meant to answer any questions in English. But somehow he couldn't. *'Ja,'* he replied, and in the same soft German, 'I'm coming back.'

'Good luck!' the man said and smiled as he backed out of the door.

What did he mean by that? Was it ironic? Was it a warning? It hadn't seemed that way, it had just sounded friendly. I must watch myself, Adler thought, not to be so over-sensitive, so suspicious – though not to be gullible either – feel my way carefully. It's not going to be easy, more difficult perhaps than I anticipated.

The customs man followed. He glanced up at the suit-cases. 'Only your personal belongings? No tea or coffee?'

'No tea or coffee,' Adler repeated, and the man passed on, closing the door of the compartment.

It was now quite dark. Adler pressed his face against the window. The mountains outside were so high and so near that there was nothing to see but blackness, with pinpoints of light here and there from the windows of some lonely house on the slopes, and one had to crane one's neck to see the faint luminosity of the sky above the rocky summits. Adler put on the light and asked the attendant to make his bed while he stood in the corridor. He had forgotten to go through to the restaurant car for dinner, had ignored the summoning bell while obsessed with remembering the scenes he had left behind. He didn't mind, he was not really hungry, but munched some chocolate: Swiss chocolate, which he had bought for old times' sake.

He went to bed and tried to make contact in his imagination with the country outside the little moving box of polished wood and upholstery in which he now lay stretched out. The province of Vorarlberg and, soon, the long tunnel of the Arlberg, and then Tyrol. Magical names! But he had not known them intimately and all he could visualise in his mind's eye was a map, the map that had hung in the classroom of his first school. For a while his imagination concentrated on that map: the outline had been roughly diamond-shaped. The top point was the most clearly outlined, surmounting as it did an embedded square, upended on one corner – the Kingdom of Bohemia. The eastern end was rounded and shapeless, the southern uneven and jagged, and the whole surface was divided up into pieces of different shapes, sizes and colours like a patchwork.

And he could remember the formula which described them: the kingdoms and lands represented in the parliament of the realm, the patrimony inherited or acquired as dowries in the course of centuries by the House of Habsburg. In the eastern half of the map, the largest, roundest monochrome expanse, embraced within two in-curving arms of a pincer, was the Kingdom of Hungary.

Strange, he commented to himself, how these early memories persist and remain untouched by later experience. For he had hardly left his primary school when the Austro-Hungarian Empire had ceased to exist and that map had been rubbed out and redrawn with different contours. He knew this one, of course, but it had never made a visual impact on his mind; whereas the other map, obsolete before he had even started on his adult life, remained indelibly imprinted on his memory.

# Two

He lay in his bed in the little box of a compartment, the shelf of the upper, unoccupied bunk over his head, his suit and overcoat swaying just within reach of his hand on a brass peg fixed to the varnished partition dividing his compartment from his neighbour's. The train swayed rhythmically as the wheels hammered out their beat each time they crossed the narrow gap which separates one length of rail from the next. Only a faint blue light shone from a tiny bulb above the door, making the darkness itself discernible by its degree of deeper blackness and moving shadows of unrecognisable shapes.

The picture of the old map, still showing dimly through drifting veils of wandering memories, conjured up the name of the small town in Moravia from which his father, as a young boy, had come to Vienna. He felt his father's arm round his shoulder and heard him describe, as he had done so many times – and he had never tired of listening – how he had come on foot, drawn by that great and glittering magnet of a city, and how he had seen for the first time, from the distance, the pointed spire of St Stephen's Cathedral. All roads in Vienna had been open then, and from all directions of the compass they had come, seeking their fortune – Czech and Pole and Croat, Magyar and Italian, and Jew of course, to mix and feed and enrich this German city, which through them became unique and truly imperial. Some had been sucked down into the morass of its lower depths, but those who were hardworking and thrifty, like himself, had made their way and become citizens, imparting and receiving that very special flavour and dye of being Viennese which was different from anything else in the world. Something, his father used to say, which you cannot lose.

In his mind's eye Adler saw his father's house, or rather his grandfather's, an old dark house in a narrow street in the very centre of the city, in the shadow of St Stephen's Cathedral. His maternal grandfather, S Kantorowicz, importer and wholesale dealer in furs, third generation of his name and trade, of solid and impeccable reputation, lived and worked there. To him his father, Simon Adler, had succeeded in being apprenticed, had become his most trusted journeyman and, there being no son, had in due course married the daughter. There was the high, arched doorway through which Kuno had passed a thousand times to and from school. It led from the street under a vaulted and paved passage into the courtyard into which the sun only shone in summer, and then only at noon. On the right was the stone staircase leading to the upper floors and the living quarters, on the left the entrance to the shop. The door to the shop had glass panels that rattled whenever the door was opened or closed. There was no shop window on the outside, nothing but a small brass plate, 'S Kantorowicz – Furrier', fixed to the wall just outside the left-hand wing of the great and ponderous dark brown nail-studded door of the main entrance to the house.

Mostly this door was folded back during the daytime; but when it was closed, a small door, cut into the thickness of the right-hand panel, with its own latch, keyhole and bolts, could give admittance to the archway and courtyard beyond. It was rather dark under that archway at the best of times, and the shop – having no access to daylight other than the glass panels of its door – always had a gaslight burning on a brass bracket fixed on the opposite wall. So inconspicuous was the notice given to would-be customers that no one who did not know where to find S Kantorowicz, Furrier, would be likely to discover him. He was not out to attract the casual passer-by. Nor was there anything to beguile the uninitiated in the little gaslit room inside the glass-panelled door, for it contained nothing but a dark brown painted counter which ran from wall to wall across the room, and the stuffed head of a seal mounted on the wall opposite the gasburner, while a stuffed baum marten climbing up a twisted barren branch on a stand was the only adornment on the counter.

The workshop was behind this little saleroom, where

Kuno remembered the great event of electric light being installed: a wonderful improvement on the gas-burners by which his father and his two or three men used to work. But that was only after his grandfather's death. Kuno also remembered his parents discussing it and deploring the old man's stubbornness in opposing what he called new-fangled ideas. The warehouses where the raw skins were stored were even further back, in the courtyard, secured from the outside by heavily barred and padlocked doors. How vivid all this was in Adler's semi-somnolent mind; it needed no effort of recollection, it was there, and he himself was there, or rather not himself, but the boy he had been, resurrected from the depths of his past. He was seeing with that boy's eyes, oh, and smelling, too! The smell in the archway was of dust and urine. It wafted down the shaft of the stone staircase opposite the glass-panelled door of the shop, for the lavatories were on the landings of each floor and their doors were often left standing open, to the annoyance of his mother. But the smell in the shop was nicer, though quite sharp. It smelled of tanned leather and of the acid essences used in the dressing and preserving of skins.

S Kantorowicz needed no shop window. His wares were not for show. The quality and workmanship of his furs, imported mainly from Russia, were such that he dealt only with customers who understood, who expected and appreciated, perfection. The purchase of a fur coat or coat-lining of sable or sealskin, of a collar, stole or muff of beaver, ermine or astrakhan, was an important transaction involving absolute trust on both sides, vendor and buyer. No one knew better than Kantorowicz that the appearance of a fur can be most cunningly deceptive. But the quality of anything he sold was never questioned, nor was the solvency of his customer. Complaints were practically unknown. It was unusual to enquire about price when ordering. Such a question could cause eyebrows to be raised in surprise and probably go unanswered, as so much depended on the number of skins required in the making and the state of the market at the particular time; and the price eventually charged, possibly a year after delivery, would always be found very reasonable. Such were the standards and the self-respect of S Kantorowicz, and the respect accorded to him in all his dealings. And if it so happened – as it would from time to time, though very rarely – that some gentleman, or lady, though highly-titled, did not comply with his standards, they would find on a subsequent occasion that S Kantorowicz, to his great regret, found himself unable to supply the particular skin required, or indeed unable to accept any order at the present time, being booked up with orders for months ahead. The old man had even been known to advise a newly-arrived financial luminary, who wished to show off his mistress in a splendid ermine cape, to go elsewhere because he was too busy to take the order; in fact he had regarded the connection as undesirable.

Professor Adler slept. Gently rocked by the rhythmic movements of the train, he slept deeply and peacefully, as if he were lying on his boyhood bed in the little room next to his parents. When he awoke, daylight was filtering round the edges of the stiff cloth blind covering the window of his compartment. He pulled it up by the metal rod that held it stretched across the thick glass pane, sat himself on the edge of the bunk and looked out. The train had left the mountains behind. The countryside was flat, green and wooded. A road ran next to the railway track, a narrow road. Beyond it: fields, a copse of fir trees, then, in the distance, a cluster of houses and a church with a steeple crowned with a bulbous top like a Turkish turban. Adler smiled as he saw it: he was sorry he had missed the more spectacular sights in darkness and sleep, but there would be plenty of time for those – when? Next year, perhaps, or the year after? He would spend his holidays walking in the mountains, at an inn in a remote valley. It was years since he had walked. The prospect gave him a thrill of pleasure. He was coming home . . .

Now the houses were closer together, they grew taller and squarer, grey and drab, showing flat, featureless faces of ennui with the suburban way of life – neither town nor country. But here *was* a town. The train ran into a station: several platforms, a long low building opposite the window, and people on the platform, men in grey loden and green felt hats, women, too, in loden or other nondescript clothes. A sign hanging from the station roof read 'St Pölten'. He hurriedly started to dress; he had not realised he was so close to his journey's end. Only an hour to Vienna. It was when they stopped at St Pölten, on their return journey from the summer holidays, that his father always began to fidget, to urge his mother to pack up what was left of their picnic, to fold the papers and put away her book and whatever he himself had been playing with. Then he had to put on his coat and gloves and sit still, for ages it seemed, while his father got down the suitcases.

Now the little stations of Vienna's outlying villages flashed by, most of them bearing long hyphenated names because they had to serve two or more small communities. Then the roofs of villas could be seen through the trees of their gardens. Suddenly there was a proliferation of tracks, and the upper storeys of town houses lining the street below glided by. Then the Western Station – or what used to be the Western Station. Formerly, there had been a long and high, cavernous, glazed-in hall into which the trains used to glide; it was old-fashioned, dingy, and yet somehow sumptuously dignified like the well-worn attire of a high-born elderly spinster who has clothed herself once and for all in her best and scorned to change her style. But now there was just – nothing: an open space where the bombed wreckage of the old station had been cleared away; stacks of building material, steel girders and concrete mixers for the new modern station under construction.

Adler experienced a violent sense of shock. It was his first actual contact with the fact to which he had hitherto not given much thought: that not everything would look the same – or be the same – as it had looked and been when he left it. I shall have to learn the lesson of the Western Station, he thought, and this phrase, repeated silently many times in the coming months, summed up and symbolised for him the situations and experiences he would be having to deal with in the course of his attempt at repatriation. Would the lessons be very hard? Had he been wise in undertaking to learn them? And he realised, to his surprise, that he could not foresee what their nature and significance was going to be.

The lesson was immediately reinforced when he crossed the platform into the open followed by his porter. It all looked so utterly different from what he remembered. Here was just an expanse of cobbled pavement and no traffic. The houses on the far side of the square, always rather nondescript – he didn't remember them exactly, of course – had at least been solid and durable. Now – if indeed they were the same houses and not something that had been hidden behind the vanished facades – they looked like a row of decayed teeth, shabby, discoloured and intermittently broken down.

Three taxis were drawn up near the exit, old square cabs, high on their wheels, their drivers wearing shapeless cloth caps and one of them a German army uniform coat without buttons. Adler was staring around in bewilderment, trying to make sense of it all.

'Where do you want to go? Will you take a taxi?' his porter was asking him for the third time, very loudly now, because he had concluded that his charge did not understand German and must therefore be shouted at. So he pointed and gesticulated, and at the same time the nearest driver got out of his cab and opened the door.

Adler turned to the porter. 'A hotel,' he said tentatively, 'I'm trying to think of a hotel.'

'Have you got a reservation?' the porter asked.

'No, no I haven't.' That was something Adler had not thought about, not with any precision. He was going to look for somewhere to live, some rooms or a small flat. He had even wondered whether he might get his old apartment back again, and then discarded the idea because it would be too big for him to live in alone. But at first he would go to a hotel. Any hotel, there were so many – he just couldn't, for the moment, remember any names of the more modest ones. Of course he wouldn't go to one of the big luxury hotels.

But the porter was saying: 'You won't get in anywhere in the centre without a reservation. The big hotels are still reserved for the Occupation Powers, and all the others are fully booked up, that I know. No reservation,' he said, turning to the taxi driver, throwing out one arm as he made this, what he considered preposterous, statement. The other only shrugged his shoulders, as if there was no more to be said.

'There used to be a Hotel K— quite near here,' Adler said, suddenly remembering a name he had heard in the distant past.

'That was bombed,' the porter answered laconically. 'But wait! There's the Hotel M—. The waiter there is a friend of mine – I might be able to get you a room. You won't like it, though.' He cast a doubtful look at Adler's overcoat, his expensive-looking American shoes. 'I could take your luggage there on a handcart, for a dollar,' he added, his eyes lighting up hungrily.

Adler hastily extracted a dollar bill from his wallet. 'Yes, please, take me there, certainly. I'm sure it will do until I find something else.'

'All right, come with me, and I'll see that you get a room – if you'll give the waiter a dollar too.'

The taxi driver had got back into his cab and slammed the door.

Adler didn't like the room. He didn't like the hotel, if indeed the place could be called a hotel, and suspected that it might be something quite different. The 'waiter' seemed to be the only person in charge. The room was diminutive and almost entirely filled with a much-too-large bed. It smelt appalling. The porter had dumped the suitcases just inside the door and left. Adler threw open the dirty little window, but as it looked out on a nauseating courtyard, the smell only intensified.

A most depressing beginning, he thought, but it will have to do for tonight. He wished he'd thought of making a reservation. But how was he to know?

Then he went out. He walked down the Mariahilfstrasse, that long, wide commercial street where he had not come very often as it was not in his district: he neither worked nor lived in it, but had driven through many times on his way to the Western Station or to more distant outskirts. And as he walked along its pavements, it aroused in him that curious ambivalent sensation which one experiences in dreams, that of knowing where one is and not knowing, of recognition and non-recognition, of the comfortingly familiar and the frighteningly strange – the sensation of déjà vu: am I really myself, experiencing this, or has it all already happened a long time ago?

He turned left into the Stiftgasse where the great barracks stood, for no other reason than an urge to change direction, to seek the protection of a narrower street, because he felt an upsurge of nausea. For a few minutes he stood in a doorway, fighting it down. Then, gritting his teeth, he went on, turning right, turning left and right again, without looking at street names, without looking anywhere, sleepwalking as it were to reach the place where he would have to wake up and look and be sure.

Finally, there he was, on the Ring: the massive pile of the Natural History Museum on his right, the ramp of the Parliament building on his left, beyond it the spire of the Town Hall, and in front of him the railings of the Volksgarten and the Burgplatz. There he was, and there it all was; though the once tree-bordered footpaths across the roadway were stripped, treeless, only a few naked trunks still standing. Otherwise it was all there. And suddenly the dislocation of time which had been dizzying him with illusions and delusions snapped into focus, and he was real, everything was real, incontrovertible fact. He was *there*. Only the trees were not there, and this comparatively trivial sign of destruction, for which he had not been prepared, caused him incommensurate grief. Hurriedly he crossed the road, entered the park gates, sat down on a bench in a deserted avenue, and wept.

# Three

A few days later, having found himself a tolerable room in a small *pension*, Adler went to call on the official at the Ministry of Education with whom he had corresponded about his return for the past six months. The exchange of letters had been dry, impersonal, official in style and tone, but in substance he had been assured that according to the law on reparation, anyone wishing to return would be reinstated in the same or equivalent position which he had held before, if it could be shown that he had been dismissed or forced to resign because of his political opinions or on the grounds of race or religion. The assurance had been adequate if not particularly encouraging. Adler had attributed the dryness to the impersonal formality of administrative language. He now glanced through his file, slipped it into his briefcase and set out for the Ministry.

The quiet little square, on which the broad, Baroque frontage of the palace which housed it looked down with ceremonious old-world dignity, was unscathed, as was the brown octagonal tower of the nearby Minorite Church. The cloudless sky showed wide stretches of blue, the sun shone kindly on the weathered stone, and a breath of spring floated on the air from the budding trees of the Volksgarten. Adler stood looking around, his heart lifted, and he felt that time, like himself, had for a moment stood still.

He had not thought of making an appointment. When he asked at the inquiry desk for the Sektionschef with whom he had been corresponding, this was of course the first question he had to answer, and when he said 'no', the clerk's mouth and shoulders assumed an even less co-operative expression than they had had in the first place. However, he pushed a slip over to him to fill in with his name and the nature of his business, and having received it, he was prepared to sink back into indifference. Then Adler produced the last letter the Sektionschef had written to him, and this at least resulted in his being conducted as far as the Herr Sektionschef's anteroom, where two other people were already waiting. This slight, foreseeable and avoidable incident at the inquiry desk had already had an unnerving effect on Adler's self-confidence, and made him aggressively defensive. He glared with hostility at the two other unfortunates who had occupied the waiting room before him. But mercifully he was almost immediately to be disarmed. The paper on which he had just registered his presence had obviously been passed into the inner sanctum: within a very few minutes the door was opened by the Sektionschef himself who, bowing slightly to the two previous arrivals and begging them to excuse him, held out his hand to Adler and drew him into his office.

'My dear Herr Professor, it is a pleasure to make your acquaintance. How are you? When did you arrive? Do please sit down,' and he pulled forward a chair for his visitor while himself retiring behind his wide, paper-strewn desk. 'I only wish you had given me notice of your intended visit. I should have had more leisure. As you saw, people are always waiting – so many interviews – so much business! But come, now you are here, let us talk as much as possible. We can get down to details another time. I have sent for your file, they will bring it in a moment.'

Words poured from his lips, soothing, ingratiating, while Adler, the light from the tall windows in his eyes, scarcely said anything and felt slightly dazed. The man opposite him was at least ten years younger than himself, fair, smooth-faced, groomed to perfection, and beaming with urbanity. He had a soft Austrian voice and his diction, perfectly cultured, seemed to caress the roundness of his vowels and the resonance of his consonants, as if consciously to distinguish his speech from the crisp, clipped enunciation used by 'foreigners' – that is North Germans. He belonged to a new generation and a new elite, very self-assured and conscious of its merits and responsibilities. He made Adler feel old, a relic, almost a stranger, and out of place in this city where he had been born and had lived for years before this blond young man had opened his eyes.

'I am delighted you have decided to come back to us, Herr Professor,' the speech continued. 'We can use all the brains, all the learning, all the experience our countrymen are able to contribute. We cannot afford to waste any of it. Such a valuable personality as yourself – let me assure you that we appreciate your return.'

Poor old fellow, he thought privately, contemplating Adler's greying hair, he does look rather pathetic. Still, we are legally bound to make reparation and I fully accept that it is our moral duty to do so.

'I could not have come back,' Adler said dryly, interrupting the flow of rhetoric, 'if I were not legally entitled to reinstatement.'

'Of course, of course, reinstatement or reparation – to the best of our ability, to the very limit that our means permit us. We are a poor country, a small country, we have suffered much destruction –' A clerk knocked at a side door, came in, and laid a file on the Sektionschef's desk.

'Ah, thank you, thank you. Yes, this is the file. We will go through it together later, and see what can be done – I mean, what you wish to do. That must, above all things, be taken into account. But now, there are people waiting whom I have promised to see.' He looked at his watch. 'I am already a little unpunctual. But never mind that. The main thing is that you have come back to us and that I have made your acquaintance.' He picked up a pencil. 'Where can I get in touch with you?' Pencil poised, he looked at Adler expectantly. But Adler, lips compressed, was staring at the floor. The Sektionschef put down the pencil and, bending forward with his hands on the arms of his chair in a gesture of rising: 'Herr Professor!' he called.

Adler looked up. 'Herr Sektionschef, I'm sorry to delay you. But I can't leave you like this. I want to *know*. I *must* know . . .' His voice sounded louder than he had meant it to be. 'I *must* know where I stand. I want to know what my situation is to be.'

'Of course, Herr Professor – that is exactly what we shall have to discuss. I realise that you must be anxious. But you, too, must realise –' He sat back again in his chair. 'You must understand, a problem like this cannot be settled in five minutes. There are difficulties, unavoidable difficulties, on both sides, on yours as well as on ours. I can put them in just two words: fifteen years. Think of them, Herr Professor. Fifteen years is a long time. We cannot wipe out fifteen years, pretend that they did not exist. A great deal has happened during those fifteen years – so much has changed. Even without all those extraordinary – and deplorable – circumstances, those most regrettable events, things do change, naturally and legitimately, in fifteen years. People grow older, young men reach maturity . . .'

Will he dare to tell me I am too old, try to pension me off? Adler wondered. Aloud, he said: 'I realise I am not as young as I used to be. But I'm scarcely fifty – a long way from the age limit if there is one in the profession of a scientist, which I doubt. And I have not lain fallow during your fifteen years. I have continued to work all the time. I am entirely up-to-date, both in information and technique.'

Why am I trying to justify myself, he thought with bitterness. I have a right to be reinstated. I am not asking for a favour.

The Sektionschef sighed and crossed his legs. His appointments would have to wait. He could not break off the interview. There must be no abruptness. The Professor must be handled gently, very gently.

'Of course, Herr Professor, we know that. We know that you have been working in the laboratory of one of the great American hospitals. It's all in my file. You are most certainly in touch with all the latest developments in your field. American research institutions are so lavishly endowed, so wonderfully well-equipped. I'm afraid we are very poor here, by comparison, and that you are making a great sacrifice in giving up all those facilities.'

'Oh, I am quite prepared to find that my laboratory' – the Sektionschef winced a little at the word 'my' – 'that my laboratory will not be as up-to-date, as streamlined, to use the American expression, as the one I have left behind. At least, for the time being. But the Institute was well up to standard when I left – fifteen years ago, as you stress – and I imagine, with all the work that had to be done during the war, it cannot have been allowed to become derelict. After all, the Germans were here, weren't they? And the Germans are nothing if not efficient. They would not have neglected a research institution when even the extermination camps, to judge by what has recently come to light, were organised with such scientific perfection.'

'Alas, Herr Professor, alas!'

'I'm sorry,' Adler continued, 'I did not intend to touch on

that terrible subject. This is neither the time nor the place to speak of it, and I hope that I shall not be called upon to discuss it again. I have made up my mind not to enquire too closely into anything that happened while I was away, or into anybody's recent past, or I could not have come back at all. But to return to my laboratory. I shall work to the best of my ability with the installations that are available, and actually my research is not as dependent on a lot of costly apparatus as it is in some other branches. I am quite prepared to improvise. It stimulates the imagination. To tell you the truth, I have found it somewhat oppressive to be governed by the necessary co-ordination of a large team working on a project which I did not, personally, consider promising – and to be dictated to, as one sometimes is, by one's own tools.

'But there, I apologise, Herr Sektionschef, you cannot be interested in the mechanics of my subject and I must not take up more of your time than is absolutely necessary. All I wanted to say, as regards the laboratory conditions which you touched on, is that one element of the admittedly complex motives which induced me to return was the hope of being more independent, more able to follow my own ideas and my own methods – for what they are worth.' Adler felt much happier having delivered himself of this declaration, and looked it. But the Sektionschef did not. However, he decided that as he could not dismiss the Professor at this stage of the proceedings, he had better deal with his case completely, and settle it.

'I see, I see, Herr Professor,' he said. 'And you have my

profound respect. The way you put it, the sacrifice you are making is less than I had feared. That is a great relief to my mind. But the other sacrifice, the material one, will, I'm afraid, be heavier.'

'You mean the financial one, I presume.'

'Exactly.'

'Well, of course I know that the scale of remuneration here cannot compare with the American.'

'There is that, also. Now let me see. You were, I believe, when you left . . .' – the Sektionschef leafed through the file before him, more to make his statement really authoritative than to inform himself of what he knew already – 'you were an Assistant at the Institute.'

'First Assistant,' Adler interrupted, 'I should have been Head of it in due course.'

'Ah, but the "due course" was interrupted, was it not? Through no fault of your own, I hasten to add, but you did choose to leave a little early. I mean, you resigned before you could be dismissed – and you left the country.'

'I should probably not be alive today if I had not done so.'

'Very probably. You were wise to act as you did, no one could blame you. But it creates a little difficulty by the letter of the law. You acted, so to speak, of your own free will, you were not actually *forced* to leave – you anticipated.'

'But for Heaven's sake, Herr Sektionschef, what difference does it make?'

'We are prepared to overlook the difference, to interpret according to the spirit, not the letter of the law – which killeth.'

'A little joke, Herr Sektionschef? Rather a grim one.'

The Sektionschef bit his lip. 'I apologise.' (How difficult all this is – things will slip out, one can't be too careful.) 'And your title of Professor was – a titular, not a substantive one.'

'Yes. So there is another Head of Department now? I suppose that was inevitable.'

'Dr Krieger is in charge of the Institute at the moment. He has not yet been formally confirmed as Head of Department. The medical faculty is partly in the process of reorganisation, as are the others. Some people have left, others are coming back. Dr Krieger is Austrian, but he spent the war years in Germany. As you know, after '38 there was a common citizenship, and these things have not been finally sorted out. All sorts of questions still have to be disentangled and investigated. Not everything has been cleared up. But Dr Krieger's case has been very thoroughly gone into and he is perfectly in the clear. A very able man indeed, as you will find when you meet him. I hope you will be able to co-operate fruitfully with him – and he with you. I'm sure that with good will on both sides, and the disinterested devotion to science which you both share –'

'So I shall, again, be an Assistant!'

'If you wish to call yourself that. You see, you will have been reinstated. But you will also be able to work quite independently, on your own projects. And your Professorship entitles you to lecture and to have pupils if any wish to enrol with you. Of course, you will be calling on the Dean of the Faculty before you start work, and discussing such matters with him. And I'll see to it that as soon as possible you receive an official document confirming your appointment and your emoluments. I beg you not to be disappointed. We are a very poor country and, unfortunately, not in a position to be lavish. We know that your merits are far in excess of the remuneration we are able to offer. And now you must really excuse me. Goodbye, Herr Professor, goodbye.'

He rose and opened the door for Adler, then held out his hand to the next caller. 'I am so very sorry to have kept you waiting . . .' Adler heard, before the door closed behind him and he was left to go out once more into the quiet little square overlooked by the brown octagonal tower of the old Minorite Church standing peacefully in the spring sunshine, to the square in which it had seemed to him that time stood still.

# Four

Back to where he had been before! That was what restitution –
what reinstatement – meant. But what one had felt to be
right, to be commensurate, to be full of promise for the future, when one was still in one's thirties, did not look the
same in one's fifties. Time had not stood still. What, he asked
himself, had he expected? The Ministry had been scrupulous, the Sektionschef had been friendly. They had put him
back where he had left off. That was what they had been
obliged to do. What had he hoped for? That he would be
welcomed with open arms, as if they had been waiting for
him for fifteen years; as if they had been longing for him to
return, enriched by experience, by accumulated knowledge,
by a deeper understanding, a more mature judgment? He
felt that now he was fit to be in a position of authority and
responsibility, to have younger men working under him. But

that was not how they saw it. He had been away too long and he was out of the running. As he had left, others had moved in and had moved up.

Slowly he retraced his steps to the small but decent *pension* in a quiet street where he had succeeded in finding a room. He was a little sadder, a little more disillusioned than he had been a few hours earlier. Not as shocked as he had been the day of his arrival, when his first, almost irresistible, impulse had been to flee. But then he had remembered what would await him if he gave up: his wife who would gloat over his disappointment and taunt him with it, and almost certainly the refusal to give him back his position at the hospital, since he had resigned it: he knew he might have held it for a few years longer, but there had already been murmurs that he was too old. And that meant that he would be entirely dependent on his wife's earnings. He would have to live on the proceeds of – corsets, on money extracted from the humiliation of rich middle-aged women. He would rather face anything than that.

So he sat down to write a letter to Melanie in which he told her of his safe arrival and that he had been courteously received at the Ministry; he had been reinstated, as was his due, in his job at the Institute, and was looking forward to starting work there shortly. He told her that Vienna had been only slightly damaged, but that everyday life was still rather difficult, weighing every word carefully so as to achieve the impression he wished to convey: that he himself was satisfied that things were no worse than he expected, but that she had been right to stay in New York. He re-read his letter and was pleased with it. So pleased was he that it would convince Melanie all was well with him, that he had almost succeeded in convincing himself, and experienced a fresh upsurge of hope and determination as he sealed it.

The next few days he spent walking about the city, once more getting the feel of the streets he knew so well but had half forgotten, trying to remember what certain houses had looked like before they had been reduced to rubble, what shops were missing – and gradually despair receded and merged into acceptance. Recognition slowly overcame estrangement, as one at first hesitatingly and then confidently recognises an old friend – however altered by the ravages of sickness and of time; and in the end one comes to cherish the enduring personality even more deeply because it has survived these changes which are at last felt to be of no account. On these solitary walks Adler found himself growing new tendrils of love for his old disfigured Vienna, and the conviction that he had been right to come took hold of him more and more strongly.

He decided to call on a few people he had known, and he went into a telephone box. There they were in the telephone directory, as they had been before. The numbers had changed – there seemed to be a different code – but the addresses were the same. That was comforting. None of them were intimate friends. He had hardly had any really intimiate friends amongst those who had stayed behind except one, an art historian whom he had known since they were boys together at the *Gymnasium*.

'Hello, this is Kuno Adler – yes, Adler – back from America. Is that you, Hermann?' And then the delight, the throat-catching emotion of hearing the answer: 'Kuno! Is it really you? How splendid! So you're back? That's really good news. You must come and see us, you and your wife. Oh, your wife is not with you? Well, I'm sure she was right to stay in New York until you see how things are shaping here.'

'It's good to hear your voice, Hermann. When can I see you?'

'Just a moment, I must look at my diary. Now let me see. Not this week, I'm afraid. I have a meeting tomorrow evening, and then I have to go to Linz to identify some pictures. What about next Sunday? Will you be free in the evening? Then come to supper if you can – just a little cold supper, Sunday evening. Oh good! You'll have such a lot to tell me. So long, Kuno.'

Sunday evening – and this was Tuesday! Fifteen years absence – so what did five more days matter? And he himself, had he not been in Vienna for more than a week without ringing up Hermann? Of course Hermann was busy. He was listed as the Director of the Contemporary Art Gallery, so it was natural that he should have a long list of engagements. He had not been waiting so impatiently for his old friend Adler's return that he would feel the urge to see him that very same day, or at the very latest tomorrow. And yet Adler felt that that was what Hermann should have said, what he had hoped he would say. Now, the spark had gone out of his pleasure. He thought that by Sunday he would not really care to go and have supper with the Helblings, that he would probably ring up and make an excuse for not going.

When he had put down the receiver he stared for a while at the telephone directory. The other two men whom he had wanted to call were doctors. One with whom he had worked in the General Hospital was now, according to the entry in the directory, Director of one of the big clinics. He decided not to ring him up. The other was a gynaecologist, although the link between him and Adler had not been medicine but music. They used to play chamber music together, and Dr Stolz had been the viola to Adler's second violin. The first violin had emigrated and the cellist, Adler knew, had died in a concentration camp. Stolz had been the only gentile member of the quartet, but he had mixed so freely and intimately with the others that he could surely never have been anti-Semitic? But now Adler could not be sure. What if he had, after all, been a Nazi? If he had felt obliged to become a party member because he had had so many Jewish friends? Or that he needed to be one for the sake of his practice? Adler felt that he could not bear another rebuff on the telephone; for Hermann's five-day postponement of their meeting had almost been a rebuff. He felt that his attempt to reestablish social contacts had not been a success, forgetting that out of the three calls he had intended to make, he had in fact only made one, and it had resulted in an invitation to supper!

On the Sunday Adler decided that, having accepted the invitation, he would after all go and see his old friend. A maid in a black dress, a little white apron and a white starched cap opened the door of the flat. It struck him as strange and old-worldly that there *was* a maid – a kind of luxury he had forgotten – but it gave him confidence too. He exchanged a few friendly words with her as she took his coat and hat, and his voice must have been heard in the living room, for the door opened and Hermann Helbling came out to greet him.

'Kuno, my old friend, how good it is to see you! Come in, come in, let's have a look at you!'

And for a moment the two men stood gazing at each other not knowing what to say. Helbling's reddish beard was powdered with grey; Adler's black hair had receded from the temples and was streaked with silver.

'You have put on weight!'

'You hardly look a day older!'

'Oh come now, that's not true!'

'Look at him, Ilse, he has hardly changed at all!'

Ilse Helbling had come into the room and shook hands with Adler. 'Hermann's right, it's extraordinary how un-changed you are! He tells me you have left Melanie over there. And your girls? They must be quite grown up. Not married, are they?'

'No, no. Not married yet, though Hilde probably will be very soon.'

And so on, still standing in the middle of the room, speaking a little too emphatically, a little too distinctly, as if reciting a conversation out of a phrase book, until Hermann said: 'Well, let's sit down,' and Ilse said: 'It's hardly worth it, I'm sure supper is ready – just a Sunday evening cold snack, Herr Professor, or,' with a little laugh, 'may I still call you Kuno? Anyway, let's go into the dining room, Mizi will just be putting some hot soup on the table.'

Eating and drinking, they all relaxed and became easier. There was a white cloth on the round table. A lamp with a silk shade hung low over its centre, making the silver cutlery gleam. Their faces were in shadow. Hermann and Ilse talked. They did all the talking. What dreadful years these had been. No one who had not been through them could have any idea. The first years of the war had not been too bad, although even when victories were being blared every day over the radio they had never believed the Germans would win; not after it became obvious the invasion of England had failed. They had always listened to the BBC: it had been dangerous to do so, but they had listened all the same. The end had been terrible: the bombing, the destruction! 'So unnecessary, wasn't it Hermann? The Germans were finished anyway – so why did the Americans have to bomb Vienna? And destroy the Opera House – the *Opera House*, I ask you! I really think they often don't know what they are doing, your new compatriots, Kuno. Then the Russian invasion, that of course was far, far worse. The looting that went on, harmless people being shot in the street, and all the women being raped –'

'Good Lord, did that happen to *you*, Ilse?'

'No, I was lucky. But scores of people I know suffered. Naturally one *knows* that the Russians are barbarians and expects the worst, while the Americans –'

'They are not my compatriots,' Adler managed to interject, 'except *pro forma*. I am Austrian, the same as you are. Nevertheless, we all have reason to be deeply grateful to the Americans, very deeply grateful, in spite of the bombing.'

Hermann tried to deflect his wife's recriminations. 'You are quite right. America is our only hope for the future, the only counterpoise against the Soviets. Without their presence, their support, we should never be able to regain our independence, or to maintain it. However, let's not get involved in politics at our first reunion. Isn't it good to have Kuno here with us again? Come, let's toast your return!'

They took their wine glasses back into the living room, and settled down in armchairs to drink and smoke. Helbling uncorked another bottle.

'One thing the Germans have done for us – they have improved our vineyards. What do you think of this Gumpoldskirchner, Kuno?'

'Excellent, I was wondering what it was.' Adler drank half his glass, then studied the label. He felt warmed and comforted. Hermann Helbling really was the old friend he had believed him to be. This was the kind of welcome he had hoped for. Now, he thought, I shall be able to tell them what these years they've been talking about have meant to me, give them the other side of the picture. And he wondered whether he should, on this first evening, speak about his estrangement from his wife, or say anything about his reception by the Sektionschef at the Ministry. There was so much, so much he wanted to talk about, such a weight of loneliness and repression on his heart as he had never acknowledged even to himself, until this moment when the prospect of some measure of alleviation seemed at hand. A blessed prospect, and he did not want to hurry. He sat smoking in silence, looking with intense pleasure round the book-lined room, the shaded lamp, the thick curtains drawn against the ill-lit mournfulness of the street outside. And so, wrapped in contemplation, and nursing his anticipation, he was too slow to seize the initiative. It eluded him – eluded him for the rest of the evening. Perhaps if he had been alone with Hermann he might still have begun to speak; and Hermann would have listened, encouraging him with a benevolent look in his kindly blue eyes and a smile half-smothered by the prickly gingery beard of a Teutonic warrior. But Adler didn't get the chance to be alone with him, or even to break the flow of conversation. Ilse was far too voluble, and she made no move to leave the two old friends alone.

As the evening drew on, the initial nagging doubt stirred again at the back of Adler's mind. Perhaps Hermann himself had said to his wife: don't leave us, I don't want to get involved in too many confidences. We don't know what Kuno's state of mind may be. He was always rather touchy, inclined to have grievances. He probably has some quite serious ones now which we might find very embarrassing. And he obviously wasn't happy in America or he wouldn't have come back. I doubt whether he is going to be happy here. These returning émigrés all have illusions. So let's just accept him and be nice to him, and leave it at that. Had Hermann, for these reasons, deliberately encouraged his wife, or was Ilse behaving spontaneously in recounting this long string of macabre incidents of the Russian occupation of Vienna – some grue-some, some quite comical – which they and their friends had experienced? At any rate, he did not interrupt her, and she herself was obviously enjoying her chance of telling them to an audience who had not heard them before. And so the evening passed quickly, in an atmosphere of physical comfort, deliberately fostered and gratefully accepted, with the tacit understanding that there had been tragedies and searing experiences in *all* their lives that could not be forgotten, but which they had survived and cauterised sufficiently to be able to sit together in a quiet room, drinking a companionable glass of excellent wine.

It was nearly midnight when Adler rose to take his leave, and make his way back to the little *pension* through the sparsely-lit, almost deserted streets. The trams had long ceased running and few people cared to be out at night in these outlying districts. He took with him the warmth and comfort of the wine and the cheerful words at parting: 'Such a pleasure to have seen you again! Let us know if we can be of any assistance. You must come again soon.' His nerves and senses felt soothed and relaxed; but as his euphoria began fading in the night air, his mind was already arguing that the Helblings, for all their friendliness, had really taken no interest in him at all.

# Five

His return to the Institute was undramatic, except for one small and irrelevant incident which he had not foreseen. He had waited until he received the official notification of his appointment, which came by post without any covering letter; that somehow disappointed him and induced him to defer, for the time being, his intended call on the Dean of the Faculty of Medicine. He would meet dryness with dryness. If all ceremony was to be omitted, he would also refrain from ceremony; so he did not write to announce his coming, but allowed a couple of days to pass in order not to be thought in a hurry. And then, one morning, he walked into the building which housed the Institute, wrapping himself in a protective indifference as if fifteen years and all that had happened in them had not interrupted the daily routine of his coming and going. But out of the corner of his eye, so to speak, and pretending to himself not to notice, he took in both the sameness and the changes that confronted him. More shabbiness, some modernisation. The hallway was the same – and the smell – that most evocative, most nostalgic of the senses, a very special smell of bricks and lingering disinfectant. Upstairs, and along a corridor, his steps sounded on the flagstones as they had always sounded, and the name of the Institute above the heavy double doors was the same. He pushed one open.

The room he entered was greatly altered, much better installed, modernised, improved, as he could not help admitting, not by American standards, but in comparison with what he remembered. The old apparatus, which he would now have called obsolete junk, was gone. The present installation was compact and streamlined. There was more room to move about. It still looked, at first glance, rather meagrely equipped compared with the big American laboratories he had come from, but that rather appealed to him. He stood on the threshold and smiled. There were several men and women in white coats busy in different parts of the long room, and they all turned their heads and looked round at him curiously as he stood there hesitating over whom to address.

Then, from a door at the side which he did not remember being there, another man in a white coat appeared and came forward with small staccato steps, holding out his hand. 'My name is Krieger,' he said. 'I'm glad to see you, Professor Adler. Please come in.' They shook hands. Dr Krieger introduced his staff, the young doctors and technicians. The women were laboratory assistants. Adler shook hands with them in turn, only glancing at their faces, barely taking in their names. His attention was fixed on Dr Krieger, the man who had taken his place. He was short and thick-set, he had very little neck and a mottled face. It looked as if the skin had been drawn too tight over its surface, so that the flesh, with its muscles and blood vessels, showed through. The eyes were hidden behind thick-lensed spectacles and his hair was cropped very close. Whether it was reddish or greyish, one couldn't tell. He is not much younger than myself, decided Adler, whose own abundant black hair lay in waves across his skull without his attempting to conceal its rich sprinkling of silver.

Krieger took Adler by the elbow and propelled him down the length of the laboratory, casually pointing to the various pieces of equipment on the way. 'The best German make – an instrument of absolute precision – we only got it last year, we were lucky, it was stored in a shelter just before the factory was bombed. But we are still without some very necessary apparatus – no hope of it at present, so we have to improvise.' Dr Krieger spoke in the same way as he moved – in short jerks. Adler looked and nodded and said nothing.

At the end of the room, encompassing the last window, a glazed partition, projecting a short way from the wall towards the middle, screened off a space into a semblance of semi-privacy. One could see it had been newly erected: the wooden base, of plain deal, was unpainted, and the glass panels freshly set. The cubicle was furnished with a sink, a writing table and chair, a rack of glass receptacles, and a steel filing cabinet. On the table there was a microscope, at which Adler glanced dubiously. He raised his eyebrows inquiringly. Krieger answered his silence. 'A little place of your own, Herr Professor, the best I could manage – to keep your notes and records. For all practical purposes, it's the general laboratory. I work there myself. Here is my own room –' and he opened the door from which he had emerged earlier: 'I have a few instruments – they are at your disposal, of course. And a reference library. There is electricity laid on here, for your use, and a gas-burner. You must tell me what you require, though many things one would like to have are unobtainable. Always the same old story: lack of money.'

As Adler still just stood there, nodding acquiescence, Krieger suddenly gave vent to his feelings of suppressed annoyance. 'What are you going to do here, Professor Adler? What are your intentions?' Why didn't the man *say* something, show some appreciation for the preparations made for him! He didn't need him, he didn't want him, he would be difficult to fit in, but he had done his best, or rather, he had done what had been required of him, and Adler ought to acknowledge it. So he repeated his question: 'What do you expect to *do*?'

At last Adler answered: 'My share of the routine work, Herr Doktor. I suppose there is enough to go round. Tests, analyses, cultures, the ancillary jobs required by the hospital. That is what is expected of me, isn't it? I shall only try to make myself useful. Later perhaps . . . but we shall see.' He broke off. 'I'll start tomorrow, if that is convenient. Auf Wiedersehen, Herr Doktor.' He walked down the long room to the door and went out. Heads turned silently to follow his progress. He felt their eyes on his back, but he did not turn round. He was glad everything had been so matter-of-fact, for he knew he was over-excited. A dose of indifference was what he prescribed for himself; but that, for the moment, was not to be.

At the bottom of the wide stone staircase the caretaker of the building, a little old man in loose trousers and a well-worn serge jacket, stood looking up at him. Short white hair, a brown wrinkled face and what had once been a trim military moustache framed a pair of very blue eyes that were now smiling under a film of tears. And the mouth under its stubbly moustache was smiling too. The whole bent figure was turned upwards, the head raised, the shoulders lifted by an inner elation shining through the aged body and the shabby clothes. Recognition was instantaneous and mutual. Adler ran down the last steps with hands outstretched, clasping the old man's hand with both his own.

'Grasboeck, you are still here! How are you? How good to find you again!'

'Oh, Herr Professor, so you have come back, you have come back!'

They could exchange nothing but exclamations, well-worn phrases, just to express, however haltingly, feelings too deep for words.

'It's been a long time – we have both grown older – but I knew you immediately – and I was so happy when I heard you were coming back to us.' And again and again: 'Such long years – such terrible years!' And they shook hands once more. Adler patted the old man on the shoulder and Grasboeck seemed to want to do a service for Adler – carry his briefcase, perhaps – but Adler had none with him, so they stood there brimming with goodwill for each other and at a loss what to do. The old man recovered himself first, stepped backwards and murmured something about having to sweep the courtyard. Adler hesitated. The impulse rose within him to say: Let's go out and have a glass of wine together, but of course Grasboeck would not be able to leave his work in the middle of the morning.

Then he remembered: Grasboeck had had a little boy who sometimes sat in his cubicle doing his homework or playing around the courtyard.

'Your son, Grasboeck, what happened to your son?'

'He was killed at the front, Herr Professor, having to fight on the *wrong* side – on the *wrong* side.'

# Six

Theophil Kanakis knew what he was looking for and he was convinced he would find it; although, when he made his first trip to Vienna very soon after the end of the war and a couple of years before Adler had decided on his attempt at repatriation, he had for a moment had his doubts. When he saw what the desultory bombing by over-zealous Americans on the verge of victory, and the vindictive shelling by desperate Germans in the throes of defeat, had done to the face of the city – the gaps in the familiar streets, the heaps of rubble where some well-remembered building had stood – he had, at first, felt that the prospect was not very promising. It was not that he grieved very deeply about the destruction he saw. It was, he thought, not really very widespread nor very severe. In fact, compared with other European cities, with London and Rotterdam, with Berlin or Munich,

Vienna had escaped with minor injuries: perhaps there was not much more fortuitous destruction there than what New York was perennially and deliberately suffering in the continual process of being pulled down in order to be rebuilt. That was a most laudable and extremely profitable process of which he thoroughly approved, for it had made him, and was still making him, a very rich man.

What made him apprehensive on this, his first return to Vienna, was not so much the destruction that he saw, but the fear of what the rebuilding – which was bound to take place sooner or later – was going to do to the character of the city. It might do a great deal of damage. And it might obliterate, if the bombing had not already done so, that very piece of property he was looking for. At this stage it was very difficult to foresee.

It was equally difficult to foresee, in the present condition of shock, bereavement and poverty, whether life in the old place would ever be the same again. If not, there was no point in continuing his quest. He must take his chance; but that he had always done, with almost incredible success, exercising his intuitive gift for investment in real estate, buying derelict buildings or promising sites for development. However, that had not been his purpose in coming to Vienna. He had not come to make money but to spend it; not to get rich, for he was already very rich indeed and, as wealth breeds wealth, getting richer all the time. Besides, what scope was there for making money, *his* kind of money, in poor little Austria? No, he had come, though this was not the time to let it be known, simply to enjoy himself.

What he was looking for was, to start with, a very vague memory, or perhaps only a figment of his imagination. Somewhere, he believed, behind the flat-faced dwelling houses of nineteenth century construction, with their street-level shopfronts and their multiple flats on the three or four landings above them, somewhere, hidden behind these squalid habitations of shopkeepers, tradesmen and clerks, he would find a small *hôtel particulier*, a pavilion of graceful eighteenth century proportions, built perhaps by some nobleman for his mistress amidst what had been at that time gardens and orchards outside the city walls. A little *palais*, the Viennese would call it; that being the designation for any private house of some elegance. Now it would only be accessible through one or more courtyards belonging to the tall utilitarian buildings which had, for many decades now, been interposed between it and the wide suburban street with its noisy pavements and clanging tramcars. A lime tree and a few little lilac bushes had possibly survived when the surrounding area was urbanised, together with a small plot of ground which might still be termed a garden. Derelict, with boarded-up windows, or used as storage, it would have fallen into ever-greater disrepair, until it would require far more money than anyone could afford for rehabilitating a house so awkwardly and inconveniently situated.

This was the house Kanakis had created in his imagination and which he believed could still be found. He racked his memory for the faint recollection of something he might have seen, or possibly only heard of, on which his fantasy had built his dream house. So clearly did he see it in his mind's eye that he felt sure he could never have seen it in actual fact without remembering where, nor could he locate it anywhere on the map. It must have been hearsay, he concluded, something someone had once mentioned in his hearing when he was a child. But he was certain that, if it still existed, it was in one of the 'inner suburbs' which, for generations, had no longer been suburbs in the real sense, but an integral part of the town which had grown and was still growing far out beyond them in every direction. They lay between the concentric circles of the Ringstrasse, which encircled the Inner City, still called '*the* City', as the heart of London still enjoys the exclusive privilege of that name – where the medieval battlements had been – and the 'belt', an irregular sequence of broad streets, a ring road which, like the rings of a tree, marked the second stage of the town's expanding growth.

Kanakis asked the hall porter for the special directory of professions and trades and carried it up to his room. He had not, like Adler, arrived in Vienna without making provision for his comfort. The town's most luxurious hotel was reserved for the staff of the American Occupation Forces and their advisers; and Kanakis, although not in uniform, had been able to secure a room there on the strength of the local knowledge he would be able to place at the disposal of the military administration. Once installed, he took the least possible notice of the busy, and often bewildered, officers, and they took none at all of him.

Leafing through the directory, Kanakis ran his finger down the list of house and estate agents, and a name caught his eye as if it had been printed in larger type than all the others on the page. Dr Franz Traumüller – not an extraordinary name in Vienna, but not a very common one either. The address of the office in one of the old narrow streets in the Inner City was a good one, promising a firm of reputable standing accustomed to dealing with exceptional properties. And 'Doktor' Traumüller indeed! The man was a university graduate, a trained lawyer – not so usual among house agents. Kanakis appreciated the name, the address and the qualification. He was sure he could not be mistaken: this could not be a mere coincidence. Franz Traumüller had been the name of the man who had been his father's bailiff, in charge of the care and the administration of the several large houses in which part of the fortune of the elder Kanakis had been invested. A descendant of the small and distinguished community of Greeks whose wealth had helped to finance Vienna's expansion and development from a small town constrained within its ancient walls into a splendid imperial city, his father had inherited three imposing apartment houses in the most elegant section of the Ringstrasse, in one of which his family occupied the whole of the vast first floor.

These houses, as well as a few others in the 'suburbs' – crowded hives of human dwellings – had been in the care, and under the supervision, of the said Franz Traumüller. He it was who collected the rents, attended to the repairs, listened to the tenants' complaints, and dealt with them only after scrupulous investigation on behalf of the landlord. He evicted the unsatisfactory and leased, as far as possible, only to the trustworthy. But he was a fair and just man, as the elder Kanakis insisted that he should be, and if he shielded his employer from all unpleasantness, he was also charged to see to it that no slur of exploitation should ever be attached to his name. Two or three times a year at stated intervals, or in a special emergency when the landlord had to be consulted personally, he came to report to Kanakis's father, who received him in his study at the far end of the suite of drawing rooms, and who was very polite to him, but a little distant and condescending.

Theophil Kanakis remembered, when he was a boy, that his father always found these visits a nuisance. He never took any detailed interest in the houses and only kept a shrewd, but distant, eye on them, as he did on his other investments. So when the butler announced the 'Herr Haus-Administrator', he used to rise with a sigh from his newspaper or his book and tell the butler curtly 'in the study' – to which Herr Traumüller would be conducted through the dining room and pantry, not through the drawing rooms. Theophil had heard his father call the man 'Traumüller', whereas *he* said 'Herr von Kanakis'. And when he himself had once met him in the hall as he was leaving, he had said 'good day, young sir', to which he had answered 'good day, Herr Traumüller', and had stood by embarrassed while Traumüller struggled into his overcoat, into which the butler did not help him as he helped his father or any other of his visitors, and saw him take his hat off the hall table, which was not held out to him, though the butler did open the door – the front door leading to the main staircase, not the back one. Herr Traumüller was, after all, not a tradesman.

And now: Dr Franz Traumüller, estate agent – properties bought and sold and administered – expert valuations. This must surely be the Herr Administrator's son, probably about the same age as himself, a man of professional standing, with a university education. Kanakis himself boasted no letters in front of or after his name. He had wasted no time on academic studies; just a short business course after leaving school (and that had been pretty useless, he mused – either you had *got* it or you hadn't – business acumen, he meant) and then, when his father died and he himself had barely come of age, he took himself off to America *with* all his fortune.

He had been pretty clever even then, for it was not easy, in those years, to transfer your assets abroad. But he had done it. And from then onwards he had made money, perhaps hundreds of times more money than had Traumüller the second, in spite of his doctorate; and now, instead of a comfortable competence like his father, he owned a really large fortune, even by American standards. Nevertheless, he recognised Traumüller's endeavour and saluted his success. He would go and see him and find out whether or not he was just the man he needed to find that dream house he had come back to find. He telephoned for an appointment in the afternoon and, after a couple of minutes during which the girl evidently consulted her employer, was given one immediately for the next morning. Obviously, the name Kanakis was as familiar to Traumüller as Traumüller had been to Kanakis.

Kanakis walked from his hotel. The Inner City is so small and compact that distances are negligible, and most of the streets are so narrow that cars are more of an encumbrance than a convenience. At that time there were very few of them about, only military vehicles, staff cars and a few taxis. Kanakis made a negative sign to the driver of one of them, who was obsequiously bowing to him at the kerb in front of the hotel. He remembered the way. Besides, he savoured the unchanged names of the old streets. They were very shabby. Paint was peeling from doors and window frames, many facades were damaged and many windows and shopfronts simply boarded up. Parts of the pavement, too, were broken, the asphalt split, paving stones lying loose.

Kanakis picked his way carefully, looking appraisingly right and left, thinking to himself that after five years of war and, in its aftermath, no money or incentive for repairs, things might have been worse. Ah, here a large building had been completely destroyed, the whole area would have to be replanned. Kanakis feared that any modern construction would be out of keeping with its surroundings. These old cities, they would be even more spoilt by improvement than by destruction. But one should have no regrets. This was a living organism, not an antiquarian showpiece. Theophil Kanakis had not been in contact with many people in Vienna before he began to sense that the *spiritus loci*, the character and spirit of the place, was going to survive and persist.

Something caught his eye on the other side of the street.

He skirted a hole in the asphalt and crossed over. The shop window opposite was covered with weatherboard, except for a small square that had been cut out and glazed; the shop was a confectioner's, and behind the small window were two trays of iced cakes, glistening with sugar and filled with cream. The price tickets, on the tiny cleft wooden sticks affixed to each row of cakes, quoted a fantastic figure, surely quite out of reach of most passers-by. In fact, nobody stopped to look at them; but Kanakis was interested. By what means had the confectioner succeeded in getting hold of the eggs, the sugar, the cream which had gone into these glamorous products of his skill? For undoubtedly they were the real thing. Kanakis saluted them with a smile. The girl behind the counter – he could only just see her through the narrow opening – looked at him hopefully and smiled back. On an impulse he went in and paid for a trayful without choosing. 'Eat them,' he said, 'take some home to your mother. No, I don't want any, but they look so good, I have enjoyed buying them.' And he went out of the shop, leaving the girl dumbfounded.

Kanakis continued on his way with a spring in his step; he was pleased there would be cakes again, that people in Vienna still had the taste for them and were able to make them. People were still the same: they liked cakes – and probably music – and all the other pleasures of the senses. His instinct had been right, the cakes confirmed it.

So it was with a new buoyancy that he went up the stone staircase to the second floor of the old house where a brass plate on the door announced that this was the office of

Dr Franz Traumüller, Estate Agent and Valuer, and a cardboard notice underneath asked clients to enter without ringing the bell. The inner sanctum must be well-guarded against intruders, Kanakis thought, but probably only fairly recently – the cardboard notice looked clean.

As he went in, there was a clatter of typewriters, and one of the three girls at work got up to ask his name. She took his card and went out of a side door to announce him, came back at once and preceded him along a passage to a room overlooking the street. This was comfortably and lavishly furnished, with tall bookcases, deep armchairs and a large writing table: more like a successful lawyer's than an estate agent's office. Two dark pictures in ponderous gold frames hung on the wall behind the desk where Dr Traumüller was seated. As his visitor entered the room, he rose and came forward with outstretched hand to greet him.

'Herr von Kanakis, this is indeed a pleasure. I shan't ask you whether you remember me because I believe we have never met, but I imagine you have come because you know who I am – as I know who you are.'

'Certainly, that is so, Herr Doktor. And I am glad to find that I was not mistaken in your identity when I found your name in the register.'

'Ah, that is how you found me! I was wondering. We have come a long way, have we not, Herr von Kanakis? But do please sit down. I mean,' he added as he saw Kanakis glance round the room, 'I mean, *I* have come a long way, as you see. Whereas you, of course – but your fame has preceded you.'

'My fame, Herr Doktor? I am not aware of being famous.'

'Well, your reputation, then. Of course, your late father – whom I well remember, having seen him on certain occasions when I was a small boy – was a man of considerable wealth. I got out my father's old files, just for curiosity's sake, after you telephoned yesterday – the files dealing with his house property. Yes, it was a substantial fortune in those days, here in Vienna. But *you*, Herr von Kanakis, well, there is no comparison, is there? American dimensions are on a different scale. I am told that everything in America is much bigger – the buildings, the distances, the rivers, even the birds, they say, are larger editions of our own, and we have only got to look at the cars. Still, I'm quite pleased with my own modest competence. May I offer you a drink? Enzian schnapps? You may not know it, I don't think it was much in evidence at the time you left us. I'm sorry I have no Scotch.'

'Thanks, I never drink in the morning, although Enzian sounds most enticing. I only know the flower – such a beautiful blue!' Kanakis leant back in his chair and looked straight at Traumüller. 'But how is it you know anything at all about me – however exaggerated your information may be – except what we both know about each other: we are our fathers' sons?'

'Well, Herr von Kanakis, Vienna is still a very small place, you know. People talk. I know a man who knows a man who . . . etc etc. Isn't that how things get about? There are so many sources of information. I must have heard about you almost the day after you arrived. We are, in a manner of speaking, in the same line of business, if I may dare to compare a molehill to a mountain, Herr von Kanakis.'

'I see.'

Herr Traumüller began fiddling with a paperknife. So far he had done all the talking, and that was not his usual method of conducting an interview. Usually he invited his client to talk, to state his business, say what he wanted to buy or sell, or any other transaction he might have in mind, and then he, Traumüller, could mention the market, the current difficulties, the high interest rates. Then, when the client had reluctantly admitted the truth of these preliminaries, Traumüller would be able to suggest tactfully that he, indeed, was the man, perhaps the only man, to overcome such obstacles. He wouldn't boast – nothing as crude as that! – but would acknowledge gratefully, almost humbly, that thanks to his connections, his reputation and, if he might say so, his expertise, his client's wishes could be met.

But this interview was not conforming to the usual pattern. Something in Kanakis's appearance, in the ease of his posture as he reclined in the deep armchair, his elegance and his tranquillity, intimidated Traumüller and inhibited him from asking Kanakis why he had come to see him. Ever since the appointment had been made the previous afternoon, Traumüller had been asking himself this question. There might be great opportunities for him here. For why had Kanakis come back to Vienna at this particular moment, after an absence of so many years? Did he plan to invest on a large scale in the rebuilding of the city? There was so much property for sale, so many building sites, so many houses whose owners would be only too glad to dispose of them if they could obtain a tempting price. And surely, if such were Kanakis's intentions, he would not want to handle this business himself? He would want a man on the spot who had all the local knowledge. But meanwhile Dr Traumüller was not at all sure how this matter ought to be approached. He knew himself to be shrewd, but possible this dark-browed man with the heavy black moustache and the blue-shadowed cheeks might be even shrewder. Or was it only the aura of wealth about him which gave him something intimidating? In spite of all the altered circumstances, his education and professional standing, Dr Traumüller felt almost as obsequious towards Theophil Kanakis as the elder Traumüller had felt towards his father.

Kanakis was taking his time. 'I see,' he said again, adding nothing to this non-commital remark, while his eyes seemed to wander dreamily round the room, feeling their way up and down the tall ebony bookcases, appraising the leather-bound volumes half-hidden by the reflecting glass of their sliding doors, caressing, as it were, the velvety surface of the tobacco-coloured suede upholstery of the two large armchairs, in one of which he was sitting. His left foot shifted a little as he settled himself more comfortably in its embrace: the slight movement might have been a testing of the quality of the Persian carpet. 'I see,' he said a third time into the silence, which seemed to Traumüller to have lasted interminably, though only a few seconds had ticked away on the big clock in its mahogany casing framed in intricate volutes of burnished bronze. These repeated 'I see's' appeared, in the end, to have a more literal application and to refer to what Kanakis was actually seeing of his surroundings rather than to the remarks Traumüller had been making about his sources of information. At any rate, their repetition, and their ambiguity, were making Traumüller more and more nervous.

At last Kanakis's eyes came to rest on the two dark, heavily-framed pictures hanging on the wall opposite his chair, and a faint smile creased his eyelids.

'Do you really recognise those pictures?' Dr Traumüller exclaimed, unable to bear this silent scrutiny any longer, and immediately cursing himself inwardly for this unwarranted suggestion. For a very unpleasant thought had entered his mind. What if Kanakis had returned to Vienna not to deal in real estate, but to recover some of the property which had been confiscated by the German Secret Police or their agents when the owners had been deported, 'liquidated' or had simply fled, abandoning all they possessed? A quick appraisal reassured him that nothing in this room could have belonged to the Kanakis family who, in fact, were not Jews, and should not have suffered confiscation, except perhaps by mistake, for the rich Jewish and the rich Greek families had been very close to each other.

'Recognise them?' Kanakis repeated with a hint of astonishment, real or simulated, in his voice. He had divined Traumüller's suspicion. 'Why? Ought I to recognise them? Did you expect me to do so? Do you mean that I must have seen them before, somewhere else?'

'No, no, of course not, it's most unlikely you would have seen them – or remembered them if you had. They are in no way outstanding or really valuable – a minor nineteenth century artist. I just thought they furnished the room, gave it a certain cachet, within the limits of what I could afford. They did in fact belong to a gentleman who was surely an acquaintance of your family, Baron E—. You might possibly have seen them at his house. Baron E— unfortunately died abroad, in England, I believe. His heirs, after they had recovered what could be traced of his property, had it all sold at auction; having no use for this old-fashioned stuff in their modern homes, I suppose. I acquired the pictures in the auction rooms, as well as most of the things you see here. All quite openly, publicly and legally, you understand. There is no great demand for this period,' he added deprecatingly, 'and there is so much of it about. But the material is magnificent and it suits my purpose.'

'There is no need to apologise, Herr Doktor,' Kanakis said, smiling broadly. 'I can only congratulate you on your bargains.'

Traumüller opened his mouth: I didn't apologise, he was going to say. How dare he insult me with such an insinuation! But he shut it again promptly. From a very rich man many things have to be accepted.

And Kanakis, sensing and enjoying this suppressed exclamation of protest, continued soothingly: 'You have most sensibly done what many, quite illustrious people have done before you: taken advantage of the reversals of fortune, shall we say, that have befallen some people of substance during recent historical events – you have purchased judiciously, and to suit your requirements. Who could possibly blame you for that? As I said, you could invoke noble precedents. Do you know that in the French Revolution, even during the Reign of Terror, the heads of several great English houses sent their agents over to Paris to acquire some fine pieces of craftsmanship for which their owners, sadly, had no further use? Most of the beautiful French furniture in England dates from those timely forays. At least it went where it was appreciated – as the contents of this room are appreciated by you, Herr Doktor.' Kanakis inclined his head towards Traumüller, as if making a little bow. 'Personally, I am not interested in the ponderous riches of our late bourgeoisie. *My* tastes, Herr Doktor, are rather narrowly defined – the eighteenth century, Maria Theresa you would say here in Vienna, and a little before and after, the Louis Quinze and Louis Seize in France. I'm afraid this taste is very widely shared, there is much demand for that period and prices are high. But I am glad to say that I can compete. There are certain advantages in being able to compete, Herr Doktor, because it means that one can usually, if not always, obtain what one likes.'

'I am not an art dealer, Herr von Kanakis, or an antique dealer. Though I could recommend you elsewhere, if that is what you want.'

'Don't be disappointed, Herr Doktor, that is not what I want from you, though later on I shall be glad to accept your offer of such introductions. No, before these become desirable, I want something which you, and I believe only you, can find for me. I remember having heard about a little gem of an eighteenth century pavilion, derelict and possibly in ruins, but still recognisable for what it once was, somewhere in one of the districts just outside the Ring. While I have been sitting here, I have remembered that it might have been your father talking about it to my father, perhaps suggesting that it was worth salvaging and might fetch a good price from an amateur. But my father was not interested, it was not his kind of thing, as you will understand if you have any memory of my father. He wanted peace and quiet – and safety above all. Safe as houses might have been his motto. Such an inappropriate comparison, as we have learned in our day, isn't that so, Herr Doktor? Every time I see a heap of rubble and a few broken walls, the tag springs to mind.

'But to return to my *pavilion d'amour*. I feel sure that something like it still exists, and I want you to find it for me. However little there may be left of it, if it is recognisable and can be reconstructed, that is what I want. You can also find me an architect who is able to do the thing in style, and with the requisite good taste. You will send me the description, you will send me the plans, and when the time comes I'll come over again and have a look. I don't expect you to find it today or tomorrow. But, please, don't take too long about it: I don't want a retreat for my old age, I want it in my prime, which is now. And your time and trouble will not go unrewarded. I know I'm asking for something rather out of the ordinary. But you think it over, Herr Doktor, and come and see me in a couple of days at my hotel so we can discuss the necessary financial arrangements. I shall be here till the end of next week and shall look forward to hearing from you. And, by the way, you might give me the address of that antique dealer you mentioned. I, too, might be able to take advantage of the reversals of fortune that have overtaken some people due to recent historical events.'

Kanakis got up from his chair to take his leave, and it was not until a few seconds later that Traumüller followed suit; as if, stunned by what he had just heard, he had needed Kanakis to move in order to come to his senses.

'But what, in heaven's name, are you going to do with this pavilion, or whatever you call it – *if* it exists and *if* I am able to find it?'

'Why, *live* in it, Herr Doktor, and enjoy myself. That's what I intend to do – enjoy myself – as one can only enjoy oneself in Vienna!'

# Seven

It looked an insignificant little shop in one of the tiny narrow streets in the Inner City, a street very close to the offices of Dr Traumüller. It was on Kanakis's second visit to Vienna that Traumüller had sent him there; the owner was, he said, the most knowledgeable and experienced antique dealer in town and, what was even more remarkable, a scrupulously honest one. 'A Jew, Herr von Kanakis, an elderly Jewish gentleman who has returned from exile and, under our restitution laws, has recovered the premises he occupied before he left. His valuable stock had, alas, been dispersed. He was only able to trace a few pieces and those were of course restored to him, but it was not very much. However, Herr Castello has had the courage to return and to start afresh. A very learned and admirable man! As you might expect, his prices are high, but he only deals in top quality, and you may be sure that anything you buy from him has been acquired legitimately – not looted, you know. I have never heard that he has sold a fake.' Dr Traumüller seemed immensely proud of the fact that Herr Castello had decided to come back and that his return had been welcomed. He perhaps over-stressed his high opinion of him because he was a Jew. He seemed to want to impress upon Kanakis that he himself and people like him were not and never had been anti-Semitic, that the horrors of the past few years were buried and forgotten on both sides: that Austrians on the whole had had nothing to do with them.

Kanakis smiled at so much disingenuousness. The issue did not touch him personally and in fact he was more interested in Castello's artistic integrity than in his commercial practices. After all, you could only build up a profitable business if you bought, as cheaply as you could, what people desired to sell, and what other people, with newly-acquired wealth, would want to buy. Kanakis could see nothing reprehensible in that.

For a little while he stood looking into the shop's one window. Through the soft translucency of old glass – no glare of bright plate-glass here – he saw the painted wooden effigy of a St Florian, the patron saint who protected houses and barns from fire, holding a house crowned with pointed yellow flames in one hand and a pitcher in the other. A piece of crimson brocade and a few folds of velvet hid the interior of the shop and set off the silver-grey gleam of a pewter jug and bowl which were the only other articles on display. Kanakis paid tribute in his mind to their sobriety, but he had no predilection for mediaeval or Renaissance art and crafts, his taste being entirely for the baroque and rococo. The shop was empty when he entered, nor was there anything to be seen there except a carved oak chest, an oak table and chairs, and a pair of tall eighteenth century pewter candlesticks. These immediately attracted his attention.

A bell had announced his arrival, and in a few moments a small grey-haired man, his head sunk rather low between his broad shoulders, giving him a slightly deformed appearance, came in from the back through a door concealed by the turn of a winding staircase. Kanakis mentioned Traumüller's name and then murmured his own, which Mr Castello was nonetheless quick to catch.

'Certainly, certainly,' the old man murmured in his turn, and together the two of them looked at the candlesticks, as if in them lay the power to reveal something of each other's purpose and intentions. 'From the church of St Severin,' Castello added in a barely audible whisper; 'there are not many like them on the market these days.' Meanwhile, he assessed Kanakis, wondering whether he was the son of old Kanakis whom he had slightly known in the old days, and whether there was anything the son wanted to sell.

But before either of them had decided whether to become more articulate, the sound of quick, light footsteps was heard on the winding staircase, and the figure of a young man appeared in the bend.

If there is such a thing as what is called in French a *coup de foudre*, an overwhelming emotional experience which originates entirely in the eyes, when what is seen carries the conviction of a revelation which no subsequent qualification or critical appraisal can refute or corrode, then this unexpected, and, for him, unprecedented experience happened to Kanakis in the moment in which the apparition of the young man on the stairs impinged on his senses. He had the porcelain figurine of a shepherdess in his hand. It was so exquisitely delicate that Kanakis felt himself catching his breath at the unconcerned manner in which the boy clasped its priceless fragility. Matters were made worse by his taking the last two steps at a leap.

'No, Mario,' he said, addressing the old man with a certain impudence by his first name. 'I'm not leaving her. I've thought it over. The price you offer is ridiculous. I'm not all that hard up. I'll see you another time.' He made for the door, and had almost reached it when he was stopped by an exclamation from Kanakis.

'Please, please, please don't go! I – I would like –' It was a weird sound, almost a shriek. Castello looked at him in surprise and the young man stopped and turned towards him. 'Yes?' he said enquiringly, while Kanakis worked his throat to regain control of his voice.

Castello instantly came to the rescue. He had already decided that Kanakis was a buyer, not a seller. 'I believe, Prince,' he said quietly, 'that Herr von Kanakis has taken a fancy to your shepherdess.'

'Indeed, yes indeed, the shepherdess,' Kanakis said, speaking now with the slow deliberation which was his habitual mode of utterance. 'Would you kindly put her down here on the table, it'll be safer. I hope you did not intend to carry her through the streets, unprotected, in your hand! It gave me quite a shock to see you.'

The boy came back and stood the figurine on the table with such controlled gentleness as entirely belied the seemingly reckless nature of his grasp. 'With pleasure,' he said, and his face lit up with a smile which again made Kanakis catch his breath.

Mario Castello understood what had happened. 'I think I ought to introduce you to each other,' he said. 'Prince Lorenzo Grein-Lauterbach – Herr von Kanakis. I'm afraid my youthful friend here is too young to have any recollection of our distinguished Greek community and the part it played in the world of finance and patronage of the arts. But you, Herr von Kanakis, are undoubtedly familiar with the name of the Princes Grein-Lauterbach. What you probably do not know, since you were not here at the time, is that, tragically, my young friend's parents were among the first victims of the Gestapo when we were invaded in '38. That he and I have both survived – in our different ways – constitutes a certain bond between us, however unlikely such a connection may seem at first sight.'

Castello went on talking, though he realised – and because he realised – that Kanakis was not listening. His head was bent over the shepherdess, whom he seemed to be studying attentively, but every so often his eyes slanted upwards to the boy who stood at ease before him, totally unembarrassed either by Kanakis's gaze or Castello's references to his person or family. He was a slight young man, rather under medium height, but so perfectly proportioned as to suggest that anyone taller or broader must inevitably be clumsy. His enchanting face was the exact replica, come to life, of the head of a young faun sculpted in the honey-coloured marble of a Greek statuette. All the outline was there, the small straight nose, the adorable mouth, the rounded chin – but all of it miraculously alive, the dark eyes sparkling, the mouth smiling a mischievous faunish smile; and the dark wavy hair, fitting close to the small head, made one involuntarily suspect that above the temples it was concealing two tiny horns which would have completed the picture.

As Kanakis started to discuss the shepherdess's merits, Castello suggested that they adjourn with the figurine to his inner sanctum, where they would not be disturbed by any chance customer entering the shop, and there they examined in detail the qualities of the paste and the glaze and decided which year and where she was made. Kanakis even tried to guess the name of the artist who had modelled her, and he and Castello gained each other's respect for their connoisseurship, while young Grein stood by, laughingly admitting his total ignorance of the subject. But he did know that luckily there was a second figure, a shepherd, to complete the pair, and if he proved to be in as perfect a condition as his lady, Kanakis was prepared to buy them for a substantial price. A meeting was therefore arranged between the three of them *and* the shepherd in Castello's shop on the following day.

Kanakis was pleased with his prospective purchase

which, with American values in mind, he considered a bargain. But bargain or no bargain, he would have paid almost any price for the chance of seeing that boy again. Meanwhile, he would have twenty-four hours in which to turn over in his mind the best way to continue the acquaintanceship. He now knew why he had come back to Vienna, and felt gratitude to the inspiration – from wherever it came – that had prompted him to do so. This was more, far more, than he had consciously had in mind. He had dreamed of a certain house, which Traumüller had since actually discovered for him and which was now in the process of being rebuilt; and he had anticipated attracting a pleasant circle of acquaintances – on different levels – by the power of his money and the kind of entertainment he would be able to offer them. He remembered his father saying that, if you had that kind of ambition, with sufficient perseverance and the necessary cash you could buy yourself into the most exclusive social circles. Yet that was not what Kanakis wanted. He was not a snob, but something far more exceptional, far more discriminating: he was a connoisseur: a connoisseur of material and workmanship in human beings as well as in artefacts. He detested cheapness and the common repetitive stamp of mass-production in people as well as in things, and while he was intensely perceptive and appreciative of people's aesthetic and intellectual qualities, he was quite indifferent to what might be called their morality, and supremely so to the position they claimed for themselves, or that was attributed to them, in society.

Now this unexpected meeting with Lorenzo Grein had,

as it were, fused all his vague expectations of an enjoyable life in Vienna into a new sense of fulfilment. One does not anticipate a *coup de foudre*, but Kanakis knew that it had happened and that it was irrevocable. However, it did not make him lose his head. Circumspection was called for. He must find out more about the boy. It was a pity, he thought at first, that he was a prince, bearing a historic name. But then he told himself: would he be what he was if he had not had such generations of breeding behind him?

Kanakis remained sitting with the antique dealer after Grein had left, and with every appearance of desultory curiosity questioned him about the young man and his history. 'I don't really know the exact details of what happened,' Castello explained, 'because I was fortunately not in Vienna at the time. Business had taken me to France, and though my instinct was to return at once to wind up my affairs, my friends in Paris were wiser than I was and insisted so vehemently that I mustn't go back that I gave in, very reluctantly I admit. I would have gone in spite of all warnings if my wife had not been with me, and that would have been the end of both of us. But she was wiser than I was, and braver – ready to face a beggarly existence in exile: in brief, I was not here, and therefore have survived.

'But the first wave of arrests carried out by the Gestapo included a few of the most prominent and most wealthy Jews and they were held for ransom rather than for political reasons. It was aimed at the Nazis' political opponents, all those who might have formed the core of an active opposition in the country, who were known to be hostile and whose hostility carried weight. Prominent among these were the Prince and Princess Grein-Lauterbach. She was born an Italian princess whose family, too, was anti-Fascist. They were arrested in their beds the first night and, as far as I know, were never heard of again. The two children, a very small boy and a girl, ten or twelve years older than he, were smuggled out of the palace by the family chaplain, a Jesuit priest who also went into hiding, and a devoted old maid. Where they spent the war years I don't know, but I understand that the girl, who was barely grown up, went out to work in some menial job in a laboratory – for she had no qualifications – in order to earn her keep. 'Bimbo' – his mother's pet name for him, and his friends still call him that – was brought up by Father Jahoda and this sister who mothered him. He is still rather in awe of her, by the way he talks, but has long since escaped her authority. I have never met her.

'His fortune? It was confiscated, and very little of it has been recovered. He is practically penniless. There is a huge old rambling castle in Lower Austria which has been restored to him and his sister, the habitable parts swarming with homeless families who have been housed there by some authority or who have simply settled there themselves. They only pay nominal rents, a fraction of what is needed even for running repairs, so he tells me, and the great ornate state-rooms have been ruined by neglect. It's a thousand pities! I believe his one aim in life is to retrieve it, and the only means of doing so is a rich marriage, a *very* rich marriage. Meanwhile, what does he do for a living? Anything he can pick up –

a commission on selling an old piece of furniture or a bibelot, acting as a guide to rich tourists who are beginning to come into the country, seeking out customers for a wine merchant – anything that doesn't involve too much work! After all, he has two very valuable assets: his title and his charm.'

# Eight

'Poldo, I've had a letter from Valery, a very long letter, about her eldest, Marie-Theres.'

And the Countess Lensveldt picked up several sheets of slightly crumpled, thin airmail paper and tried to hand them across the table to her husband, who had just finished peeling an apple at the end of his luncheon. The scene was the dining room in the Lensveldts' castle of Wald in Upper Austria.

'Marie-Theres seems to be a difficult girl,' the Countess continued, 'a *problem* girl is what Valery calls her on one page, on the next she says that she is absolutely normal and very sweet-natured. That is meant to reassure us. I can't make head or tail of what she means. Will you read the letter?'

'Certainly not,' the Count replied, 'you know I don't like

reading complicated letters, and I can't read Valery's hand-writing.' The Countess put the sheets down next to her plate with a sigh. 'Not that she has treated us to much of it,' the Count continued, 'as she might have done since postal communications have been re-established.'

'Valery has always been out of touch with us,' the Countess said thoughtfully.

'Well, what does she say now? What does she want? I suppose she wants something, or she wouldn't have written. And why do you say we need reassurance?'

'Yes, the gist of it is that she wants to send Marie-Theres over here and she asks whether we would have her here at Wald – for a few months.'

'For a few months! A difficult child! For you to cope with!' the Count exploded.

'Well, Valery says the difficulty does not lie so much in the girl herself, but that American life does not seem to suit her. She thinks a change of surroundings and *our* way of living here in the country would do her a great deal of good.'

'Oh, she does, does she! But she doesn't suggest coming over herself, after all these years, to see us, to see you and Fini. That would have been normal. But she always was eccentric, marrying a total stranger, going off to America with him, and now she's got a problem daughter. I suppose the girl has got herself into a scrape with some young man. It can't just be "surroundings".'

'Well, there does seem to be a boy in the background, but he's not involved in the way you would think. I shall have to write and try to find out what all this is about. What she says is very confusing, for instance that Marie-Theres doesn't like boys, and that her schoolteacher thinks that's unnatural and has made Peter very angry by saying so. Anyway, here are some pictures of her.'

Count Lensveldt looked at the photos one after the other and then looked more closely. 'She seems to be very pretty. How old is she?'

'Let me see, she was, I think, two years old when Valery and Peter went to America. She must be about eighteen.'

The Count was studying the snapshots. They were in colour, a development which was not yet in use in Austria. 'She's certainly extremely pretty, more than pretty – beautiful. I can imagine all kinds of complications with those looks.'

The Countess smiled. 'So you would agree to have her? By the way, Valery says that Peter will pay for her keep.'

'Will he indeed! She's your *niece*. We're not paupers yet. When we have to take paying guests, we'll have paying *guests*, not family. They must just let her have pocket money. Tell your sister *that*.' The Count picked up the photographs and put them in his pocket.

As the Countess Lensveldt sat down to write to Valery, she thought about her sister's strange marriage and the circumstances leading up to it. For it had not been predictable that Valery Altmannsdorf and Peter Larsen would get married, but the very unlikelihood of their meeting confirmed Valery in her unshakeable conviction that she had been meant to marry Peter. This was a source of great strength to her and coloured her whole outlook on life, which was positive and unquestioning, but it also closed her mind to the doubts and difficulties of others. She had no time and no sympathy for other people's misgivings and uncertainties, which she was inclined to regard as nonsense, and that estranged her especially – and unhappily – from her eldest daughter.

Valery Larsen was the youngest of three sisters – Francisca who was writing to her was the middle one – who were the daughters of the late Prince Altmannsdorf. He had once owned vast estates in Bohemia, but he had never lived in any of his different castles, except during the shooting season, as he much preferred town life in the Palais Altmannsdorf in Vienna. He had left the administration of his estates to a cousin, who might have expected to become his heir since he himself had no son; the only positive interest he had taken in what he owned was in his forests and his game. Among his employees, he only knew his gamekeepers, and his head forester, whom he valued and trusted, was the only one with whom he had a personal relationship. Between seasons this man often came to Vienna to talk things over, bringing with him a smell of wood smoke and pipe tobacco even in his town clothes, and a sense of wind and open spaces on his weather-beaten, bearded face. 'Old Anreither' the young princesses called him; he was almost one of the family and they loved him.

When, in 1918, the Austrian Empire fell apart, the cousin was left to take on citizenship of the new state of Czechoslovakia and to wrestle with its decrees concerning the large estates within its borders, and Prince Altmannsdorf in Vienna was, for a while at least, cut off from the source of his revenues. Valery, his youngest child, was four years old at the time. Born during the war, she had from the start been a sickly baby, and the lack of adequate food during the last disastrous year had reduced her to such a featherweight scrap that her parents decided to swallow their pride and apply for her to be included in the parties of children which generous people in Holland and the Scandinavian countries were offering to receive into their homes to save them from starvation. Valery had been taken to Denmark and had spent two years with the family of a farmer, living with his numerous children. They had loved her and she had loved them and, young as they were, a very tender friendship had developed between her and a little boy of her own age. When at last she went home, strong and healthy and speaking nothing but Danish, little Jens pined to have her back again in the summer holidays. She had been so happy and the Altmannsdorfs were so grateful that they could not refuse to send her. Gradually it came to be accepted by both families that Valery would spend a couple of months with the Larsens every other year during her childhood and adolescence, while Jens or one of his sisters occasionally came to Vienna.

Then suddenly, as such things happen, Peter, the eldest of the Larsen sons, fell in love with her and she with him. He was an exceptionally brilliant young man who had taken a first-class degree in chemistry in Berlin and had come on to do postgraduate work in Vienna under a well-known professor. The two of them became engaged, but as he refused to convert to Catholicism, being as firmly wedded to his agnostic views as any devoutly religious man to the tenets of his faith, they were, after a great deal of bitterness, eventually married from Peter's home in Denmark, at the local town hall, and received their matrimonial blessing in the adjacent Lutheran church. Valery insisted on this ceremony, feeling, rather inconsistently, that a heretical ceremony was better than none at all or, perhaps, that unless she had been inside some kind of church she would not be properly married. Her mother and sisters did not attend the wedding. Her father had died and her mother refused to recognise the marriage, until the prospect of Valery's emigration to America, and her own failing health, made her fear that she might not see her secretly most beloved daughter again.

For Peter Larsen's years of study in Germany, which coincided with the rise of Hitler's party and his coming to power, had convinced him that a major war in Europe was becoming unavoidable. In the mid-thirties he started making enquiries in the United States, and having been offered, on the strength of the papers he had published in scientific journals, a research post in one of the major chemical companies, he decided to take his wife and small daughter across the Atlantic. However, before leaving Europe, Valery went to Vienna for a month to see her mother and sisters and to show them her little girl, whom she had christened Marie-Theres. It was her mother's name. She had chosen it as a token of love for her, as a gesture of asking forgiveness, of a hope of reconciliation. As such, the old Princess had accepted it and had once again received her errant daughter into her heart and home. But to Valery herself the name had meant more than filial piety. It embodied everything she wished to remember of the old Austria, of her country's and her family's greatness, as a tiny phial of concentrated scent may preserve and penetrate for years to come alien fabrics and alien habitations with the faint but unmistakable memory of its odour.

Yet those last weeks in Vienna had been far from happy. They had been full of discordant thoughts and emotions, heightened by a sense of finality, with the accent alternating between escape and regret. Escape, however, predominated. Valery was already estranged from the views and opinions of her relations and former friends. She no longer had any desire to live amongst them. Her life with Peter had changed her. She saw them now as he saw them, as narrow-minded and blind to the realities of the world. It was all she could do to keep her temper when her sisters and their husbands ridiculed the 'panic' which had seized Peter Larsen and impelled him to 'take refuge' in America. They shrugged off the notion that Nazism would spread to Austria, and some of their friends even thought that it would not be such a bad thing if it did, so little did they understand its sinister implications. Nor did any of them believe in the danger of war. They were quite out of sympathy with the apocalyptic vision, as they called it, which she had acquired from Peter, and they teased her for going around, as they said, in a mood of gloom and foreboding, looking at everything as if she were seeing it for the last time. Only the certainty that she was going away with Peter, that wherever he and she were together all would be well with her, prevented the outbreak of another and final quarrel to spoil the underlying tenderness of leave-taking.

The leave-taking she did indulge in, and indulged in all the more consciously because she was already determinedly looking forward to her new life, was the parting from places rather than from people. As the last days before her departure went by, gathering speed as the final moment approached, she endeavoured to avoid the repetition of discussions which only tended to become acrimonious, and equally the effusions of emotion which were losing their sincerity and beginning to cloy. Instead she went out for walks with Marie-Theres, spending her afternoons in the gardens and parks where she herself had been taken as a child, only wishing that her little girl were old enough to glean some impressions to remember. It was here that Valery said goodbye to Vienna before turning her face resolutely to the New World.

In America, both Peter and Valery Larsen were almost immediately a complete success, because they were both absolutely single-minded. Peter was single-minded about his work, which dominated all his thoughts, and Valery was single-minded about her husband, who dominated all her emotions. The rock of their marriage was so secure that the problems which bedevilled other people's lives seemed to her extraneous and insignificant. Peter's career progressed rapidly. He was a man of brilliant gifts, wholly dedicated to his work; in a very few years he was head of the research department of his firm and was offered a visiting lectureship at the Massachusetts Institute of Technology. Valery had from the first embraced American life wholeheartedly and with zest. In the beginning they had moved with their few possessions from house to house and from district to district, until Peter's increased income had led to their settling in a ranch-style house in Eden Rise.

Valery had taken it all in her stride – the moves, the initial hardships, the readjustments – with a mixture of curiosity and amusement, hardly realising that all her surroundings, both people and places, were to her so interchangeable that they scarcely impinged on the core of her life – the happiness of her marriage. Everything to her was easy because of Peter. His presence, his voice, his touch, were the substance of her existence and even later, when they were already living in Eden Rise and he sometimes had to be away from home for days, he was still there, even in his absence, and he was always and unshakeably hers. Marie-Theres came through those first financially-restricted years as a small child always alone with her mother, in her arms or by her side, almost physically part of her. And to her, when Peter was not at home, Valery talked all day in her native German, while Peter and she spoke mostly Danish to each other; until, imperceptibly, the language of their host country took over.

As soon as they were more settled, Carl and then Anna were born. Marie-Theres was no longer an only child. Valery coped with her babies and with her housekeeping by trial and error and with her healthy, uncomplicated common sense. She managed with washing machines and dishwash-

ers instead of with cooks and housemaids, she learned to
drive a car, to shop at the supermarket. She exchanged small
talk with the other wives and mothers and was liked by all
of them because she was friendly, cheerful and completely
unpretentious. Social ambitions in the context of American
society were meaningless to her. When Peter occasionally
brought home a member of his team, and these men were
accompanied by their wives, Valery was equally pleasant to
them all.

Peter sometimes marvelled at how unaware she was of
anything that could be described as 'social position' or 'status', and he gave her credit for a broader idealism and liberal-
ity of outlook which she did not really quite deserve; for to
her, née Princess Altmannsdorf, there did not seem much to
choose between anyone she met in America except as mea-
sured in terms of money, and that was a scale that had no
meaning for her other than that of convenience. She found
that when they moved to a 'better' district and a more spacious house, which they did as soon as they could manage
it financially, and bought a second car so that she could be
more independent, then one lost sight of one's former
'friends' and made new ones. It just happened that way. One
tended to associate with people who shared the same living
standards, lived in the same kind of house, ran the same
kind of car. Anything else would have been awkward. As a
child and young girl Valery had witnessed various vicissi-
tudes in her family's fortunes. They had been exceedingly
rich, then, when she was quite little, very poor. That was

why she had been sent to Denmark. Later, things had recovered, though the great castles and estates had never been regained.

But all these changes had made no difference to the fact that she was a Princess, that she had her sixteen quarterings – sixteen ancestors of noble birth. Social superiors did not exist for her. This certainty was so ingrained in her that she was quite unconscious of it and she would have been astonished if anyone had told her that this was the reason why everybody else, whatever their background, seemed to be on the same level. That was also the reason why she unhesitatingly conformed in outward appearance to the standards of dress, make-up and vocabulary of the women with whom she associated in daily life. She was so sure of herself, so utterly without a doubt as to who she was and always would be, under whatever circumstances, that she was only anxious to conform, to look and seem like everybody else, thus avoiding all questioning and curiosity about herself which she would have felt to be embarrassing and – it must be admitted – impertinent. Even her husband, who admired and loved her ease and affability, her total lack of self-assertiveness, had not penetrated the deepest truth – that this very conduct and behaviour on the part of his wife expressed the most subtle and exquisite form of pride.

Yet Marie-Theres did not see her mother in that light. To her she just seemed smug and self-satisfied and at one with the glossy, enamelled surface of suburban life which she herself found both exhausting and boring: exhausting because she was expected to be always on the go, always doing something, going somewhere, taking part in something else, never at rest, and this put a strain on her vitality which, albeit unconsciously, she needed for her inward growth, her silent struggle to come to terms with herself. And all this activity was so boring, pointless and repetitive, it felt at times to be almost too burdensome to bear. But how to talk to her mother about it? Her mother enjoyed this kind of life, she would not understand. Inarticulate as she was, how could she find words to confide in a mother who would not have the faintest idea of what she would be trying to say? Alas, those early days of intimacy, when Marie-Theres was a baby and Valery had been feeling her way into a new life, had long gone. Then, Valery had done all the talking, communing with herself rather than with the small child who had been but a passively listening companion. Now Valery had made her life and enjoyed it and Marie-Theres was on her own – wondering how to make hers.

Eden Rise, where they lived, was one of the new suburbs carefully planned to suit the lifestyle of people such as themselves. What Valery and Marie-Theres looked out upon from their adjoining bedrooms in the morning meant to the mother achievement and security, to the daughter monotony and oppression. What they saw was a carefully groomed strip of garden consisting of lawn and low shrubs that merged in a curve into other similar bands of grass and shrubs. Cement footpaths and driveways leading to garages formed a repetitive pattern between the road and the fronts of the houses. Across the road a similar fringe of gardens and the same ranch-type houses, brightly painted wood over concrete foundations, each with its wide plate-glass window on the ground floor, exposing the depths of its living space to the light of the skies and the gaze of neighbours and passers-by alike. One end of the road curved downwards to rows of more closely-clustered houses at the foot of the rise, the less expensive ones, of course. The other climbed upward, divided and looped round the summit. There were trees up there, visible over the roof-tops, the gardens were larger, the houses newer and more spacious and more secluded. Some had swimming pools. The Larsens would move up there one day.

Marie-Theres foresaw that her own life would conform to the same pattern. If she married Budd Gresham they would start by living in a small house at the bottom of the hill, and then they would move up – halfway as her parents were living now – and at last, perhaps, to the top. *If* she married Budd Gresham. *If* she married him. Budd was nice, she was very fond of him. But she didn't want to marry him – though she probably would. What else was there to do? However, he had now left school and gone away to college and Marie-Theres was on her own.

And it was at this point that Valery became aware of her daughter as a problem. Marie-Theres had been lazy and dreamy since she had begun to grow up, although that was nothing remarkable in a fast-growing child. But now she was sullen, listless and, Valery felt, sometimes positively hostile to her. She refused to take an interest in anything. Valery had not noticed it so much while Budd was around. He had always called for her and taken her out to picnics, to dances, to watch a game. Now that he was gone, it appeared that she had no other friends, she belonged to no clubs, took part in no sports, refused the invitations of other boys, and declared all the usual activities of her contemporaries to be boring. After school hours or at weekends she just sat around or lay on her bed with a book or listened to a record picked up at random, while she seemed to be asleep with her eyes open and no one knew what went on in her mind.

Valery was sure that she was not pining for Budd, that she was not in love with him. That she would have understood. Valery knew what love was. What she did not understand, and what irritated her almost beyond endurance, was this indifference, this deadness in a girl so young and so lovely, with every kind of amusement and opportunity within her reach – as she pointed out to her again and again – only to be met with a blank expression and a shrug or sigh. It was becoming a burden on Valery's own life. It was difficult to go out and play golf or bridge, to go to a club meeting or to a film with a friend, all things she looked forward to, if she knew that Marie-Theres, who ought to be enjoying life as much as she did, or at least to be doing something interesting or useful, was moping alone in her room. Sometimes she tried taking her with her, to the golf club, to a lecture or the cinema, but of course Marie-Theres did not fit in with the people in her own set, who belonged to an older generation, and it soon became clear to her that the presence of a girl tagging along with her mother was both incongruous and a nuisance. Besides, Marie-Theres's obvious reluctance and bored expression on such occasions was enough to destroy all the pleasure she herself would have experienced.

In fact, Marie-Theres's silent disapproval – if it was disapproval – was making Valery's social life impossible. Carl and Anna were no problem. They always had something to do, friends to be with, at home, or at friends' houses, or at holiday camps. They were children like everyone else's children. But Marie-Theres? Valery had tried to talk to Peter about her, but here, in her turn, she had met with total incomprehension. What fault could she find in Marie-Theres? She did not get involved in undesirable company, she did not stay out late, her boyfriend was the nicest possible boy, a very promising young man. Well, yes, he was away at college just now, but he would come back in the vacation, they wrote to each other, didn't they, or rather he wrote to her, and she didn't pick up with anyone else in his absence. Was she to blame for that? Besides, Valery soon felt that it would be unwise to complain about Marie-Theres to Peter, for he was almost infatuated with his beautiful daughter.

Thus Marie-Theres was the one person who might conceivably come between them, and on no account must Valery allow even a hint of disagreement about their daughter to interfere with her perfect relationship with Peter. He was such a single-minded man, so 'innocent' she called it in spite of his cleverness; he was so totally absorbed in his work, and took his domestic life so much for granted, that only a major crisis would justify her in disturbing his peace of mind – not these rather intangible perplexities, which she found diffi-

cult to put into words and which she sometimes thought
might be all in her imagination. So she dropped the subject
almost before she had broached it. Perhaps there was nothing unusual in Marie-Theres's behaviour, perhaps she was
just going through a 'phase' in her adolescence and she would
grow out of it, and perhaps she, Valery, *was* making a problem out of what was only an inconvenience. But then a crisis
arose where she had least expected it and in a shape she had
not foreseen: Miss Bates, Marie-Theres's form mistress, came
and spoke to her.

Miss Bates was rather a formidable woman and a highly
competent schoolteacher. About the same age as Valery, there
could be no greater contrast than between the two women.
She was everything that Valery was not: professional where
Valery was amateur, disciplined where Valery was easy-
going, with a sense of her own superiority based consciously
on education and achievement, while Valery's was unconscious and inbred. Valery admired her enormously for being
so essentially American and 'modern', while Miss Bates
thought herself entitled to look down a little on Mrs Larsen
who, she knew, was a 'princess' and must therefore be rather
degenerate and lacking in moral fibre. The contrast did not
make communication between the two women easy, and
Valery had often reproached herself for not taking sufficient
interest in Marie-Theres's schoolwork and not keeping in
closer touch with her teacher. But now she felt that the one
person she could and should speak to about her daughter
was Miss Bates.

However, she forestalled her. This is where Valery took

up the tale in a long rambling letter to her sister, the letter which the Countess Lensveldt had before her as she was writing her reply. Miss Bates, it seems, had come to see Valery to talk about Marie-Theres. She had expected to hear complaints about the girl's schoolwork and she thought they would probably be quite justified. But Miss Bates had taken quite a different line. She had started by saying that she had taken a fancy to Theresa (as she called her), that Theresa had attracted her special attention because – well, because of her looks. In a room full of growing girls, dark or fair, fat or angular, round-faced or freckled, all nice enough but none particularly distinguished, Theresa stood out like a work of art. She seemed to belong to a different race.

And the more closely Miss Bates observed her, the more set apart she appeared in more ways than just in looks. She did not mix with the others, she did not conform, and by the studied politeness in her manners she seemed to surround herself with a kind of vacuum which she allowed no one to penetrate. All, of course, except young Gresham, but there again their relationship had been different from a normal boy-and-girl friendship. Gresham had seemed to worship her in a romantic, subservient sort of way, hardly daring to touch her. Miss Bates had said she thought he had never even given her a kiss and this she found disconcerting. There was something wrong there. It also impinged on the girl's work, which was not as good as it ought to be, for Theresa was far from stupid. Well, wrote Valery, now came the bombshell. Marie-Theres was suffering from a 'blockage' – Miss Bates's expression – and she should see a psychiatrist: Miss

Bates was prepared to recommend one who would go into Marie-Theres's difficulties and help her to become 'normal'. Valery said that she had never been so taken aback in her life. Although she had heard plenty of talk about psychiatrists since she had been in America, it had never crossed her mind that anyone from her own family might have anything to do with one. Nobody amongst *their* relations had been mad.

Valery had almost laughed at Miss Bates, but fortunately had been able to control herself in time, for the poor woman would have been mortally offended, she was so serious. However, when she told Peter about it, he didn't laugh but became very angry. She had never seen him so angry, he had marched up and down the room and stormed at her, as he did now and again when he had to let off steam. Of course she knew that he was not raving at her but at whoever it was who had given him cause for anger, in this case Miss Bates, and she was only acting as a lightning conductor who happened to be present to take the charge. But when the storm had settled and she and Peter had talked the matter over quietly, they had decided that when Marie-Theres left school at the end of term she should not go to college, where there might again be threats of psychiatrists, but should have a complete change of surroundings. Therefore – and the letter reverted to the opening request – would they have Marie-Theres at Wald?

# Nine

Wald, Upper Austria
20<sup>th</sup> June 195–

My dear Valery,

Your girl has now been with us for three weeks and I'm sure you will be anxious to hear how she is settling down and what our impressions are of her, now that we have got to know her a little better. So far I've only dashed off those few lines to you the day after she arrived, telling you that we were all rather taken aback by her appearance. We were not prepared for anyone quite so lovely and quite so smart. As I said, it gave me and the girls rather a fright, we wondered whether we should be able to cope with her, whether she was not going to be even more discontented here than you say she was at home, seeing what a simple life we lead.

I must go back to those first impressions in order to explain how mistaken we were in our conclusions and how very different Resi is from what she at first appeared. By the way, we call her Resi, though she asked at first to be called Marie-Theres, but we find that too much of a mouthful so I suggested Resi which is what, as you know, most Thereses are called in Austria, and she accepted this with perfectly good grace.

Well, you know, my girls are really very good-looking, though Helen, since her tragic loss, is not quite as fresh as she used to be, and that grieves me a lot. But our family have always been blessed with strong, healthy figures and pleasant faces, bright eyes, clear complexions and thick hair. Hanni has them all. But it must be your Peter who gave her her elongated figure, so straight and narrow, almost too tall for a girl, that delicate nose and mouth, and those extraordinary pencilled eyebrows, which give her, more than anything else I think, such a look of a Florentine Madonna. Naturally her clothes, too, distinguished her from anybody we had seen in this part of the world for many years; the girls had never seen anything like them, what with the war and, worse still, these post-war years, when there wasn't a stitch to be had and not much money to buy anything anyway. And those sheer nylons, and those long slender legs to show them off! Next to such elegance, the girls looked like country bumpkins and felt like it too on the station platform. I saw it all at a glance. There was a dreadful moment of silence, Resi standing there very stiffly and superior-looking and in reality terribly shy, and then Hanni, who is the most good-natured and spontaneous girl in the world, laughed and embraced her cousin, then Helen did so too, and I kissed her and we all drove away. But Poldo – you should have seen Poldo, how his eyes popped out the moment he caught sight of her, he simply gobbled her up, old sinner that he is. And I can't help chuckling to myself when I see how he still melts each time she comes into the room. But does Resi notice? Not she, she doesn't even treat him like a grandfather (he wouldn't mind that if she put a little playful tenderness into it) but like a grandfather clock, like a venerable piece of furniture, something that isn't really alive. Poor Poldo, and he's so delighted to have such a pretty niece about the house.

And Resi herself? As far as I can judge she is perfectly happy. I can't quite make her out yet for she is very reserved, but she makes herself pleasant and is no trouble to anybody. Hanni really likes her and intends to draw her out, little by little, to find out what goes on inside her head. I have urged her to write you a little more than the occasional postcard she has been sending, and she has promised to do so.

So at last, after several gentle promptings, Marie-Theres delivered herself of the following:

Upper Austria
Schloss Wald

Dear Mama and Papa,

I have written to you twice already to say I had a good trip and that the country is very beautiful and that the family are nice to me. But you say I should tell you more, particularly how I find the place and the people. Well, Mama, you know what it's like, though you were here a long time ago, so I shall describe it as best I can for Papa's sake, and for you in case you've forgotten some of it.

You said the house was a castle, and it's called Schloss, but I don't think it's at all like a castle. I thought a castle had towers, and a moat and draw-bridge, and a great big hall. Wald is simply a house. It's true it's very big and full of long corridors, but it's not high, only one storey, except for the attics, and there is just one tower, a square stumpy one with nothing but a clock in it just under the roof. The house is built round two courtyards, where there are big flat stones with grass growing between them; some of the upstairs rooms look out onto it and have balconies. The downstairs rooms are on three sides, and on the fourth there are large doors with store-rooms behind them. Aunt Franzi says they used to be stables for horses, and a place for harnesses and horse-carriages, but now there are no horses and only two broken-down carriages. I like to go and explore there because there are all kinds of things, such as stone figures with no heads or with heads and no arms. The living rooms downstairs are rather dark because the walls are terribly thick and because of the trees outside. The windowsills are so deep you can sit in them with your legs drawn up, like on a table. I sit there sometimes – they are like hiding places, you can see and not be seen. From upstairs there's a lovely view, especially from Aunt Franzi's bedroom. You can look over the treetops down the hill and there's the lake and the steep rocky mountains over on the other side of it. You can't see the road along the lake, or the village under the hill, but you *can* see a loop of the road going up to the house, so you can see if anyone is coming.

My room is very nice though it doesn't have a view. At first I was sorry but now I think I like it better that way. It's upstairs along a stone passage and it looks out onto the small courtyard which has a tree in it and the stone basin of a fountain that doesn't work. The sun shines in at the window in the morning and I can hear the birds singing. There isn't a shower in the house, but there's a bathroom along the passage with a tin bath painted white, although the water for it has to be heated in a kind of stove by lighting a wood fire underneath, so it's quite a job to have a bath and we have to take it in turns. Uncle Poldo says that when the new electricity plant is

built in the mountains he will have some real bathrooms put in, but then he also says he won't have
enough money for them anyhow and Aunt Franzi
says she doesn't mind, she's so used to this and they
may as well go on as they are.

I like Aunt Franzi best of all the people here. She's
easy and kind and, well – I suppose I should say moth-
erly. Her hair is quite white, she doesn't look at all like
you and I think she must be a lot older, not just a few
years like you said. Helen is rather prim and old-
maidish, well of course she's thirty, but Hanni is very
jolly. She talks to me a lot and treats me like a real
friend, though she's twenty-two already. We go swimming together in the lake. Helen has a job in a sawmill a
few miles away where, I think, she keeps accounts and
writes letters, so she's out most of the day and when
she's at home she does all Uncle Poldo's letters for him.
Uncle Poldo doesn't seem to do *anything*. Hanni had a
job in Vienna but she's given it up and is spending the
summer here. Then in the fall she's going back there
and will look for another job. In Vienna she lives with
our Aunt Josephine, or Fini as she calls her. I'm to go
there for the winter too. Aunt Franzi's son, Franzl,
hasn't come yet, so I don't know him. I don't like Uncle
Poldo much. He makes silly jokes and laughs at them
himself but I don't think they're funny at all.

Lots of love to you both and Carl and Anna. I hope
you think I've written enough now but I'll finish by

saying that I'm very glad I've come here, and you needn't worry about me, ever, any more. What's so nice here is that people are not in a hurry. Love again,

Marie-Theres.

Valery read both these letters with immense relief, and as for Peter they also gave him a good deal of satisfaction. Valery felt that a burden had been lifted off her shoulders: her sister had accepted Marie-Theres and found her 'no trouble', and Marie-Theres seemed to like her aunt very much. Altogether she seemed to like a great deal there, while at home she had never liked anything at all. For a few minutes Valery thought over that strange last sentence at the end of the girl's letter, about people not being in a hurry. It gave her an inkling that Marie-Theres had been temperamentally out of tune with the busy atmosphere she herself found so exhilarating. To her mind, the girl had been simply and offensively lazy, but at Wald nobody was finding fault with her on that account and possibly they did not even notice it. Therefore, mercifully, all was well and, as Marie-Theres wrote, her mother need not worry about her any more. She overlooked the insignificant little word 'ever'. Peter said that both letters were delightful and where was Miss Bates and her psychiatrist now, he would like to know! But he told Valery not to show her Marie-Theres's letter.

# Ten

That year there was a wonderful June in the lake and mountain country around Schloss Wald. Day after day the sun shone in a cloudless sky, night after night stars trembled clearly in the dark depths of the sky. Except for that one sustained effort of writing her long letter to her parents, Marie-Theres, or Resi as she was called at Wald, lived semi-unconsciously in a smooth alternating rhythm of waking and sleeping. She had never been so happy before. Like an insubstantial bubble, weightless and shimmering, she floated on the broad unruffled stream of life as it was lived at Wald.

How the hours passed she hardly knew. In the mornings she would lie in the grass where an angle of the castle wall made a square of shade for her head and her long bare legs were stretched out to the warm caress of the sun; lying with her eyes half-closed, she would watch the butterflies fluttering between the tall grasses, settling and spreading their wings on a patch of pink clover or balancing on the purple flower-head of a wild scabious. She loved this corner, but she had not mentioned it in her letter. Returning there again and again, it had begun to feel like her own, a safe and secret possession and refuge, hidden not by any visible fence or shelter but only by her own secret happiness.

Her Aunt Francisca was the only one who knew where she was, and seemed to understand what she felt about it without ever saying so. Then, later in the morning, 'Resi my child, where are you?' she would call, emerging from the wide shady archway in a faded blue linen dress with enormous pockets bulging with two pairs of secateurs, hanks of twine and other garden paraphernalia. 'Come out of your hiding place, lazybones, and help me cut the flowers for the house.'

'Yes, Aunt Franzi, I'm coming.' Resi would scramble to her feet, slip on her sandals and follow her aunt down the path towards the little wooden gate into the kitchen garden. The path ran through a meadow of long grasses and wild flowers, which only when it had been scythed looked, in colour at least if not in texture, like a lawn. Her aunt walked slowly, remarking as Resi caught up with her, that she must really persuade Amberger that it was time to cut this hay-field. Her voice was gentle with a warm, intimate inflexion in it.

Resi took the Countess's wicker basket from her arm and they went first to the flower garden. The flowers were not grown in borders for display and decoration around the house, but in a glorious jumble of shape and colour without plan or pattern, for cutting only. Here the Countess stood critically surveying her field of operation. There were the huge sunflowers and tall hollyhocks that would stand in the dark corners of the library; brilliant multi-coloured zinnias to fill a copper bowl on the hall table where the westering sun would catch them; and the more delicate petunias and stocks for the bedrooms. Sweet peas in pastel shades the Countess kept for her own boudoir, 'you see how selfish I am' she laughed, 'I keep the best for myself – what would you like for your room today, Resi? The marigolds you had last time must be faded by now. It's so nice to have flowers to look at while you're dressing, I always think. We'll give these pinks to Hanni, they're her favourites. Where *is* she, by the way? Have you seen her this morning?'

'Oh yes. I think she's driven out with Uncle Poldo. But she said she would go swimming with me this afternoon.'

'I hope you do go. The lake ought to be quite warm after the sun's been on it all morning.' And she added, 'I'm afraid it's very boring for you, poor child, with just us. But next month it will be different – more young people around.'

'Oh no, Aunt Franzi, I'm not bored, and I don't want anything to be different.' The Countess straightened up from her flower cutting and gave her niece a long questioning look. No, the child was not being polite, she was simply and sincerely stating a fact. 'I'm very happy,' she murmured, and, unaccountably, her eyes filled with tears.

The Countess felt moved, she patted the girl's arm, and bent again to finish cutting the flowers. Resi gathered them up and laid them carefully, stem by stem, in the wicker basket. But her enthusiasm for busying herself in the garden – her aunt's main interest and occupation – never lasted very long. When the Countess went over to the vegetables, where the lettuces, beans, peas, carrots and cabbages were laid out in orderly rectangles, Resi drifted off to inspect the strawberry beds and the currant bushes, all carefully netted and inaccessible to the casual pilferer. She knew her aunt would now spend a long time conferring with Amberger, the old gardener, who would be hoeing between the bean rows, or talking to one of the women stooped over their weeding, and she found the local dialect difficult to understand. She also had no inclination to exert herself and would pretend to be out of earshot if her aunt called her, teasingly, to suggest that she help with the spinach for lunch or do some other useful task. Instead she would seem intent on examining the little green plums on the plum trees, as hard as stones and as green as olives, which would take many more weeks to ripen into deep blue, luscious fruit. And the Countess would turn with a tolerant little laugh to the village woman she happened to be speaking to and say, 'the girl's not used to our kind of life. But give her time and she'll come round to it by and by.'

'Maybe they don't *have* gardens or vegetables in America, Frau Gräfin. I've heard that they eat everything out of tins there,' the woman answered.

Resi felt her aunt's occasional suggestions that she should do one thing or another were meant kindly but not seriously, and that it would not be taken amiss if she passed them by.

She loved watching her at her various comings and goings and enjoyed simply being near her. There was so much natural dignity, together with warmth and simplicity, in the older woman that it gave the girl a feeling of trust and security such as she had never known before. She liked everything about her aunt – the way she wore her hair, swept up smoothly from her temples and the nape of her neck and held in place by beautiful honey-coloured combs. She liked the clothes she wore, her faded gardening clothes as well as her formal dresses – rather old-fashioned, as she had hardly bought anything for years, and yet so elegant and becoming. And she simply loved her face, sunburnt and only faintly lined, innocent of all make-up, and kindly blue eyes, firm mouth and magnificent teeth that gleamed when she smiled. 'Of course they're my own, child! Do you think I'd wear false teeth? I'm not as decrepit as that, and I trust I never shall be!'

Inevitably Resi compared her aunt with her mother. She found it difficult to believe that they were sisters, although she did sometimes catch a resemblance in a tilt of the head or a movement of the hand and, quite startlingly, in an inflexion of the voice. Francisca Lensveldt was only six or seven years older than Valery Larsen, but in appearance and manner they might have been a generation apart. To Resi, her aunt at fifty seemed genuinely and comfortingly old, while her mother in her early forties was incongruously and artificially young. Only now, with her aunt for comparison, did Resi recognise that she disliked her mother's studied youthfulness, her slim figure achieved by severe dieting, her ultrafashionable clinging clothes, her plucked eyebrows. They went well, of course, with her restless activity, with her ceaseless pursuit of a host of 'futile occupations' – which was what Resi felt them to be. Aunt Franzi's figure was ample, her expression, though energetic and purposeful, was calm and her movements seemed to be a mixture of strength and repose. Resi never though *her* occupations 'futile'.

Her Uncle Poldo was rather less of a pleasure. He was stout, spoke in a loud voice and laughed a lot. That was harmless enough, and he certainly meant to be kind. Only sometimes she caught him looking at her in what she felt an embarrassing manner, difficult to describe. And then, every evening at 'good night time' there was a little ceremony in which he insisted on kissing her. There was no means of escaping it. He would put his arms round her, draw her very close to him so that she felt the soft bulge of his stomach and implant a kiss as near to her nose and mouth as he could manage, though she twisted her head as much as possible without appearing positively discourteous. For, after all, he was an elderly gentleman and her uncle, and her aunt, who was always present, seemed to think it all perfectly natural. He then rounded off his little performance, still holding her, by humming or whistling a few notes of a tune which, she learned, were taken from a popular song beginning 'Girls are made to be kissed'. Her involuntary blushing and stiffening as he held her tight surely added a touch of spice to his secret enjoyment, had she but known it; and perhaps he would have been less insistent if she had been more acquiescent. Then, releasing her at last, he would heave a theatrical sigh: 'Ah, to be young again', or some such sentiment, and with 'sweet dreams, my child' and 'good night, Uncle Poldo' the evening ordeal would be over.

On the whole she was able to ignore him and forget about those few uncomfortable moments as soon as they were past. They cast only a very fleeting shadow on her happiness. But Budd's letters were a different matter. They nagged at her conscience and made her feel guilty. And it was impossible to ignore them because everyone knew she received them, although, to her shame, she did not read them. Budd wrote regularly every week. Whenever she saw an envelope in his handwriting on the hall table where the postman left the letters, she would pick it up and hurriedly retreat to her room. If Hanni or her aunt happened to be present, they surely assumed she was taking them there to read undisturbed. What she actually did was to push them unopened right into the back of her drawer, and try to forget them. There were several in it already, and as the little pile grew, so also the sense of her own injustice towards Budd, of a kind of betrayal of him, grew within her. She tried to argue herself out of it for, she thought, she had never promised him anything, never tied herself to him in any way. Then why was she so reluctant to read his letters? He was so *good*. But why, oh why was he so persistent, why couldn't he leave her alone, allow her to be free! Later perhaps, some other time, she would read those letters and possibly even answer them if she felt like it, but not *now*, not *now*.

She would have liked to put Budd right out of her mind, but that was not possible because Hanni was too curious about him. When she was not with her aunt she spent most of her time with Hanni and she liked her too. It was impossible not to like her. She was so jolly, full of life and warmth, overflowing with cheerfulness. Although four years older than Resi, it was flattering that she treated her as an equal and took her into her confidence. She seemed to have so much experience and knowledge about life and its problems, only to her they were not problems, just interesting situations, to be talked about endlessly. And all these invariably revolved around the one and only subject; love. There were infinite variations to this theme: love undying, love light-hearted, love as a vocation, love as a pastime, and on all these Hanni would pontificate seriously as if arguing a philosophical thesis. But not for very long, for then laughter would break in and she would pass from the general to the particular and illustrate her thesis with concrete examples: what made a certain young man attractive, why one girl she knew had a string of successes and another had none, poor creature. It was all very fascinating for Resi but especially so when Hanni talked about herself, which she did for the sheer enjoyment of making confidences to an impressionable and admiring listener and at the same time doing something for her young cousin's education.

These talks usually took place down by the lake after they had both had a swim and lay sunning themselves on the wide strip of grass belonging to the bathing place. The Lensveldt family had their own cabin in the long low wooden building on the edge of the water, from which stepladders gave direct access to the dark depths of the lake. There was also an artificial swimming pool embedded in the shore, where children and less experienced bathers could safely splash about, for the waters of the lake were very deep even at the edge and gave no foothold anywhere. Hanni, of course, was an excellent swimmer and was delighted to see that Resi, who had learned to swim but had only been used to pools, soon overcame her hesitation and followed her into deep water. Afterwards they lay on the grass, drying, eyes half-closed, completely happy.

'Now, Resi, it's your turn to talk. Tell me about your boyfriend. Out with it! Don't be so secretive. I've a right to know, haven't I?'

'What boyfriend, Hanni?'

'The one who writes to you. Now don't pretend! I've seen his letters – always the same handwriting, and it's not a girl's. What's his name?'

'Oh, you mean Budd.'

'That's not his *real* name, surely?'

'No, it's Harcourt.'

'I mean his *first* name, his Christian name.'

'That *is* his first name, he's Harcourt Gresham, but everyone calls him Budd.'

'What extraordinary first names Americans have! Dwight, Averil, Woodrow – Harcourt – so un-Christian! But never mind. Tell me all about him. What's he like?

'He's very nice.'

'I don't doubt it. But that's not very informative. Let's put the question differently. Are you very fond of him?'

'Yes – I mean: no. I don't know.'

'So you're not in love with him?'

'Oh, no!'

'All right. *That*'s what I've wanted to get clear about for a long time. In what way has it got to do with 'Budd', as you call him, your coming away like this for a year? So it's not because you want to marry him, and your parents don't want you to either because they think you're too young or for some other reason? Is it because *they* want you to marry him and *you* don't, or you're not sure and you want to think it over? Or because you want to break off the friendship altogether? Is that it? Anyway, I see that you let him write to you, but I haven't noticed any letters of yours waiting to be posted.'

'Oh Hanni, you ask so many questions at once! I don't know how to answer them. I think that Budd *thinks* I'm going to marry him some day, but he has never asked me because he knows I'd say no. Anyway, he hasn't finished college yet, and after that he's going to study and be a scientist like Papa. I know Papa likes him very much and would be pleased if I married him because then he'd have a son after his own heart. But he hasn't told me so. One feels that kind of thing, doesn't one? I'm sure Papa loves my brother Carl, but Carl isn't going to be a scientist. He's only interested in baseball.'

'In any case you wouldn't marry Budd just to please your father!'

'No, I'm not going to marry him – or anybody else. I don't think I'm going to get married at all.'

'Why, good heavens, Resi, of course you are, some day. You're not the kind of girl to stay on the shelf. You'll change your mind when you fall in love. Must I believe that it's never happened to you yet?'

'No, I don't think I'm made that way. I can't even imagine what it's like.'

'That's nonsense!'

'Have you fallen in love – often, Hanni?'

'Of course, dozens of times. No,' she corrected herself laughing, 'that's not true. Really and truly: four times.'

'Are you in love now?'

'Yes, I am with Georg. You'll meet him, he's coming here soon with my brother Franzl. I'm sure – I'm almost sure – that I really do love him – that he's the *right* one. I wanted to see him *here,* then I shall know for certain, and we can get engaged.'

'You mean you are really in love with him and he with you?'

'Yes.'

'Then he must be somebody very special, very exciting. You're lucky, Hanni, I never find anybody exciting like that. All the boys *I* know are just ordinary – even Budd who is so nice and so good and whom I like very much.'

'You don't look like a girl who will pine in vain. Now let's hurry up and dress or we shall be late.'

# Eleven

Towards the end of July there was a change of rhythm in the life of Wald, as the Countess had told Resi there would be. Visitors came and went, some just for the day on their way to other places, some staying for a night or two. But the main arrivals who came to stay were the son of the house and the friend he brought with him. The young Count Franz Lensveldt, halfway in age between his two sisters, came with Georg von Corvinus, who was courting Hanni and almost definitely accepted by her as her fiancé. The Count and Countess, with Hanni, went out into the courtyard to greet them as Franz's old car rumbled through the archway.

The cook and the maids were also there, hovering in the background, for the young Count was a great favourite with them and they were curious to catch a first glimpse of the man to whom, the rumour was, the Countess Hanni was about to be engaged. As the sound of the two young men's laughter reverberated under the archway and in the hall, the whole atmosphere of the house changed. The Countess beamed and squeezed the arm of her son, the Count grunted some welcoming words at Corvinus, Hanni's voice rose to a higher pitch, and the maids hurried forward to seize the suitcases, in spite of the young men's protests, taking the opportunity to look them up and down with dancing eyes.

Georg von Corvinus, after taking his law degree, was destined to enter the diplomatic service. In due course he could look forward to being sent abroad. Meticulously groomed, and wearing the traditional grey loden suit with the small green stand-up collar, green lapels and antler-horn buttons on the jacket, with broad green stripes down the trouser legs, his ease and polish were at once marvellously contrived and perfectly natural. His manner towards his host and hostess, as he entertained them immediately with a flow of *faits divers*, struck the exact balance between deference and intimacy. One felt that whatever the situation he would never be awkward or embarrassed; in fact, it was a pleasure to see him function – for he functioned rather than behaved. Hanni felt a glow of satisfaction, she saw herself as a future ambassadress, and when her mother put an arm round her shoulders in a gesture of tacit approval, she knew that everything was going to be all right.

'But wherever is Resi?' the Countess asked, and at that moment Hanni realised she had completely forgotten her cousin. A wave of panic swept over her, and she thought of all the talks they'd been having and how she had been trying to teach Resi how to fall in love. Oh God, what if Georg, so terribly, terribly attractive, and Resi herself . . . ?

They all turned round at the sound of the door opening and Resi came drifting in from the garden, smoothing her rather crumpled cotton frock with both hands. There was the faraway look in her eyes which she had when she had been dreaming in her favourite retreat. She smiled, and the Countess made the introductions.

'Your cousin Franzl,' she said, 'and Herr von Corvinus.' For his benefit she added, 'Resi is my American niece. My sister emigrated, you know, with her husband before the war.'

Franz shook hands with her vigorously. 'Splendid,' he said, 'a cousin worth having,' but Georg, under Hanni's apprehensive eye, bowed ceremoniously and made a few conventional remarks to her in English, asking whether this was her first visit to Europe and whether she was enjoying her stay.

Resi scarcely glanced at him. 'I'm sorry, Aunt Franzi,' she said to her aunt in German, 'I was at the other end of the house and didn't hear the car.'

'Oh good!' said Franz, 'she speaks German, that will make things much easier. My English is sketchy!'

'So is my German,' she said, turning to him. Of the two young men, it was Franz she immediately liked, because he was so like Hanni. Georg, she felt, was intimidating. He, too, stiffened, feeling slightly annoyed at being denied the opportunity of showing off his linguistic accomplishments. But he very politely complimented her, in German, on hers. 'Mama used to speak it to me when I was little,' she explained, 'and I had nearly forgotten it all, but it has come

back to me since I've been here and have had some practice.'
And that, to Hanni's infinite relief, was all that passed between Resi and Corvinus, nor, during the days that followed,
did they take more than the most superficial notice of each
other. That Georg was too completely infatuated with her
to look elsewhere Hanni found most comforting and satis-
factory, but she would have liked to have heard some spontaneous remark of appreciation – possibly slightly tinged
with envy – from Resi about the incomparable perfection of
her lover. No such remark was forthcoming and when at last
Hanni could not forbear from asking for her opinion, all
Resi could find to say was that she thought Georg 'very nice'
which, to judge from the flat tone of voice in which she said
it, really meant 'quite ordinary'.

But her cousin Franz she really did find 'very nice' and
genuinely meant all that those words implied. He was, she
felt, so much like Hanni, jolly, cheerful and light-hearted,
friendly and companionable – like a big brother she would
have said, if she had thought of putting their relationship
into words. She was completely at ease with him, probably
because Franz felt exactly the same towards her. He was surprised by this, for as a rule he was not slow to make up to any
young female who, as he used to put it, 'had all the right
curves'. But though he thought his new cousin pretty – in
fact, more than pretty, quite beautiful – he felt not the slightest temptation to fall in love with her. Perhaps Resi was too
slim and straight, mentally as well as physically, for his taste.
'Too classical,' was what he told his mother, to her great
amusement – 'too, too – untouchable.'

Now, for the first time since she had come to Wald, Resi felt the freedom she had so much enjoyed becoming a little oppressive, in that she felt at a loose end. Hanni had no time for her – she spent the whole day with Georg, and when they went swimming, even if she was asked to 'come along', Resi was reluctant to intrude, or pretended to prefer to stay at home. She would have liked to spend more time with Franz, but he seemed totally absorbed in his shooting. He was out every day before sunrise, sometimes accompanied in those early hours by Georg, and again in the late afternoons he went alone, while for the rest of the day he was immersed in interminable discussions with his father or the gamekeeper about the minutiae of his sport.

Count Lensveldt had been forced by straitened circumstances to sell a large part of the forest to the State, but he still possessed a substantial acreage and derived his income from its yield in timber. As for the shooting rights, he had retained all of them. There was thus a large area in which Franz and his friends could go stalking. The game was chiefly fallow deer, but also sometimes a stag, and – high up in the mountains, after an arduous ascent which meant spending the night in a log cabin – chamois. There were also capercaillie, blackcock and, in the right season, snipe.

Game was Franz's overriding passion, the only thing in life he took really seriously. He not only went out with a gun every day he was at Wald, he also talked about it constantly. Georg was just sufficiently experienced and interested to be able to participate, which was fortunate, as he would have felt disqualified in the eyes of his future father-in-law if he had not been able to comment knowledgeably on the trophies adorning the hall walls, and also to describe the excellent buck he himself had shot at his brother-in-law's place in Styria.

One morning, coming along the passage from her room, Resi caught sight of an open door that she had not noticed before, assuming it was a broom cupboard. When she looked in she saw Franz in his shirtsleeves, with several guns on a large table and an array of cleaning materials, brushes, oily rags, leathers and polish scattered around.

'What are you doing, Franzl?'

'Hello, Winter Sunshine! Come in and keep me company at my labours. I want someone to talk to. As you see, I'm cleaning the guns.'

Resi went in and glanced over the table.

'Why do you call me Winter Sunshine?'

'It seems such a good name for you. Do you mind? I called you that the first moment I set eyes on you. It describes you, you know. You're not offended, I hope.'

Resi laughed. 'No, I rather like it. I mean, because it is *you* who said it, Franzl.'

'That's all right then. Now look at these guns, especially this pair. Aren't they beautiful? My father bought them years ago, from Purdey's in London. There's nothing to touch them. He hardly ever goes out after roebuck now, which is a pity as he's becoming overweight. But he lets me use his guns, which is good luck for me. And the least I can do is to look after them, for he doesn't, and our gamekeeper doesn't have time.' Resi stood watching him as he drew a rag through the long gleaming steel barrels and polished the shapely stock. Then he opened and closed the breech, carefully oiling the hinge and the trigger. Resi pointed to another gun on the table.

'Why has that one got two barrels?'

'The double-barrelled one is for shot, little pellets of lead in a cartridge like this.' He showed her one. 'You shoot birds with it – game birds, I mean, capercaillie, snipe, pheasants or hares and rabbits – the shot spreads like spray. These hunting rifles are for bullets. Look, there's a telescope fitted along the top of this barrel, to allow you to shoot with complete precision at the right spot on a big animal, a buck or stag, in order to kill instantly if possible, rather than wounding or disabling. A clean death is not cruel, if that's what you're thinking, but an inept, wounding shot is a disgrace. And it's far more cruel to allow a wild animal to die of hunger or old age, which would happen if they were not controlled. Do you see what I mean?'

'Yes, Franz, I do.' He was still handling the rifles. 'Will you show me how they work?'

'Like this' – he was as keen to initiate a new and eager listener into the intricacies of his obsessional passion and its instruments as Hanni had been when talking about her love affairs. He showed her the cartridges and where they were placed, but removed them again immediately. 'You must never load a gun in the house,' he said, 'and never before you are actually going to use it. Never carry it loaded, except with the breech open. Then it cannot go off accidentally. Now, unloaded, I'll show you how one shoots. You close the breech, draw back the spring called the cock, and when you pull the trigger it releases the sharp point that hits the charge of the cartridge and sets the shot or the bullet flying.' Lovingly, with his fingertips, he caressed each part of his treasured weapon, delighting in the precision of its workmanship, its smooth soundless action, the barely audible click as the barrel closed on the stock. He rubbed his cheek against its satiny surface.

'May I hold the gun?' Resi asked.

'You can try. The shape of the shaft fits your shoulder, your right hand close to the trigger, left arm extended to hold the barrel steady – look through the telescope at your target. You will see crossed lines on the lens. You will be aiming at the exact spot where they meet.'

'Goodness! How heavy it is!' She let the gun sink as Franz withdrew his supporting hand. He wiped his hands on a rag. There seemed no more to say, but he was debating within himself and suddenly he came to a decision. 'Resi,' he asked, 'would you like to come stalking with me this evening? Have you got strong shoes? Mama can lend you a dark cloak. You would have to make no sound, walk very softly: ask no questions. I mean that.'

'Oh, Franzl! I'd love to. I'll promise everything you've said.'

'Just before sunset, then. Ask Mama about a cloak.'

The Countess watched them set out together with astonishment. She had never known Franz to take anyone with him when he went stalking. It was a solitary pursuit. But Resi will share his solitude without disturbing his concentration, she thought, and she was right. She felt the same when Resi was with her.

They drove in the old Volkswagen a little way beyond the village and then turned up a side road which, after a short while, became a stony track along which the sturdy car jolted its way at a snail's pace. At another turning, the track widened and a little stream of clear water came tumbling over mossy stones. Here there was a flat space, just large enough to park the car, and they got out. With his gun under his arm, barrel pointing downwards, Franz led the way into the forest up a barely discernible footpath. Resi followed without a word. The trees stood tall and silent and so close that it was almost dark. On a carpet of pine needles, moss and dead beech leaves they walked without a sound. The breath of the forest was cool and fragrant.

In quarter of an hour they reached a clearing where trees had been felled and grass grew between the stumps. A roughly-built platform of logs on tall stilt-like legs stood half-concealed on the edge of the clearing. Franz climbed the ladder leading up to it and motioned Resi to follow. He scanned the landscape with his field glasses. Resi wrapped herself more closely in the dark-green rough woollen cloak her aunt had lent her and looked around. It was lighter out here in the open, the sky pearly-grey with a hint of rose, the edge of the forest in darkness.

Franz touched her arm, pointed, and produced a second, smaller pair of field glasses for her to look through. On the edge of the wood, on a strip of grassland opposite the platform, was a dappled doe and a tiny fawn by her side, grazing and lifting her head between whiles. Then there was another, with little spiky antlers and, emerging from a different direction, several more. It was getting dark. Silently, Franz lifted his gun. Resi felt her heart beating and, looking with her glasses for his target, she saw, just above some tall grasses, a pair of spreading antlers rising and disappearing. Franz waited a moment and then put his gun down again. 'He's too far away and it's too dark now,' he said. They were the first words he'd spoken since they'd left the house. 'I never shoot unless I am quite, quite sure,' he added. They climbed down the ladder and began to make their way back to the car. Franz was talking now. 'He was a capital fellow. Never mind, I'll get him another time. One has to be patient. Did you enjoy yourself?'

'Very much. I'm glad, though, that you didn't shoot.'

'I knew you'd say that. You were very good, very quiet. If you like, you can come again. But another time I might shoot, at least I hope so.'

As they drove home the moon, a thin silver sickle, rose over the black tips of the fir trees and cast faint ripples of light onto the lake. Franz, driving carefully over the loose stones, shot quick glances at the girl beside him. She seemed lost in thought. When the rough track evened out onto the smooth road, he took his right hand off the steering wheel and felt for hers. But there was no responding movement. She was gazing at the lake and the sky. Franz smiled to himself, gave his whole attention to the road and pressed the accelerator.

# Twelve

Again the rhythm of life at Wald changed. Franz left to return to his office in Vienna, saying that he hoped to be back for another week at the end of September. Resi had gone out with him several times more to different places in the woods, and he had shot three bucks. The 'capital fellow' they had seen on their first evening, who had been spared because the light had been failing, had been shot the following morning at sunrise when Franz had gone out with the gamekeeper while the rest of the household was still asleep. He was brought in at breakfast time in the boot of the car and laid on the flagstones in the courtyard, a beautiful honey-coloured animal crowned with upright, sixfold branching antlers. The Count and Corvinus came down to inspect him and the men stood around for a long time, discussing, measuring, reminiscing, and comparing his various points. Resi joined them later unnoticed and stooped to stroke the soft woollen coat. It astonished her to find the body still warm, but there was no visible blood. The shot was at the base of the neck and had killed instantaneously: any haemorrhage had been internal. Then, as she straightened up, Franz had looked at her inquiringly.

'Well?' he asked.

'You must be very proud of him,' she answered.

'I am,' and he patted her shoulder approvingly. She had not been squeamish and had instinctively said the right words. Had she reacted differently, there would have been no more of those silent and enthralling expeditions at sundown into the depths of the forest.

But now Franz was gone. Hanni and Georg were understood to be engaged, although no announcement was to be made until Georg had passed one more important examination which he still needed to launch him on his career as a diplomat. At dinner they had all drunk a special bottle of wine which the Count had himself brought up from the cellar on the evening before Franz's departure, and the Countess had kissed her future son-in-law on both cheeks. That was all.

The following week Georg and Hanni were to go and stay with Georg's sister and her husband in Styria. But before they went two other visitors arrived in Wald who were both to have a considerable influence on Resi's life and destiny. The first to come was a friend of Helen's, who drove to the mainline railway station, where Resi herself had arrived, in order to fetch her. She was a quiet girl, short, dark and somewhat foreign-looking among the tall, fair-skinned Lens-veldts. Resi did not think of her as a girl at all but as a middle-aged woman. This was her youthful bias and did not do justice to Nina's quick, nervously-controlled movements and the intense fire of her eyes. Her figure was stocky, but she had small hands and feet with finely-shaped wrists and ankles. Her eyebrows were thick and she wore her black hair twisted into a voluminous knot at the nape of her neck. Her strong features would have been imposing on a tall girl, but even so, without the advantage of height, her presence was that of a personality, but one that made no impression on Resi, ex-cept, as soon became apparent, in a negative way, in that she absorbed the special attention of her uncle and aunt. The Count treated her with a kind of courtesy that was almost deference and the Countess with affectionate solicitude. Resi saw her uncle put his hand under Nina's elbow to lead her into the dining room and draw out a chair for her at his right hand. He not only rose when she came into the room, but would see to it that she was comfortable before he sat down again, and asked her leave before he lit his cigar. He also gave up his little demonstrative embrace and good night kiss of an evening, contenting himself with a wave of the hand and a nod of dismissal, while accompanying Nina to the door and wishing her a peaceful night's rest.

All this Resi noticed and was far from resenting. But it was Aunt Franzi's behaviour to Nina that was hurtful; for it was to her that her aunt now called to come into the garden and help her choose and cut the flowers, her advice she sought in arranging them in vases, and with her she sat in the afternoon at the long table at the back of the house stripping the red currants off their stalks and picking over the raspberries for jam. They talked and talked, of people and of things Resi knew nothing about, and though they did not discourage her from joining them, they also did not actively invite her. Aunt Franzi, who had once been so concerned that she should not be lonely or bored, now did not seem to give her a thought.

So instead of drifting dreamily and happily through the summer days, Resi began to wish that something would happen. Something did and was, of course, somebody. The somebody was Lucas Anreither. He irrupted early one Sunday afternoon into the late-summer somnolence of Schloss Wald, with the energy of his youth and the irreverence of his opinions. His appearance was heralded by the roar and splutter of a motorcycle being ridden at top speed up the hill, then by its more subdued entry under the archway into the courtyard. Everyone was sitting rather drowsily in the big drawing room after luncheon, with the green shutters half-closed against the blazing sun. The Count, with the newspaper on his knees, had unashamedly gone to sleep, the Countess had taken her embroidery frame and was passing her needle very slowly through the canvas, finding it difficult in the half-light to see what she was doing. Helen and Nina had retired to their rooms. Hanni and Georg, sitting very close to each other on the sofa, were speaking in whispers, ostensibly in order not to disturb her father, while Resi had ensconced herself on one of the wide windowsills, her legs drawn up and folded under her. Through the slats of the shutters she was the first to see the young man enter the house. He neither rang nor knocked since, being familiar with the household, he knew that on a Sunday afternoon the maids would not be on duty. Hanni disentangled herself from Georg's arm and went to the door, but before she had time to turn the handle, it was thrown open vigorously, almost in her face.

'*Servus*, Lucas,' she said, using a familiar form of greeting to the young man who stood on the threshold. 'Well, come in,' she added, laughing, 'nobody's going to eat you!'

The young man's exuberance was slightly muted by the half-light. He came in hesitantly, looked round and approached the Countess. He bent over her hand and she looked up at him with a smile. 'Well, Lucas,' she said, 'it's nice to see you. How are your grandparents? And your parents, too? I hope they are all well.'

And to the Count, who had opened his eyes sleepily and let the newspaper slip to the floor, 'Poldo,' she said, 'Lucas Anreither is here.'

'So I see,' he answered, 'and a damn noise he made, too.' Corvinus got up from the sofa and picked up the paper for the Count. The two young men stood looking at each other awkwardly and a current of mutual dislike passed almost tangibly from one to the other. No attempt at introduction being made, they just stared. Corvinus sat down again. Hanni took Lucas by the sleeve and said: 'Here's a surprise for you. Come and meet my American cousin, Resi. She speaks German, so you can talk to her.' So saying, she planted Lucas firmly in front of Resi and with the other hand gave a vigorous push to the shutter so that the brightness of the day suddenly shone upon her. The effect, of course, was startling, as Hanni had meant it to be, and she watched with amusement the look of speechless amazement on Lucas's face. 'This is Lucas Anreither, Resi, a very old friend of mine. I'll leave you to get to know each other.'

So saying she returned to the sofa. 'Who is he?' Georg wanted to know. 'He came in as if the place belonged to him!'

'You must ask Mama,' Hanni said, 'but actually he *is* almost one of the family.' She felt that an explanation from the Countess would do much to dispel the antagonism which had surfaced in the tone of her fiancé's question. The Countess, too, had noticed it.

'He's got a rather self-assertive manner,' she admitted, 'but really it's a kind of shyness. The place does *not* belong to him, naturally, but he belongs to the place, or rather, to us. We've inherited him. His grandfather, old Anreither, was my father's head-forester and gamekeeper. My father set great store by him, and we girls, my sisters and I, all loved him. His son and daughter were our playmates. The son studied agriculture and is now in the Forestry Commission in Vienna. It so happened that he married a farmer's daughter in this district and they have a bit of land in the neighbourhood. Lucas is their only child. He spends most of his summer holidays with his mother's family here, so he, in his turn, has been a playmate of Hanni's and Franzl's. Third generation, you see. But he is a student at the University and is going to be a lawyer, I understand, very clever, very ambitious, very "modern", but still good old Anreither stock. Nothing wrong with him.'

'That's what you always say,' said the Count from the depths of his armchair. 'I've never much relished him myself. Georg is quite right, he does behave as if he owns the place. But he doesn't, not yet at least. And now Hanni's getting married he won't have so much inducement to come up here all the time.'

'Won't he?' said the Countess, and turned to look at the far end of the long room, where Lucas had hitched himself up into the other corner of the window seat opposite Resi and was holding forth to her with vigour and enthusiasm.

'I'm afraid he won't get very far if he talks politics to Resi,' she remarked. 'Such a dull subject, anyway. Perhaps she'll help him find out they are not the only things that matter in the world. It'll do him good.'

# Thirteen

The days passed. 'Must we have that fellow here *every* day?'
the Count asked irritably, looking out of the window as the
motorcycle with Lucas astride it spluttered once more into
the courtyard. 'He's a Red, and I don't see why I should have
a Red sitting at my table day after day, looking at me with
that ironical smile of his every time I express an opinion he
disapproves of. And that proletarian check jacket and blue
shirt he wears! His father's a countryman and his mother's a
farmer's daughter, so why can't he dress properly and wear
loden when he's in the country like everyone else? Advertis-
ing his class-consciousness!'

'Oh politics!' said the Countess soothingly. 'Politics are
not all that important. *People* are important. And Lucas is
not just "that fellow". He's old Lucas Anreither's grandson
and we've known him all his life. What would my father

have thought if I refused to have his devoted Anreither's grandson in the house? Old Anreither was practically one of the family. And the boy is a decent chap and hasn't done anything wrong.'

'Old Anreither was your father's forester,' the Count answered, 'and he didn't have him at his dinner table, for all the trust and mutual attachment there was between them. He wouldn't have dreamed of it, nor would Anreither himself.'

'Things are different now,' said the Countess defensively. 'Anreither's son is a councillor in the Ministry of Agriculture and Forestry and young Lucas is a law student. I suppose one could say the family have come up in the world.'

'Up or down! You do have queer ideas, Franzi. I'd say down! But whichever way it is, he's a Red – and I don't like him.'

'But Poldo, he behaves himself. His manners are good, he never contradicts you, even when you express quite extreme opinions which I know you don't really mean, only to provoke him, and I can see he can hardly swallow his indignation.'

The Countess was laughing, but the Count was not in a mood to be amused.

'I wish he *would* lose his temper and be rude to me. Then I'd have an excuse to throw him out.'

'Well, you won't have to endure him much longer. He'll be going back to town in a week or two. Please don't let's have a scene now. You never used to object to him when he was a child and used to come and play robbers and gendarmes, or whatever they did play, with Franzl and Hanni. He's doing no harm now and he's being very useful.'

'Useful! I'd like to know what you mean by useful! Because he and Hanni played together as children, he still speaks to her with the same kind of uninhibited intimacy – as if it were his right to do so. And she, being as sentimental about the Anreither family as you are, allows him to do so. And I can tell you that Corvinus doesn't like it, and he's right. I don't know whether *she* thinks or whether *you* think that making Corvinus jealous or just angry is going to hasten their marriage, but *I* say it will make him break it off. And I'm pleased to have Georg Corvinus for a son-in-law, but I wouldn't have Anreither under any circumstances. If she wanted to marry *him*, I'd never speak to her again.'

The Count made as if to leave the room, but the Countess was too quick for him. She slipped between him and the door and lifting both her hands to his shoulders and her smiling face to his sullen one, she gently made him bend towards her.

'My beloved old Poldo, you've got it all wrong. There's nothing whatsoever between Lucas and Hanni and never has been. Of course such a marriage would be unthinkable and neither he nor she have ever thought of it. Don't you know that if there had been the slightest hint of an attachment, I should have put a stop to it? And I feel sure that Georg Corvinus will very soon ask formally for your consent to their engagement, why, they are as good as engaged already. Don't you realise that if Lucas comes here everyday now, it's because of a quite different attraction? He's falling in love with Resi, oh not very seriously and she's certainly not giving him any encouragement, poor fellow, but I do think it's good for her to have someone to make up to her and give her some practice in being courted, so to speak. She's far too reserved. Perhaps poor Lucas will succeed in breaking down her defences a bit. No harm will come of it because, as I said to you, he really is an awfully decent chap. That's why I think he's useful.'

'How cynical you women are! You'll have a young chap come to the house, in spite of all his damn socialist ideas, because his grandfather was your father's servant, yes, my dear, of course he was his servant and he never thought of himself as anything else, nor did the Prince – but you'll encourage him to court your sister's daughter, and she half a child still, though you don't mean her to take him seriously. That's all too devious for my simple mind. What if she *does* take him seriously and he *does* want to marry her? What would you say to your sister then?'

'It's just a little childish flirtation, Poldo – no thought of marriage! Besides,' the Countess added reflectively, 'what would Valery have to object to? She knows who Lucas Anreither is. Not much difference between his background and Peter's. And if they went to America, what difference would it make over there? But good gracious, Poldo, no need to speculate about it. It won't happen.'

Resi did not, of course, overhear this conversation between her uncle and aunt, but she did hear her uncle refer to Lucas several times as a 'Red'. She found the notion disturbing. It made Lucas, who seemed such an ordinary person, rather mysterious and sinister. Her uncle obviously disapproved of him, but her aunt, whom she trusted implicitly, treated him as one of the family, as did Hanni. It was so contradictory. She decided to ask him a direct question.

'Lucas, are you really a communist?' They were walking one evening along the footpath above the house, where there was a fine view of the lake between the pine trees. She stopped to face him, feeling very daring, as if she were handling an explosive charge that might go off at the slightest touch. But Lucas did not explode. Instead, he gave a little laugh and said quite calmly, 'No, I'm not a communist. Who gave you that idea?'

'Uncle Poldo says you are a "Red".'

'Well so I am, what *he* calls a Red. I'm a Socialist.'

'What's the difference?'

'My dear girl, there's a world of difference. In the first place, I'm a Democrat.'

Resi felt relieved, but puzzled. 'A lot of people are Democrats, there's nothing wrong with that. Our neighbours in Eden Rise are Democrats. We see quite a lot of them, though my father's a Republican himself. I don't know what *I* am, I haven't thought about it much yet. But if you say being "Red" in this country doesn't mean you're a communist, why does Uncle Poldo object to you and yet allow you to come to the house all the time?'

'I know he doesn't like me and I really ought to stay away. I often tell myself that it would be more dignified if I did.

But the Countess is kind to me, and she's very fond of my parents and my grandparents, who are deeply attached to her family. Franz and Hanni and I – we played together as children and that friendship hasn't changed since we've grown up and I've formed my own political opinions.'

'Then your parents are not "Red" like you?'

'Good heavens no! They're Black.'

'Black!' Resi stared at him in utter bewilderment. 'Black?' she repeated. 'They can't be, Lucas, not with you being so fair-haired and white-skinned,' she murmured.

It was Lucas's turn to stare, then his eyes twinkled, his mouth creased and he began to shake with laughter. 'No, no,' he gasped at last, 'not what *you* mean by Black. Black is what *we* call the "clerical" party, the *Christian*-socialists, on account of the clergy and their black cassocks, you know.'

But Resi was starting to grow bored. 'No, I don't know and I don't want to know. You call Christians Black and your-selves Red, but not a communist, it's all very complicated and I don't really care about what you are.' She found Lucas very tiring to talk to. He was always asking her things about America that she couldn't answer, about what he called 'so-cial conditions', or about the kind of work her father did, of which she could only say it had to do with chemistry. In a way Lucas was rather like Budd, not like him as a person, but behaving like him in always being *there*. If she were sitting in the garden he sat down beside her; if she were going to walk down to the village he would walk with her. He even tried to persuade her to ride behind him on his motorcycle, but this she refused, saying that she didn't think she would care for it. It was very difficult to find a defence against his gentle persistence without being outspokenly rude to him and this she could not bring herself to do. She would have had to shut herself up in her room if she had really wished to avoid him, and then probably her aunt would have called her and she would have had to explain, which would be embarrassing, as she would have to give a reason without having one – or pretend not to feel well, and that would cause a fuss. So all she could do was smile at Lucas, inwardly regretting that the absolutely cloudless days of drifting and dreaming, of chatter with Hanni, of basking in the mellow ambiance of her aunt, and the cool, silent evening vigils in forest clearings with her friendly, undemanding cousin Franz had come to an end.

In any case, summer was waning, the days were getting shorter, and when autumn came she was to go to Vienna, a city of which her mother spoke sometimes with nostalgia and sometimes with distaste, which on some occasions she would describe with words of heartache, and on others with contempt, a city which she craved to see once more and at the same time vowed she would never set foot in again, so that in Resi's imagination it seemed to be a place out of a story book, invented, not real, and she wondered what it was going to be like actually to live there.

The time for that was not yet ripe, though the end of long leave or holidays or vacation – or whatever in the language of offices, academies and laboratories the summer respite was called – was in sight, and plans that had been suggested, discussed and then postponed for one reason or another had to be carried out at once, if they were to be carried out at all. Helen proposed that before returning to work at the saw-mill, and before Nina went back to her Institute in Vienna, they go up to the Bichl Alm. This was a high pasture on a mountain on the other side of the lake, just below the glacier one could see from the upper windows of the castle and just above the limit of the tree growth. It was exactly the right moment for the excursion: the weather was settled, the cows would still be up there but would soon be coming down, there would be no more tourists, and the Sennerinnen, the women who looked after the cows, would put them up in their wooden cabins, the Alm-Hutte, if they decided to stay the night and see the sunrise.

'Resi ought to join you,' the Countess said, 'she's been here all summer and hasn't seen anything of the mountains except from a distance. She hasn't seen any Enzian growing, or any Alpenrosen, and hasn't heard any cowbells. That is something she mustn't miss, or when she goes back to America no one will believe she has been in Austria at all.'

'Won't it be too strenuous for her?' Helen did not relish the idea of having to look after a possibly straggling and footsore Resi: she and Nina were experienced climbers and did not want to be encumbered. But Lucas, who of course was present when the expedition was discussed, left her no time to oppose the suggestion.

'Oh, I'm sure she'll be all right. It's not really a climb, it's a walk up to the Bichl Alm and not a difficult one. I know every inch of the way. Oh Resi, you'll see how wonderful the mountains are, how grand it is when you get up on the heights and have a whole panorama spread out beneath you – so different from being down here and, as the Frau Gräfin says, it's an experience you mustn't miss. If we take two days to do it, with a night's rest in between, why, it's child's play.'

So Lucas was going too, that of course was inevitable. The thing seemed to be settled. Resi had not expressed an opinion one way or the other. Her aunt had said that it was the right thing for her to do, so perhaps it was. If Helen had stood by her opposition she could have said she preferred to stay at home. Those two older women, Helen and Nina, were rather formidable, she was sure *they* would not have wanted her company. However, if Lucas were going too, what was she to say? But Helen said it instead of her: 'All right, Lucas, if you come we shall be four and you can help Resi on the difficult bits, so that solves the problem.'

'What problem is that?' asked Hanni, who at that moment came into the room followed by Georg Corvinus.

'Nina and I are going up to the Bichl Alm tomorrow,' Helen said, 'And it seems that Resi and Lucas want to join us.'

'I'd love to come,' said Hanni. 'Oh Georg, would you go up to the Alm with us, with me, I mean? Instead of going stalking for once. We'd see the sunrise on the snowfields, the pale dawn, the pink flush in the sky . . .'

Corvinus did not at first welcome the suggestion. He looked across at Lucas with distaste. But Hanni had slipped her arm through his and pressed it. Her eyes, as she looked up at him, seemed to hold a promise. 'Pale dawn, pink flush,' he repeated half mockingly. 'How poetical you are, Hanni, irresistibly poetical. Very well then, if your sister and Princess Nina don't object . . .'

'Of course not,' said Helen, 'all the better. Another man to cope with Resi if she gets into difficulties.'

'She won't,' said Lucas decisively, 'I'll see to that.'

Resi herself said nothing. She had not been asked. She didn't know.

# Fourteen

Crossing the lake on the little steamer that plied between the villages dotting its shores had been unadulterated pleasure, as had the walk along a path through meadows to the foot of the mountain where the climb began. There was a little wooden sign post attached to a tree which pointed the way to the Bichl Alm, and the tree also bore a red and white painted ring round its trunk, a sign Resi was to see many times as the track wound its way up the mountainside.

The ascent was gentle in the beginning and the little group kept fairly close together, Helen and Nina in the lead, followed by Hanni and Georg, while Resi brought up the rear with Lucas behind her, all walking in single file. Then the path became steeper and the pace of the walkers began to change and differ from each other. There was silence between the two older girls as they concentrated on the rhythm of their movements carrying them at a steady pace to the high pasture above. For a while there was some chatter and light laughter between Hanni and Georg, until they too fell silent with only a word or exclamation here and there.

Resi was silent from the start. She looked up at the soaring pine trees with the sunlight gleaming copper red on their majestic trunks and the ecstatic shafts of light between their branches – and her heart lifted with joy at the sight. But the path had become stony and slippery and she was forced to keep her eyes down most of the time so as not to stumble. Although she inhaled draughts of cool sweet resin-scented air, her breath was growing short and hard as the climb grew steeper. Worst of all were her feet. She had never worn heavy boots before, but had been told she must put them on today. There must have been a crease in one of her socks and a blister was forming.

Then suddenly there was a respite. They came out of the wood and emerged onto a meadow that hardly sloped at all, a heavenly meadow with soft, springy grass underfoot, starred with deep blue flowers, deeper blue even than the sky. Lucas came up to walk beside her now that the path was wider. She had almost forgotten he was behind her, and seeing how the distance between herself and the others was increasing she was thankful that he had not left her alone. She turned and smiled at him, one of her rare, radiant smiles, and he smiled in return, his heart suffused with happiness. He suggested that they pause for a few minutes to look around, although not for too long in order not to lose the impetus still needed for the remaining climb. Resi wanted to stop and pick some of the blue flowers that so enchanted her; from this he gently discouraged her, not saying, as indeed was the case, that the picking of Alpine flowers was forbidden, but only that it was useless as they would quickly wilt in her hot hands. Leave them where they belong, look and don't *grab*. It was a word that stayed in her mind for a long time and she liked Lucas the better for having said it.

But now the climb began again, and steeper than before. They were out of the forest and its shade, walking not on pine needles but on short turf and pebbles, between boulders and outcrops of rock. The sun was hot on her neck, sweat began running down her face, and the boots felt heavier and heavier. That crease in her left sock, it cut like a knife at every step. She wanted to sit down, take off the boot and shift it, but that was impossible, for there was now no room to sit down between the high rock-face above and the steep slope covered with prickly bushes below. She felt sick and dizzy and a dreadful urge overcame her to let herself fall down, down into that abyss. But Lucas was there. He put one hand under her elbow, the other on her waist. His voice was close to her ear. 'Don't look down,' he said, 'keep your eyes on the path, just take one step after the other, we're nearly there now, only ten minutes more.' Ten minutes of agony to Resi, they seemed like an hour, and for the last steps he almost had her in his arms. Then just round a bend there was a dip in the ground and a wide grass basin spread out before them. There was the tinkle of cowbells and a group of wooden buildings, one with a verandah along its front, was only a hundred yards away. It was the Alm and the end of the excursion.

The others were already sitting on benches on either side of a wooden table. They had unwrapped their sausages and slices of bacon, and the Sennerin, the cow woman, had brought out a large jug of milk, loaves of dark brown bread and a huge dollop of butter. Resi sank gratefully onto the bench; she was almost too exhausted to eat. Hanni greeted her with laughter. 'So you've got here at last – congratulations – well done', praise which sounded more derisive than appreciative, while Helen said kindly, 'Was it *very* hard work? Drink some milk and you'll soon feel better.' She and Nina seemed as cool and unruffled as if they had just been for a stroll instead of an arduous climb. But Lucas, who now sat beside her, looked round at them all angrily. 'You needn't laugh at her, she has done remarkably well for a first effort. You forget that she has had no training. When she has had some practice, she'll take this in her stride as easily as the rest of us.'

Dear Lucas, yes indeed, dear Lucas, you *are* like Budd, comforting and understanding. I wish you *were* Budd, that it was Budd here next to me now, and by a strange substitution of the imagination a feeling of tenderness for distant, long-neglected Budd welled up in her, and it was him she saw in her mind's eye as she laid her hand on Lucas's arm and smiled at him. But how was Lucas to know?

After they had eaten, Helen and Nina said they would lie on the grass and sunbathe, while Georg and Hanni decided, for privacy, to walk round a shoulder of rock to get a view of the mountain range beyond. Resi wanted to take off her boots, but Hanni advised against it, she would not be able to put them on again if she did, and she would have to tackle the descent barefoot like the women who looked after the cows! She should simply rest her feet and their throbbing would subside. Resi reluctantly obeyed, hoping Hanni was right. She hobbled about looking for a place where she could lie down, but it was difficult to find one where she could stretch out in comfort because of the cow-pats swarming with flies, some of them quite vicious ones which stung. The cows themselves were wandering all over the place, they looked and sounded nice from a distance but were terrifying if they came too close.

At last she found a hollow behind a small hillock where the grass was longer and greener, there were no cow-pats and the cows were out of sight. A safe place. She lay down and half-closed her eyes. But it was not long before Lucas came and sat down beside her. She pretended to be asleep, however, she looked at him between her eyelids. He had taken off his shirt, his chest was red with sunburn and glistening with sweat. He was very close, she could hear him breathe, smell his body. She shut her eyes tightly, perhaps he would go away. Suddenly the sun was off her face, he had bent over her, she was in his shadow. She lifted her hands to push him off, but he had put his hands on her shoulders and his mouth was on her mouth. She felt his lips, hot and moist, and as she pressed her own lips together, denying him the response he expected, she felt his hard teeth bruising them. It lasted only a moment, for bewildered, hurt by this unsuccessful attempt at a kiss, he sat up again and looked down at her sheepishly, half-ashamed. And she looked up at him without a word while a sob rose in her throat and tears filled those beautiful blue eyes and ran silently down her face.

He was at a loss, he couldn't understand her: only a short while ago she had smiled at him so kindly, and on that last steep bit of the climb when she had felt dizzy she had let him put his arms round her, he had felt the softness of her body, he had practically carried her. But now she was crying.

'Darling,' he said, 'what's the matter? Have you never been kissed before? Do you dislike me so much?'

She only shook her head. 'No, no, no,' was all she managed to say, although it was not clear which question she was answering, and she said nothing more. He lingered a little and then rose to go. Brushing the tears from her cheek, she rolled over and sank into a deep sleep.

It was late afternoon and the shadows were lengthening when she rejoined the others, who were debating whether to stay the night and sleep on straw pallets in the cabin or to make the descent before dark. Hanni and Georg decided to stay and watch the sunrise. Resi, with unwonted decisiveness, voted to go down and go home, and Nina, looking at the girl's drawn face, agreed. This time they all stayed together, Lucas leading the way, Nina or Helen lending Resi a steadying hand until, in a much shorter time than it had taken for the climb, they reached the lake shore and caught the last boat across to Wald.

# Part Two

# Fifteen

Grasboeck had welcomed him back! It had seemed only a small, insignificant incident, those few minutes he had spent with him in the hallway of the Institute, but they sank into Adler's consciousness and gave him unexpected solace. For days he wondered why it was that they meant so much to him. And as he pondered, an understanding grew and ripened in him that if he was, once more, to grow roots and become established in this country to which he wanted to belong, then he must feel his way down to the roots and sink them into the earth, the deep, dark subsoil of the mind where they would be safe and invulnerable. It would not be enough to renew connections with former acquaintances, or even to try to re-establish mutual affection with old friends. Social relationships were at best superficial, they could be pleasant if treated lightheartedly, they could easily be hurtful if too much was expected of them. And even with such old friends as Herman Helbling – it was good to see them from time to time, but their experiences had been too different. Nor in the realm of social intercourse would he find the security of belonging, and if he could not be sure of belonging, there would be no sense in his having returned; he must go to the roots, the roots.

The month was October, a month of shortening days but of golden light from sunrise to sunset. There was not much time before winter set in, yet in that time he would start growing his roots.

He abandoned the too-familiar Inner City and on Saturdays and Sundays set out to walk through districts he had not seen during the years he lived near them. He walked along streets of which he had never known or only barely remembered the name, but tending always outwards, westwards or southwards, towards the vineyards and the hills where the fringes of the city were gradually engulfing the little outlying villages.

Lost in these neighbourhoods, he looked with tenderness at time-worn facades, peeped into wide-open doorways that often revealed inner courtyards surrounding a lime tree whose leaves were beginning to fall and were clothed with a crimson climbing vine. He read the names over shabby shopfronts displaying cheap underwear, groceries or ironmongery. Humble and out-of-date, and not very alluring, nevertheless the names had a familiar ring, names derived from farms and their husbandry, interspersed now and again with the Czech or Polish which contributes so much to

Vienna's inimitable flavour. And familiar, too, were the voices of the passers-by when he caught snatches of their conversation in a dialect he had to retrain his ear to understand. Some rebuilding, repainting and repaving was already going on, and no doubt, in time, concrete and plate-glass would take the place of wood and stucco, and asphalt would supersede the 'cat's head' cobblestones.

If Sunday morning was fine he would take a tram to the end of the line and then begin the climb along a straggling village street, between cottage gardens and vineyards, into the wooded hills. For years now he had not walked at all, and at first he got so tired that he wondered whether, at his age, his muscles would ever regain the strength necessary to carry him on such day-long wanderings. But his delight in feeling the earth beneath his feet, and the moss and the stones, of seeing shafts of sunlight between the trees, the shadows of clouds on the grass of the meadows, and of breathing the smell of resin and fallen leaves – all this impelled him to persevere, and rewarded him with gradually increasing strength. When, in an open-neck shirt and dusty boots, he finished his day with a meal of black bread, sausage and beer in a humble inn, then rumbled back into town in a crowded tram, he felt as anonymous, as inconspicuous and unselfconscious as any indigenous citizen of his native city, physically exhausted but spiritually free, lonely but at peace.

He *was* lonely, but he was coming to terms with his loneliness, which was of a different kind from the loneliness he had experienced in exile. His loneliness over there had been like an incurable disease which held no hope of alleviation and no comforting prospect except death. But his present solitude, he was beginning to understand, was simply a concomitant of ageing, of ripening, and if there were deprivations there would also be compensation and enrichment.

His daily work at the Institute was routine, but it left him leisure to think. If it did not fall to him to inaugurate research projects, he could still follow up a few ideas inspired by past experience, and seek to connect various trains of thought that had flickered through his mind over the years but about which he had never had the time to think profoundly. And in his spare time, when it was no longer possible to spend hours wandering out of doors, he occasionally went to a concert in the evening or called on the Helblings, who always welcomed him most kindly, all the more so as they felt he was no longer making any particular demands on their sympathy. On the contrary: when he went to see them, he went deliberately to forget about himself and avoided all references to his own past and problems.

He had become a good listener, and found a special kind of detached enjoyment in his listening. There were often a number of quite interesting people at their flat, art historians, musicians, architects and journalists, and their talk was mostly of personalities, their ambitions, jealousies, quarrels and frustrations and not least of their love affairs, and in listening to them with benevolent amusement he was glad he had not, by speaking of himself, placed his own affairs on the same level.

For Kuno Adler was changing. He was becoming less

vulnerable to things that used to burden or irritate him, less sensitive to what he once might have imagined to be slights and innuendos, and more ready to accept people at their own valuation without suspecting them of hypocrisy or deception. And this inner change gradually made itself felt in his relationships with the other workers at the Institute. It was an inner change that scarcely found any expression in outward occurrences, but rather in imponderables, in a shift of emphasis, an alteration of balance. Adler continued as he had begun, to perform his share of the routine tasks of the Institute, carrying out tests and writing reports for the hospitals, never interfering, never asserting himself, never criticising.

Occasionally he would approach one of the younger men with a request to double-check a result in order to confirm or correct his conclusions, or he would enlist the assistance of one of the technicians to perform a delicate manoeuvre. It was all done most courteously on both sides, but if in the first weeks and months the younger staff were inclined to regard him as an elderly, slightly out-of-date outsider to be treated with kindly tolerance, they gradually came to recognise that they had amongst them a man of wide and ripe experience from whom it would be profitable to learn if only he were willing to teach. This, however, Adler never volunteered to do, and would only express an opinion or give advice if he was specifically consulted. Otherwise he held himself aloof and confined himself strictly to his own tasks. This behaviour on Adler's part avoided, as far as possible within the framework of one institution, any closer contact between himself and Dr Krieger.

In the beginning Dr Krieger was pleased that this should be so. He had, very reluctantly, been forced to accept the re-appointment of the returned émigré, albeit in the subordinate position of an assistant, but having had this man forced upon him against his will, he had decided to cloak his reluctance with a show of good grace and even with enthusiasm. Then, after his first gesture of welcome, he had thought that the easiest way to come to terms with the new arrival would be to leave him to his own devices and to ignore him. To his great satisfaction it then appeared that Adler would not make this difficult: he did not assert himself, as Krieger had feared he would, but seemed content just to be tolerated, probably humbled by the bitter experiences he obviously must have suffered abroad, for why, otherwise, had he chosen to come back?

Adler, on his part, did his best to keep out of Dr Krieger's way in a kind of self-protective reaction against having an authority set over him which he did not intend to challenge yet hoped to notice as little as possible. But he also admitted to himself that he had taken an instinctive dislike to Dr Krieger as a person, for imponderable reasons which he assured himself had nothing to do with the fact that the latter was occupying the place which should have been his own.

The months passed, the work progressed, and imperceptibly a shift in the balance of Adler's relationship to the rest of the staff began to take place. His prestige grew, he was treated with greater deference, and though his own unassuming habits never altered, he certainly felt inwardly more at ease. Finding he had time to spare from his routine work he quietly began a small research project of his own, using such equipment as was available at times when it was not otherwise in use. The little cubicle that had been installed for him, but had so far seemed to have no particular purpose, now became useful for keeping his private slides and test-tubes and for writing and filing his notes. He had also had an idea for a piece of electrical machinery for use in his research; and his old friend Grasboeck had put him in touch with an instrument maker who had his own workshop. Here Adler spent many happy evening hours getting the thing built and tested to the mutual delight of the inventor and the craftsman, whom he was able to pay for his skill and materials out of his small reserve of private savings – for at this time his dollars represented incomparable wealth in his now-impoverished country. This small apparatus, too, was installed in Adler's cubicle.

Dr Krieger was not a sensitive man, but even he could not help noticing a change in Professor Adler's standing within the Institute. It was difficult to say what it consisted of, but it showed itself in the manner in which he was spoken to by younger men and by the way the technicians were prepared to help him, especially one of the young women, who seemed to have taken it upon herself to look after him by cleaning his instruments and tidying up for him as if she were his own personal assistant. Yet he kept himself very much to himself, never gave any directions to anyone and so could not be accused of allocating to himself any authority in rivalry to Dr Krieger's own.

Nevertheless, Dr Krieger did feel that his authority was

no longer as absolute as it ought to be, that a rival source of power existed within his domain, and it irked him beyond endurance. However, as there was nothing tangible with which to approach his opponent, he had not known how to tackle him. Perhaps this new piece of machinery Adler had installed without his permission, without even notifying him or explaining its uses, might provide him with the longed-for opportunity. He decided to proceed diplomatically.

'Am I disturbing you, my dear colleague?' Dr Krieger asked in his most suave manner, pushing open the door that led from his private room into the semi-partitioned work-space where Adler was sitting at his desk making notes in his almost illegible handwriting on a small scribbling-pad. He had obviously been tearing off one page after another regardless of where they came to rest: some had landed on the floor. It was early afternoon, but the winter day was already darkening and the neon tubes above the workbenches on the other side of the partition had already been switched on. Adler only had a green-shaded standard lamp on his writing table. 'One moment, Herr Doktor,' Adler said, finishing an entry in a notebook and getting up from his chair. 'Of course you are not disturbing me. What can I do for you?'

'I think it is time you and I had a little talk.'

'Certainly, Herr Doktor, if you wish it. Do please sit down.' He turned the chair on which he had been sitting and offered it to Krieger. There was only one other chair in the place and that was stacked high with papers, scientific journals and reports, mostly American. The table, too, was littered with all kinds of paraphernalia. While Krieger contemplated the disorder with evident distaste, Adler cleared one corner of the table with the sweep of an arm and hitched up onto it with one thigh, the other foot resting on the floor.

'Sorry I'm in such a mess here,' he said apologetically. 'What do you wish to talk about?' He was completely relaxed, in spite of his uncomfortable position, while Krieger, sitting rigidly upright on his chair, looked as tense as he always did because of his tight skin, closely cropped hair and pebbly eyes behind rimless spectacles.

Actually Krieger was at rather a loss about where to begin. He bent down and picked up one of Adler's loose leaves that had fallen near his chair, glanced at it, shook his head and handed it back to its author with a smile of deliberate politeness. Adler said 'thank you'.

But Krieger had found his opening. 'I see you write your notes in English,' he said. 'I suppose it has become more familiar to you over the years than the language of your schooldays. And all those American publications to which you subscribe' – he pointed to the stack of papers which filled the shelves and overflowed into the other chair – 'you keep in touch with all the most recent developments – over there. No doubt you also correspond with your former colleagues?'

'There is little occasion for that, and if I did, would there be any objection?' said Adler. 'I am writing a paper in English because I think this journal, to which I have contributed before, will print it. I have not yet made contact with any of the German language papers, but actually, as you know, the language itself is of secondary importance. The technical terms are international and the connecting text is easily translatable.'

Krieger continued: 'Of course, living there for so many years, your ties with America must have become very close. And what about this little contraption here?' – he pointed to Adler's newly-installed apparatus – 'I was afraid from the start that you would find our equipment inadequate, so you had it sent over to you – as a present, I presume, for your private use? It doesn't figure on our budget, does it? For in that case you would have to request it through our proper channels and that is in the first place through me. But I don't remember being consulted. In any case I don't think any supplementary expenditure would have been approved in the present state of our finances. There are many things the Institute is badly in need of, but I haven't been able to get them passed.'

'This little machine, Herr Doktor? No, it didn't come from America and it certainly has not burdened your budget. I had it built locally at my own expense. It didn't cost much, I can assure you. If you wish to see its purpose I shall be glad to demonstrate it to you at any time. As for the little course of research I am carrying out on the side, I had understood from the authorities when I took up this appointment that I should be free to work on my own if I liked. I clearly remember the Sektionschef saying so at the interview I had with him. Perhaps it ought to have been put in writing. I didn't anticipate there would be any objections. Or are you suggesting that I neglect the work allocated to me in the day-to-day duties of the Institute? If you have any complaint of that kind to make against me, will you please say so unequivocally.'

'No, I have no complaint of that kind. How could I have? It is only that your general attitude and behaviour ever since you came here have more and more made me wonder. You hold yourself so aloof, so unapproachable – with one exception of which I will speak in a moment, about your private research project – you communicate with no one – again with the one exception, and certainly not with me who, I believe, should be the first to know about it. But to me, to me personally you are hostile, Herr Professor, you want nothing to do with me. You even write in English so that I should not understand. So why, why on earth, Professor Adler, did you come back?'

'The answer to that is very simple, Dr Krieger. I came home. I am an Austrian. I belong here.'

'Do you? And you didn't like America? You were not happy there?'

'I didn't say anything about America, I only mean that I didn't like being in exile. I prefer to live at home.'

'And do you feel at home – now? When I see you working so much on your own, so aloof, avoiding contact, as much as possible, with the others, but especially with me, I wonder whether you are not more of an exile here than you were over there. Of course you make one exception – which I find significant. Fräulein Grein.'

'Fräulein Grein?'

'She is the only one of the Institute's personnel who is openly hostile to me, who avoids me as much as she dares, who is scarcely polite. She was here years before I was appointed, and I'd find it very difficult to have her removed, much as I should wish to do so. And she is the only person to whom you have attached yourself, with whom you make a team. That is not a pleasant situation for me and does not make for a profitable collaboration between us.'

Adler was genuinely surprised. He lifted himself off the table and went and stood by the window. It was quite dark outside now. Through the glass partition the assistants and technicians in their white coats, the girls in their white overalls, looked pallid and greenish in the hard diffused light of the neon tubes, as they bent over some delicate operation or moved from one place to another. Their voices, if they were speaking to one another, were inaudible. It struck Adler that the silent gleaming laboratory seemed to be suspended in the darkness of space. In New York, he thought, there would have been walls of light all around, across the street, across the courtyard, over the neighbouring roofs. Here the houses opposite had closed their eyes and in doing so had, paradoxically, made themselves invisible. The two feeble yellow globules of the street lamps down below never penetrated the surrounding haze.

Then Adler turned back to face his interlocutor. 'To tell you the truth, Dr Krieger, I don't know what you are talking about.'

'Oh, come now, my dear colleague. Fräulein Grein must have gossiped to you about me?'

'Fräulein Grein has never gossiped about you or anyone else. We have hardly exchanged any words at all, and the few we have spoken have been concerned only with our work. She is the last person one might suspect of gossiping, she is so reserved, so reticent.'

'She certainly is so with me, but with you I should have thought it would be otherwise.'

'And why should you think that?'

'Well, she might expect some sympathy from you. She might expect you to listen to whatever tales she thinks fit to tell about me, slanderous tales, without any vestige of truth in them, but damaging nevertheless, and disruptive of good relations between us.'

'I still don't know what you are talking about.'

'That is difficult for me to believe, especially in view of your – to put it mildly – unfriendly attitude towards me. Do you mean to tell me that she – or perhaps it was someone else? – has not told you that I have been accused of what our enemies have been pleased to call "war crimes", medical war crimes in my case, and that I have had to defend myself before a tribunal? But if that is what you have been told, you must also have been told that I was acquitted – acquitted and vindicated.

'If you insist,' Krieger continued, 'that Fräulein Grein hasn't told you anything about me, then I will tell you myself. Because I want you to know. You have undoubtedly heard of the "Doktor's Tribunal", the so-called court of law set up by our enemies after the war in order to prosecute medical men, more-or-less eminent ones, for alleged "crimes" against the inmates of certain institutions. The proceedings were based on the denunciations of a motley crowd of people who described themselves as "victims". I was among the accused – and I was acquitted.' Dr Krieger raised his voice a little as he repeated, 'I was acquitted, officially, judicially found innocent by judges who were certainly not prejudiced in my favour. I can show you the transcript of the judgment if you wish.'

'Ah,' said Adler, 'now I understand what the Sektionschef meant when he told me of your appointment here. He said you had been thoroughly investigated. You were employed in what you so euphemistically call "certain institutions". Concentration camps, I suppose.'

'As I've just told you, I was completely exonerated. Nothing I did, no experiments I undertook, no tests I carried out, no treatments I applied were found to be contrary to the interests of science, to the pursuit of pure knowledge. So I was acquitted. What more can you want?'

'You are telling me something I did not know,' replied Adler. 'No one has talked to me about you, or about what you did or did not do. I am hearing it for the first time from your own lips, Dr Krieger. You say you were acquitted: I assume you would not be the Director of this Institute if you had not been. That is sufficient for me. I see no reason why I should make any further inquiries about you or your activities, whatever they were. I can only repeat that neither Fräulein Grein nor any one else has said anything slanderous about you in my presence. And I also don't know why you should especially suspect Fräulein Grein, nor why you accuse me of what you term unfriendliness towards you. This is not a pleasant or profitable conversation, Dr Krieger. I suggest that we break it off, I don't understand why you started it in the first place.'

'Because, Herr Dr Adler, Herr Professor I should say – I want to clear the air. And I want to make some basic principles clear. You call yourself a scientist, Dr Adler? And what is a scientist? A man who devotes himself to science – that is, to knowledge. That is an overriding aim: we strive to know. That is all that matters. You are not a Christian, I presume? Neither am I. You do not adhere to any dogmatic religion, neither do I. So we neither of us have any prejudices which inhibit our pursuit of knowledge. Now let me tell you that I was working during recent years in surroundings, in circumstances, which were ideally favourable to the gaining of pure scientific knowledge. My colleagues and I had the opportunity of carrying out experiments, testing and researching with the only biological material that can yield convincing results in the field of medical science: not with rats and mice and rabbits – but with live human subjects. Some of my colleagues, I won't deny it, sometimes overstepped the limits of what was strictly necessary to achieve an objective result. I was careful never to do so, and as I have said, no fault could be found with me. I have no regrets, except that in the foreseeable future such opportunities will probably not be available again.'

Krieger went on: 'Of course you have prejudices. That is natural in your case. Although I ought to point out that a true scientist should have no prejudices, but should approach every field of investigation without preconceptions. But we are all more or less conditioned by our traditions and environments. I have myself admitted to humanitarian considerations which in my case have saved me from unpleasant consequences. I was acquitted. But I can tell you for your comfort that our material – I mean my colleagues' material – were not Jews. They were Gypsies.'

'And you say this to comfort me! Good God! Material! Living men and women, whoever they were!'

'Well, I suppose I should not have told you! I was carried away. I'm sorry.'

'Don't be sorry. It is a satisfaction to me to have met at least one self-confessed, unrepentant Nazi. There must be many of them. Where have they got to? They all seem to have disappeared. One goes about amongst people, wondering. It is so harassing to have to suspect, looking for signs, listening for unpremeditated, revealing remarks, and perhaps being unfair to people whom one may have wrongly suspected. So I am pleased to have met one openly, face-to-face. I can only thank you for being so frank. I can also understand now why you asked me why I came back. I am one of those, Dr Krieger, whom you didn't get rid of.'

# Sixteen

The summer waned, it was October and Marie-Theres had been at Wald for nearly four months – was it not time that she went home to America? Had not the purpose of her having been sent abroad been accomplished? Valery and Peter discussed the problem – it was still the same one, namely what was their daughter to do? Valery did not feel they were any nearer a solution. And Marie-Theres herself was reluctant to return. She wrote that Hanni was going to Vienna, she had a new job, she was going to be secretary to the Director of the Gallery of Modern Art, she was going back to live with their aunt, Baroness Josephine Simovic, the Countess Lensveldt's and Valery's eldest sister. Couldn't Resi go there too? She was anxious to see for herself the city her mother used to talk about so much, sometimes with nostalgia, dwelling on the old streets, the old houses, the palaces, the churches, and then in a sudden change of mood, with bitterness for the sentimentality which the mere mention of its name seemed to evoke. Marie-Theres, in her letters, begged to be allowed to go and find out for herself.

So now she was there, sharing with Hanni the one spare bedroom in her Aunt Fini's flat in the seedier part of the third district. The street and the house were shabby, but the third district was a good address and not very far from the area which housed the Embassies and many important private houses. The Baroness Josephine Simovic, née Princess Altmannsdorf, was the widow of a General in the one-time Imperial Army. She had lost her husband between the two wars and now had to live on her tiny widow's pension, so that Hanni's small contribution to the housekeeping budget, and Peter Larsen's ample provision for his daughter, eschewed by Count Lensveldt on his country estate, was gratefully accepted.

Aunt Fini was a very different person from Aunt Franzi, and when Marie-Theres first saw her she was filled with misgivings. Where Aunt Franzi was all expansive warmth, tall and broad in her person and wearing comfortable, colourful if somewhat faded linen dresses, country-style woollen skirts with large pockets and green or brown silk blouses, Aunt Fini was thin and one would have called her erect rather than tall. She always wore black, mourning for her husband even after all those years, just a touch of white at the neck and a black velvet ribbon round her throat. She also wore a long chain of jet beads with a tiny silver cross at the end. Her face was very pale and deeply-lined, her lips bloodless, her white hands veined with blue. To Marie-Theres, who had never seen an old lady who *looked* like an old lady, she was a daunting figure indeed, but she smiled at her young niece and her voice was soft as she welcomed her to Vienna and to her home. This was also something the girl had never seen before: such a lot of furniture, so many overstuffed chairs, and so many small tables covered with unrecognisable small ornaments and faded photographs in heavy frames, the tall window that might have let in light had it not been for the long velvet curtains framing the intricate lace ones.

But the bedroom she was to share with Hanni was more austere. Two brass bedsteads, the same kind of chest of drawers with jug and basin as she had had at Wald, and a courtyard outside, although without tree or fountain, just naked paving stones and the back view of the neighbouring houses. Was this Vienna? Marie-Theres endured a few hours of panic. Oh no, oh no, she felt, this is terrible, I had much better have gone home. I can't possibly stay here. But then there was tea in the cluttered drawing room where the curtains were drawn and the lamps were lit under their funny green shades, there were beautiful thin tea cups and painted plates and a delicious cake. And it was reassuring not to see any sign of the distress she felt on Hanni's face: she was chattering away to her aunt about events at Wald and laughing as she always did, and the severe aunt herself seemed nothing like as forbidding as she had at first appeared, but kindly and full of interest in what she was being told. So gradually Marie-Theres's panic subsided and she was able to answer Aunt Fini's questions about herself, and how her mother was, and even to laugh with Hanni about her own surprise at these, to her, strange surroundings.

When, later that evening, they retired to bed, Hanni was full of sympathy for the shock to her cousin's feelings in encountering her severe-looking aunt and the apparent discomfort of their bedroom. 'It's not as bad as it looks,' she assured her, 'and we're very lucky to have somewhere to stay in Vienna at all, it's almost impossible to find a room, so much has been destroyed. Anyway, we won't be here for long, I hope I shall be able to get married in the spring, and who knows what's in store for you? Perhaps you'll get engaged, or you can always go home if you don't like it here. Meanwhile, you can go out and see the town and meet people: Georg has found just the thing to keep you occupied.' And she went on to tell her cousin about a course of lectures and guided tours which had been laid on for young foreigners who, for one reason or another, happened to be in Vienna – chiefly the families of the military or civil members of the missions of the occupying powers stationed there. At the Foreign Office Georg had found out all about this, he had even had a hand in setting it up. Resi would be able to learn something about Austria's history and history of art, and be taken sightseeing, and as she would be one of those who understood the language, she could also be taken to the theatre. 'And,' said Hanni, 'you will meet young Americans, French and British and you will be sure to make friends.'

'I don't make friends,' Marie-Theres whispered, rather

sullenly, under her breath. 'And it sounds very much like school all over again.' But Hanni had already turned over and gone to sleep and so Marie-Theres did too.

It was, indeed, very much like school all over again. The next day Hanni had taken her to the University by tram, shown her where to get on and off, had helped her to register and find her way up wide shallow staircases and steep winding ones hidden away in corners, along broad corridors and through narrow passageways to the lecture room where the courses were being given. There was a small gathering of students, the lecture had already begun, and the lecturer was speaking voluble and fluent, but strongly accented, English. Hanni, not wishing to interrupt, had pushed her in through the door, whispering that she would fetch her this first day to go home for lunch, and left her. All heads had turned towards her as she came in, so she quickly sat down in the nearest empty place in order to hide her embarrassment. What the talk was about she did not take in.

Two or three days went by, two or three of the other students tried to speak to her, but she looked so aloof, in fact some thought she looked haughty, that they felt rebuffed and left her alone. And then on the third day of what she felt to be her ordeal, as she was coming out of the lecture room with her books under her arm, who should be coming along the corridor towards her but Lucas Anreither! He held out both his hands towards her, one to grasp hers, the other to relieve her of her books.

'Resi, what a surprise to find *you* here! Fancy you being in the University. I should never have imagined it. Come along, where shall we go?' In fact Lucas's surprise was disingenuous. He had found out that Resi was in Vienna and what she was doing and he had come to find her, cunningly waiting a couple of days for her to feel bewildered and out of her depth, as indeed she did. A smile and a warm greeting were his reward.

'Oh, Lucas, how nice to see you!' Here was a familiar face, an anchor in an unknown sea. He drew her arm through his.

'It's a lovely day, let's go and walk in the gardens.'

Some of the other young people who had made unsuccessful attempts to strike up an acquaintance watched them go. 'So that was who she was waiting for – that young man was Austrian.'

The two of them sat on a bench in the gardens next to the University and chatted as old friends. Resi was happy. She knew Lucas, he was someone from Wald, someone with whom she felt at home. Then he took her into the Inner City and showed her quaint little streets and street corners, the 'real Vienna', he called it, 'I'll leave the monuments and showplaces to your sightseeing guides,' he said. Lastly, he took her to a coffee house and they sat in the window drinking coffee out of small cups which was served with accompanying glasses of water. It was real coffee which Lucas had ordered at an exorbitant price, but it was worth it to him just to be with her.

From now on they would walk about the town every afternoon and almost always end their strolls in a coffee house. Without Lucas, Marie-Theres would probably never have had any experience of Vienna, never overcome her bewilderment, she would have rejected her surroundings almost without taking them in. For in those early post-war years, and in the autumn, the city was grey, in the public gardens the trees were shedding their leaves. But with Lucas at her side Resi felt safe. Her anxiety at being alone was allayed, her fear subsided and made way for curiosity, even for the willingness to take in what she saw. She began to understand what her mother had told her and to search within herself for the affinities she had inherited. 'This is the Palais Altmannsdorf,' Lucas had said on one of the first days of these wanderings, and she had stood looking up at the wide grey facade, with its high shuttered windows and the crumbling corner of its damaged roof, fearfully as if she was seeing a ghost. After that she had insisted on walking past there again and again. Fear and attraction, some obscure stirring of the blood, arose within her when they turned into that narrow street, and she would press Lucas's arm, as if to steady herself until they were out again on the broader thoroughfare where there were shops and people on the pavement.

Lucas was delighted to feel this token of her dependence on him. Ever since that day on the Bichl Alm, his love for her had deepened from a mere summer flirtation to an intense, incandescent passion, and he was determined to woo her. He was elated not only by being 'in love', but by a sense of mission and historical fulfilment. He saw Resi in the context of her background and himself in the context of his own. He, too, looked up at the imposing façade of the Palais Altmannsdorf. Resi was a daughter of this house, only two generations removed from the grand old man, her grand-father, who had been the master of his own grandfather. Yes, they had been master and servant, that was the stark truth, however much the relationship had been mellowed by benevolence into the semblance of 'almost' friendship. 'Al-most', that was the poisonous word in which his parents still revelled and which he so bitterly hated. 'Almost', that was why he himself was treated by the princesses, the daughters, almost as an equal, almost as one of the family. 'Almost', what a hidden sting there was in that word. It had been newly envenomed only a few days ago when he had asked Resi: 'Have you told your aunt that you are seeing so much of me, that you go out with me almost every day? Doesn't she object?'

'Oh, yes,' Resi replied, 'I have told her, why not? She doesn't object at all, she's pleased. You see she knows who you are. She's far more suspicious of the people I meet at my lectures, she's always asking Georg Corvinus, Hanni's fiancé, to find out who their families are, in case I get involved with one of them. She says that's because she is "responsible" for me. She keeps on saying that. But she knows who *you* are, Lucas.'

Indeed she does, thought Lucas, I'm old Anreither's grandson and as safe to be her niece's escort as a footman would be. An Altmannsdorf couldn't get 'involved', as you call it, with *me*. But you are mistaken, my lady, I, the grand-son of Prince Altmannsdorf's forester, am going to *marry* the Prince's granddaughter and become one of the family as of right and as an equal, not *almost*.

There was a slight tinge of disappointment for him in the fact that the road had been smoothed for him by Resi's father, who himself was not a nobleman, but, as he heard, a farmer's son. It would not give him quite the same satisfaction to say to Mr Larsen, 'I want to marry your daughter', as if the father had been a Prince Altmannsdorf or a Count Lensveldt, as Hanni's father was. It was actually Count Lensveldt whom Lucas had in his mind's eye when he pictured the scene in which he would be demanding Resi's hand in marriage, not a nebulous American scientist who would probably not realise the boldness and the implications of the request. If he ever did stop to think that Peter Larsen, as a young man, had taken this same bold step in marrying an Altmannsdorf daughter, he explained it away by telling himself that Larsen had been a foreigner and that the circumstances leading to that match had been exceptional and peculiar, due to the upheavals of the First World War. And he also knew, through his close association with the Lensveldts, that for many years Resi's mother had been an outcast, that reconciliation had only come about when she and her husband emigrated to America. Also, that they had married abroad.

That was not going to happen to Lucas. He would not go to America to marry Resi, he would marry her here in Vienna, or better still in the village church at Wald. A charming little church, whitewashed inside and out, with as much paint and gilt on its saints and around the altar as the village could afford, and in which, from his early childhood, he knew every carved pew-end, every crack in the flagstone floor, and how the light fell on the Sunday mornings on the brass of the altar rail. Now, of course, he was a socialist, an agnostic, a 'Red' as Count Lensveldt called him, but his parents were 'Black' church-going people. How delighted they would be about the marriage, how they would enjoy the wedding, and how he himself would chuckle inwardly at this little footnote to the dialectic of history.

Meanwhile, with such thoughts at the back of his mind, Lucas looked lovingly at Resi, who looked back at him with her candid blue eyes and not many thoughts behind them except that he was as nice to be with as Budd had been. In fact, while she was with Lucas her thoughts often strayed to Budd, and she promised herself to make an effort to write to him in answer to some of those unopened letters which she really must – *must* – open one of these days.

They were again sitting by the window in Lucas's favourite coffee house, looking out on the broad avenue of the Ring where the trees had now all shed their leaves and the light was failing earlier every day. 'I shall have to go home,' Resi said, 'my aunt does not like me to be out alone in the dark and I am frightened. The Parkgasse is so badly lit.'

'You will not be alone, I'll take you right up to your front door, so we still have plenty of time.'

'Then if you have plenty of time, Lucas, why don't you come up to my aunt's apartment? I'm sure she wouldn't mind if you came – she knows who you are.'

'She does, but I don't want her to know me on those terms. And I don't want you to think of me as your aunt does. I want to be my own real self and I want you to understand me as I really am. We never talk about serious things, and I couldn't talk about them in your aunt's room, even if she invited me in. So let me try to tell you about them now, and I'll try to explain in the simplest words I can, and if you'll have patience and listen to me, you will begin to see the world as I do and that will mean so much to me. So very, very much, Resi.'

Thus, on that afternoon and on many following ones, Lucas attempted to woo Resi by teaching her the philosophy of historical materialism. 'You are being taught history, Austrian history, I suppose, in that lecture room of yours, all about the dukes and counts and archdukes, their wars and marriages amongst themselves and with foreign princes and princesses; but all these things are not important, they are but the ripples on the surface of history. It is the social conditions and the economic forces which shape the world. Power lies in the hands of those who own the means of production. And in the old days, when the nobility seemed so important, it was land, land that brought forth the crops and it was the nobility who owned the land.'

These were the words and other dry ones like them that he spoke with his lips, but his eyes burned with passion as he discoursed on the feudal system long since superseded and of which only empty symbols remained. All that, he said, was done away with in the French Revolution and was never transplanted into America where, as your glorious constitution declares, all men are born equal. But alas, the economic forces had their way and the power that was wrested from the nobility fell into the hands of those who owned money, the capitalists.

'Yes,' said Resi dreamily, getting a little bit bored with this kind of talk, but trying her best to make some response to the efforts she felt Lucas was making on her behalf, 'yes, I suppose it's not quite true that all men are born equal, because some have rich parents and some have poor. But then everyone can get rich, even if they are born poor, but not everyone can be a prince if he is born that way.'

'What do you know about princes, Resi? Aren't they just ordinary people, like you and me? I know your grandfather was a prince, and your aunts are princesses, and your mother too, but isn't she proud of being just an ordinary American citizen? Mrs Larsen? And your uncle and aunt at Wald who are just nice people, do you think they are so very special because they are a Count and Countess? They have no *power*. They are just ordinary people. A prince doesn't mean anything, nowadays.'

'I do know a prince, and he is not at all ordinary,' said Resi.

'And who is he?'

'Nina's brother, Bimbo Grein.'

'Oh, so you have met Lori Grein, have you? That degenerate playboy.'

'What does "degenerate" mean? It's something unpleasant, by the way you say it. And you don't know him, because you call him Lori. None of his friends do.'

'No, I don't know him, and I don't want to. It's a good thing he and his like are no longer of any account in the world. It's the money-men who have their power now, the capitalists.

It needs another revolution to get rid of them, like the Russian Revolution.'

Oh, Resi, adorable Resi, Lucas said in his heart, I wish I could just say how much I loved you instead of trying to make you understand. It is only when you understand my view of the world and are able to share my thoughts that there will be no barrier between us and you will be able to love me as I love you.

It was his way of wooing her, this teaching of economic history, for he believed that only when he had made her think as he did would she accept love from him. 'No, my dear,' he said, 'it's a question of power. Those who have money, the capitalists, own the means of production, and they exploit the poor who have nothing but the work of their hands to live on. It needed a revolution to get rid of the feudal system; it needed another revolution to get rid of capitalism: the Russian Revolution. They have abolished the money-power, the capitalists in their country. That is what we must strive for now in the world, that is how history moves on.'

But here Lucas had done his cause a signal disservice. For at the mere mention of the Russians, Resi was roused from the dreamy acquiescence with which she had been half-listening to Lucas's dissertation and looked up at him with dismay.

'Oh no Lucas, not the Russians, not what they have done, not what they want to do. If you believe that, then you really are a Red as Uncle Poldo said. Then you are – dangerous.' And she looked around the peaceful coffee house where only two elderly gentlemen and a harmless-looking couple were sitting with their coffee cups, reading the newspapers on bamboo frames. Did Lucas carry a bomb in his brief case? Lucas bit his lip. He had allowed himself to be carried away by his own logic, or rather by the logic of his theory, and by the simplifications forced on him by the use of such elementary language as he felt Resi could understand. He put out his hand to touch her arm and gave an awkward little laugh.

'Of course I'm not dangerous. I'm not a revolutionary myself, I was speaking in general terms, to explain to you what history is about, that's all. All I want to do is to vote at elections to abolish the iniquitous money-power, the capitalist system, and if that is what Count Lensveldt calls being a Red, well, so be it. In time you will come to understand.'

But Resi, though she did not understand, thought that it might be better if she saw a little less of Lucas, however nice he was, and she began to make excuses to avoid meeting him quite so often, with the result that his love for her grew even more passionate. He had not known how much he loved her. What at Wald had seemed a delightful, affectionate, slightly amusing attachment to this beautiful girl, amusing because of her naivety and ignorance of the most elementary facts of the modern world, was developing into a burning, soul-searching love, a desire to possess her body and soul, but soul even more than body, to make her his own by impregnating her with his own mind and ideas and views of life. She was malleable, she could be formed, indeed she *would* be formed by any man who could capture her imagination and win her love. And he was determined he would be that man.

# Seventeen

(The first page of this chapter is missing from the original typescript.)

The hall of Kanakis's house, paved in squares of black and white marble, panelled in white and rising from the ground through the floor above to a ceiling of opaque glass panes, contained a semi-circular staircase with a wrought-iron balustrade leading to a little balcony of a similar design above the central door in the hall opposite the main entrance. The hall was the only part of the house to be brightly lit by candles in gilt sconces round the walls. The other rooms, the long central one with its three French windows giving onto the tiny garden (but now closely curtained) and the two others to the right and left of it, were all dim and subdued, though each in a different way. The larger room on the right had a polished parquet floor, chairs along two sides, and an American record player at the back, a long, smooth, discreet cabinet made of some exotic wood, elegant and unobtrusive, equipped with every technical perfection to diffuse dance music, sentimental songs, syncopated or lilting rhythms.

The lighting came from above, hidden behind cornices, and the room was filled with a diffused, hazy glow, cool and caressing as if at the bottom of the sea. This impression was reinforced by the trailing green plants which hung or climbed about the room, gently swaying in scarcely notice-able draughts. The smaller room on the left was the light-est; it contained a buffet and a bar. But in the central room Kanakis had achieved the extraordinary feat of marrying the delicate elegance of the eighteenth century with modern comfort. Silk panels and exquisite stucco mouldings, inlaid cabinets and bronze sconces, but no delicate chairs or vola-tile tables, only a deep blue Savonnerie carpet on the floor, couches and cushions in groups half-hidden behind screens, a scattering of pink-shaded lamps, and in one corner a large low table surrounded by three semi-circular sofas where Kanakis himself liked to sit with his closest friends.

Surprise and delight were the successive emotions which awaited the guests to Theophil Kanakis's 'little palace'. He had not found it difficult to collect first a small, then a wid-ening, circle of friends to fill his rooms. Bimbo Grein had brought the younger set. Artists, actors and men of letters soon found means of being introduced. It all began by special invitation, and then became a weekly institution throughout the winters of the early 1950s when, after the terrors of per-secution, the barbarities of occupation and all the privations of the period, luxuries were still rare and lavish hospitality the greatest luxury of all. As a result Kanakis, with the help of Bimbo and one or two of his older friends, had to be very careful to select and limit the number of people admitted to his Thursday evenings, to avoid both overcrowding of the limited space and too obvious discrepancies of tastes and affinities among the guests.

Although the range of social background and age was wide and varied, it was Kanakis himself who insisted on maintaining the accent on youth. He enjoyed the company of the generation younger than himself in whose eyes he could see the reflection of his prestige, of his secure maturity, and of his personality enhanced by the mysterious aura of his wealth. This aura surrounded him in almost the same manner as, in olden days, 'a dignity surrounded the king': a magnetic and indefinable use of power to confer benefits, to dispense comforts and enjoyments, warmth and light to anyone within reach of his influence. Kanakis was perfectly aware of the source and power of this influence. It enabled him to indulge in an emotion of which he approved in himself and enjoyed as one of his own virtues, the emotion of benevolence. He enjoyed smiling at his young friends and making them feel happy. Their enjoyment of his beautiful house was a necessary and complementary ingredient of his own possessions; their pleasure in his lavish hospitality added the final touch of polish and delight to his consciousness of providing it.

In this there was nothing ignoble, for he had no vanity wanting to be gratified, no self-importance for which he desired flattery. What he sought was the purely aesthetic, and in a sense moral, pleasure of indulging his taste and his sensuous predilections and to do so without giving offence. At the same time, he had the judgment and sufficient command of his feelings to avoid being exploited. He would not invest financially in any scheme or person or idea because, as he invariably told applicants, he was not interested in financial returns. He would make no loans, as he wished to avoid both gratitude and ingratitude as the most insidious poison to personal relations, and he had no ambition to 'cut a figure' either in politics, in industry or even in the cultural life of the country to which he had temporarily returned; although he took a lively, if completely detached and, as he would say, impartial, interest in all these aspects of its progress.

Most of the young set came in couples, the young man or girl bringing the partner with whom they happened to be going out at the time, but as they were all more or less interrelated or had known each other for years, these were also groups of three or four who came together, broke up and reformed, danced or sat out as attractions or curiosity moved them. The dining room, with its table laden with delicacies not seen for years, and the dancing room with its subaqueous lighting, were the greatest centre of attraction in the early evening; but sooner or later the flow was reversed and there was a drift back into the long drawing room, especially towards its far corner where Kanakis himself sat talking. He was a wonderful talker and entertainer and an equally good listener if he had recruited someone else to do the storytelling. To drink he served only wine and no hard liquor, declaring that in a country blessed with the delicate fragrance of the grape it would be a crime to assault the pal-

ate with the blunt instruments of gin or whisky, let alone
vodka. By this means he also endeavoured to heighten the
company's spirits without allowing them to rise tumultu-
ously or to degenerate and become maudlin. And as he also
kept the record player low-pitched, he would repeatedly explain that for obvious reasons he wished to avoid sound or
light from penetrating to the outside world and disturbing
people sleeping after a day's work.

Marie-Theres first came to one of these evenings with
Hanni and Georg von Corvinus. They found Bimbo acting
as a master of ceremonies for Kanakis, a kind of Puck serv-
ing Oberon, his king, ministering to his tastes and whims,
but far too impudently independent to be subservient to
them himself. He brought with him a friend, a distant
cousin, a schoolfellow, or just a boy he had met somewhere
by chance and whom he presented to Kanakis as suitable to
help carry a tray of glasses or a plate of sandwiches. For himself, he always brought a girl, not always the same one, on
whom he would on that particular evening lavish the most
unremitting attention – in spite of which he seemed to have
his eyes and ears alert for everything that went on in the
room. He was everywhere, moving with the grace of a cat,
smooth as silk, and with the energy of a coiled spring, and
Kanakis, however interesting and fascinating he found his
companion, always remained conscious of Bimbo's presence
somewhere in the background.

To Marie-Theres, these evenings at Kanakis's 'little palace' revealed a world totally new to her, mysterious, baffling
and intensely fascinating. She was lost in a strange country

without a map or compass, in which words had unfamiliar meaning and behaviour was unpredictable. To a certain extent she recognised the country of romance for which, in the boredom of her adolescence, she had secretly yearned but had never been able to envisage. On entering the brightly-lit hall, with its golden sconces and shining marble floor, its scent of camellias and orange blossom from the little potted trees, it had seemed like a dream. Kanakis had come out to see who was arriving and had seen her standing there, her violet-blue eyes wide open and that rare childlike smile on her lips as she looked around her in amazed delight.

'Countess Hanni, will you present me please?'

Hanni, still extricating herself from her coat and scarf, said: 'Resi, here is our kind host, Herr von Kanakis. You see, I told you what a privilege it was to be invited to his lovely house. Herr von Kanakis, this is Resi Larsen, my cousin from America, a daughter of Mama's youngest sister, a fellow-citizen of yours. I felt sure you would allow me to bring her even without a special invitation.'

'Indeed! I am honoured, what an acquisition!' And opening the door to the long drawing room he called, "Bimbo, my dear fellow, see whom we have here, an Austro-American cousin of Countess Hanni Lensveldt. Is she not exquisite?'

From this moment Resi entered an unknown country. Bimbo rose from the low couch on which he had been sitting half-entwined with a dark-haired girl and dutifully came forward. His first glance told him that this girl was strikingly beautiful and his senses warned him even more immediately that she was not as other girls were. As a result, he bowed with rather ironical ceremony, which made Hanni laugh and say, 'Well, Bimbo, she is not an Imperial Highness, you know,' and to Resi, 'This is Lorenzo Grein, Nina's brother, we all call him Bimbo. Mind you don't fall in love with him, though I expect you will. We all do, it's like catching measles. We get over it and then we're immune.'

Bimbo took no notice of her. 'I'll introduce you to someone who speaks English,' he said to Resi in English, but before she could answer, Hanni said, 'No need, my dear, she manages perfectly in our own lingo – spoke it at her mother's knee.'

'Ah, all the better, then I'll leave her to you and Georg,' he said, and sloped back to where the dark-haired girl was waving to him with one upraised arm while vigorously defending the cushion against any attempted encroachment with the other. Hanni and Georg Corvinus were greeting friends right and left, and a group round a low table covered with wineglasses beckoned to them to come over. They nodded towards them and looked round at Resi, whose eyes were following Bimbo's retreating figure in a kind of trance.

'Would you like to dance?' asked Kanakis who, unnoticed, had suddenly appeared at her side. 'I'm not as young as I used to be, but I'm still capable of a few passable steps. And I must show you my aquarium.' He took her hand, and leading her half a step behind him, he threaded his way past and between the poufs and cushions that littered the floor to the door that stood ajar at the further end of the long room. Opening it, they plunged from the warm, rose-coloured half-light into a deeper, blue-tinted darkness, and the rhythmical beat of dance music, coming from an invisible source, grew louder. Three or four couples were swaying or jerking silently to its syncopated rhythm. Kanakis put his arm round Resi's waist and proved himself a consummate performer of those prescribed ritualistic contortions. Stranger and stranger. To Marie-Theres, dance music, as she had known it at school or club dances, had always been hot and strident, hammering loudly at the senses. Here it was muted, insinuating, whispering and confidential, secretively exciting. Kanakis saw the perplexity on her face. 'I can't have it played more loudly,' he said apologetically, 'as I don't want it to be heard outside. I don't want anyone to complain; people all around want to sleep. I have tested the volume very carefully myself, standing in the street to listen, and like this not a sound comes through. So I'm afraid it is not as stimulating as it might be.'

'Oh, I like it like this.' She had dropped her voice to a whisper, to comply with the ambience, as if she, too, feared that her normal speech might be heard beyond the enclosing walls. 'I like it like this, and dancing with you. You're a wonderful dancer, Mr . . . er . . .'

'My name is Theophil,' he interrupted, 'much easier. I haven't danced for years, you have refreshed my taste for it. But now let me get you something to eat and drink and we'll go to the other room. Unless you would like to dance again. I'll go and find you a partner.' But she didn't want to be left alone and she followed him.

She went to the corner table, where he sat in the seat he had occupied before he got up to dance with her, next to a tall, sinuous woman with hair drawn back sleekly from her forehead and large circular golden earrings like suns, that caught the lamplight and glittered.

'What was it you were saying?' he asked, stroking her bare arm with two fingers. 'Don't tell me I have missed one of your *boutades*, I couldn't bear it. You'll have to repeat it for my benefit if I have.'

'My dear Kanakis, I'm sure you've already heard the story of what the great Crivelli said to Goering when he was presented to her at the big reception in '42? After she had sung *Tosca* so divinely? "Ah, Reichsmarschall," she said, "I thought I had finished with murderers for this evening." I can tell you, all of us who heard it, our hearts missed a beat. But he pretended to take it as a joke, though his face looked like thunder, and he laughed loudly.'

'And nothing happened to her afterwards?'

'She fainted. She must have frightened herself to death. But no, nothing happened to her. Her voice and her reputation saved her, I suppose. She is coming to sing at the reopening of the Opera. What an ovation she will get!'

Resi sat in a corner of the sofa opposite, now and again nibbling the sandwich and sipping the wine one of the young men had brought her unasked. Everyone around her was either listening to the sleek-haired woman with the gold earrings (a Burgtheater actress), or talking in low voices. She did not understand anything that was being said. She tried to look over her shoulder to where Bimbo Grein had been sitting, but he was no longer there. Perhaps he had gone into the other room to dance with his partner. Kanakis, too, though paying marked attention to his neighbour, was searching the room under half-closed eyelids. Resi thought these looked like little grey canopies with black fringes and she found herself wondering whether grey was their real colour or whether it was the effect of shadow. Everything seemed to become hazy and insubstantial around her and for a moment she thought she was dreaming and would suddenly wake up in the little white room at home in Eden Rise or at Aunt Fini's with Hanni in the other bed. And then panic rising, tears overwhelming her, everyone seemed to stand up at the same time, in one concerted movement, tensions relaxed, voices changed their resonance, they were all saying good night and goodbye, shaking hands and discussing prosaically how to get home.

# Eighteen

Kanakis searched the telephone directory for the number of the Baroness Simovic. That was where that pretty American girl was staying, the one who had seemed so shy, or rather a little stiff, at his party. She had said the Baroness Simovic was her aunt. The name was not in the book – can't afford a telephone, poor woman. He would have to find out where she lived and go and call on her, which was a nuisance, but perhaps just as well. She would be all the more benevolent and co-operative if the old-fashioned proprieties were observed. Kanakis called at four o'clock and sent in his card by the elderly woman in a black apron who opened the door. A relic of days gone by, an old factotum, but still – a servant, probably by now almost a companion. At any rate, the Baroness did not have to open the door herself.

He stood in the narrow dimly-lit hall and heard the two

women's voices through the half-open door. The maid's was emphatic, the Baroness's a little apprehensive.

'A very elegant gentleman,' said the woman.

'Of course, of course, show him in at once.'

The lady wore black and looked much older than her years, in her seventies rather than her early sixties. The hand she held out to Kanakis was thin and blue veined. She shook her head a little with a slight nervous tic. He bent over her hand and kissed it, actually doing so, not just making the gesture.

'I believe you will have heard of me, Baroness?'

'Certainly, certainly – it is most considerate of you to call. I'm afraid my niece is not at home. She works, you know, the girls all do nowadays. She is a secretary.'

'Is she? I am surprised. I should not have thought so. I believed she was only here on a visit.'

'Oh, you mean my niece Resi – Marie-Theres I should say. I thought you meant my other niece Hanni Lensveldt. It is she who is a secretary – to the Director of the Modern Art Gallery, Dr Helbling. She has spoken to me about you and about your wonderful parties. I thought, when you were announced, that it was her you wanted to see. But Resi – it's true, she is also my niece, my youngest sister's daughter who lives in America. I think she's out too. I'll ask Kathi.' The Baroness half-rose to go to the door, 'no bells any more,' she murmured, but Kanakis interrupted her.

'Please don't trouble yourself, I came to make myself known to you, so kind of you to receive me.'

'I'm very pleased . . .' and, inconsequently, 'Resi is such a child.'

Kanakis smiled. She's thinking: 'He's too old for her,' but he assented: 'Yes, quite, very young indeed and very lovely.'

'Hanni, you know, is engaged,' the Baroness went on, by way of making conversation, 'to Georg Corvinus – you know him, perhaps? A grandson of General von Corvinus. My husband served under him when he was a young subaltern. In a garrison in Galicia. But you wouldn't know about that – it was long before your time, Herr von – Kanakis.' The Baroness had glanced at the card that lay before her, to make sure she got the name right.

'Indeed, I do know about it, Baroness,' he smiled, 'I am of old Viennese stock, you know, strange as it may seem to you. And I happen to know Georg Corvinus too. Come to think of it, he came to my house with both your nieces, the Countess Hanni and Fräulein Marie-Theres. It was he who brought them. I'd made his acquaintance before that through a mutual friend. And now will you permit me to put my request to you, the request I came to make? I have taken a box at the Opera for next Thursday, at the Theater an der Wien of course, as the Opera itself is not rebuilt yet, and I should like to invite Fräulein Marie-Theres, and the Countess Hanni too, if she would care to come. I have a young man also, to keep the young ladies company. I confess that I love young people. They give me the greatest pleasure. I feel like a kind of uncle towards them, old bachelor that I am.'

'Indeed, it is exceedingly kind of you, Herr von Kanakis,

a most generous, rather unusual invitation. I'm sure the girls would be delighted. They don't often get the chance of going to the theatre. Tickets are so difficult to get – and so expensive. Resi has been taken to the Burgtheater once with her class – her study group I mean, to see a Grillparzer play. She didn't want to go, she said she didn't like organised parties, but I persuaded her. I thought she ought to make the most of all her opportunities to educate herself – that is what she is here for – but she didn't enjoy it. The language was probably too difficult for her.'

'But you will allow her to come to the Opera with me – with *us*, I mean, won't you? It's not a difficult opera. Tchaikovsky. I'm sure she'll enjoy it, and she'll be with friends. I'll chaperone her!'

The Baroness laughed. 'You – a chaperone, Herr von Kanakis, I can't see you in that capacity. A young man like you! But still, if you are going to be a party – although I don't know about Hanni – I agree, of course. Besides, I have no illusions, girls do very much as they like nowadays – Hanni went out with Georg long before they were engaged – I don't imagine that my approval or disapproval of what they do makes much difference. But Resi is so young and so far away from her parents. You see, I am responsible for her, I *feel* responsible.'

'No harm will come to her, Baroness, you may rest assured. I'll call for her, and the other young lady, if she wants to come, on Thursday then. And please don't wait up for them. We shall want to have something to eat after the performance and I'll see that they get home safely.'

* * *

The four people gathered in the box on the first tier of the Theater an der Wien looked a well-composed, perfectly attuned quartet. The broad-shouldered, swarthy-complexioned man of forty, in a discreet dark suit of unquestionable perfection, was obviously the host and the dominant personality. His note was power and restraint. The one highlight in his appearance was the very large black pearl which he wore in his grey tie. He sat well back in the box on a slightly higher chair, which allowed him to see over the heads of those in front.

Immediately in front of him, with her arm resting on the red velvet ledge of the box, was a young woman with dark hair looped in a thick bang across her forehead and gathered in a heavy bun at the nape of her neck. Her complexion was dark, and one might have been tempted to look for some resemblance with the man above and behind her, until one noticed that an indefinable luminosity in her eyes and a sweetness around her mouth set her off from him as being of an entirely different breed. It would have taken a more prolonged and concentrated study of her face to discover the beauty of those features, but no observer's glance would have lingered long enough for that discovery because the two other people in the front of the box would immediately have claimed all his attention. Next to the dark girl sat the enchanting figure of a young faun, a boy of the same colouring and texture as his sister, but in his case sparkling with darting gleams of fire, the embodiment of the laughter dancing in his eyes. And next to him, tall and upright, sat a golden girl, her Nordic fairness enhanced by the dark trio of her companions, the light blue she was wearing reflecting the colour of her eyes, a blush on her cheeks from the excitement of her surroundings.

A truly remarkable quartet even to the casual onlooker, if such a person happened to be present amongst the audience that crammed the theatre tier upon tier and row behind row for what promised to be a dazzling performance of *Eugene Onegin*. While the great Opera House on the Ringstrasse was still being rebuilt, this old theatre, which had been the scene for generations of innumerable operettas, was giving a temporary home to grand opera, and doing so with the charm of a famous soubrette long retired and grown old, receiving with unpretentious but becoming adornment, and a dignity all her own, the visit of a great noble lady calling on her in state and wearing all her diamonds. The sense of this meeting of ranks, and the perfectly self-possessed ease with which both parties carried themselves, gave to an opera performance in these surroundings the peculiarly festive atmosphere of a special occasion which was very touching. The audience obviously responded to it with emotion, into which the release from years of fear, and delight in the revival of this most beloved art of musical drama, also flowed and swelled. Of the four members of our quartet, Kanakis was the most consciously and sensitively aware of this. He studied the people in the stalls below him with fascination. Most of the women were wearing a new dress, or one they had refashioned for just such an evening as this, and one could see that both they and their men had groomed and prepared themselves to be at their best. And when the music began they were all rapt in concentration.

Nina Grein, the girl in the dark dress, her thick eyebrows almost meeting over her nose, the one feature that obtruded itself in her face and distracted the beholder from recognising the beauty of her eyes and mouth, was the one most totally absorbed and most deeply moved by the coming together of music, audience and theatre. She was too poor, too sad and too lonely, since the disappearance of her parents, even to attempt to buy a ticket, or even to wish to do so, and too fearful also, had she been offered one (as had occasionally happened), of coming into contact with some black-uniformed, jack-booted SS officer who might be among the audience; also, because of her name, she had of necessity lived as inconspicuously as possible, continuing her work, her religion and her devotion to her young brother, for whom she had tried to make a home. She had given him her all, but felt it was too little, or rather, unacceptable. Had their beautiful mother and their resplendent father lived, Lorenzo would have been overshadowed by their personalities and have taken his measure from their standards. But she was only an awkward older sister to whom he had no reason to look up, too young for respect, too old and too severe for intimacy. All he gave her was a rather condescending affection which both touched and hurt her at the same time.

However, it was to him that she owed her presence this evening, through the invitation of his new friend Theophil Kanakis, although she had at first hesitated to accept, as she could not quite make out what had prompted it. Bimbo had been seeing a lot of this Kanakis recently, for whom he had been buying antiques. Why shouldn't she accept his invitation, he had asked impatiently: Kanakis liked going to the opera and to the theatre, but he didn't like going alone. He liked taking boxes and inviting people; he could very well afford it, so why shouldn't he do what gave him pleasure? And then Bimbo mentioned that he had also invited Marie-Theres Larsen, that half-American girl who was staying at her aunt's, the old Baroness Simovic. Ah, Nina thought, now she understood. That was the girl she had met last summer at Wald. Of course, it was now obvious to her that she was being asked to make up a foursome. Once I should have been called a chaperone, Nina remarked wryly to herself, thirty-four and elderly, because I am unmarried. And that girl is only a child. Nina wondered for whose sake she was being asked to chaperone her – not Bimbo's surely since he could have taken her out by himself if he wanted to, but not like this, to the Opera, which he could not afford. Kanakis himself? She had not met him, but she was puzzled that a man of his age should be interested in an empty-headed little girl however lovely to look at. But then – all men were alike, a fair face was what attracted them, nothing else mattered.

Then the lights went out and the curtain parted and was swept up on either side of the stage. The girls in the garden sang. Suddenly Nina's eyes were brimming. Some protective armour she had been unconsciously wearing round her heart had been breached and she knew herself to be vulnerable again; as she had not been for many years. Life was not only

work, austerity, self-denial; there was also music, the magic
of an opera house, there was opera. She laid both her arms
on the ledge of the box and bowed her head over them to
hide her tears. Kanakis leaned forward and whispered in her
ear, 'Are you all right? Are you not feeling well?' She had
thought that in the darkness no one would notice her moment of weakness, and she quickly sat up and turned to look
at him. He was evidently not engrossed in what was happen-
ing on the stage; for him the performance was a mere setting
for the little company he had gathered in his box and it was
them he was watching rather than the singers. Her own
over-dramatic gesture of self-abandonment had drawn his
attention to herself; he would not have noticed it if his eyes
had been on the brightly-lit garden scene.

'I'm quite well, thank you,' she whispered in return. 'It
was the music – I am enjoying it so much.' And she turned
again, replacing her hands stiffly in her lap. But now her attention, too, was deflected to the other occupants of the
box. Resi's face was in profile, her exquisite nose outlined
against the summer sunlit sky, her lips parted in a smile of
utter bliss, as from time to time she glanced sideways at
Bimbo sitting beside and slightly further back from her to
make room for his legs, which he had crossed, his hands
clasping his knee at the level of the box's velvet ledge. His
lips were pursed as if he were whistling the melody to the
accompaniment of the orchestra, but though his whistling
was soundless, he glanced mischievously right and left,
inwardly enjoying his own performance and challenging
everyone near him to detect his unwarranted contribution

to the score. In fact, two or three people sitting in the stalls just in front of him did notice his antics and frowned, at which he grinned and winked at them, then resumed his pretended whistling. But he did not respond to Resi's obviously adoring glances; not once did Nina observe his eyes meeting hers; he was quite pointedly ignoring her. Several times Resi tried with inconspicuous gestures to attract his attention, brushing against his hand as she smoothed her dress, bending forward so as to obscure his view of the stage, and then quickly straightening up again and sitting back, apologising with a smile for the unintentional inconvenience she had caused.

Onegin and Tatiana, Olga and Lenski, were walking in the garden, Olga and Lenski accepted lovers, Tatiana proceeding ceremoniously, listening intently to the interesting conversation of the stranger from a world beyond her experience. Onegin was politely indifferent to the looks cast in his direction. So was Bimbo. That, to Nina, was not surprising; undoubtedly he would later report to her laughingly how the 'new' girl had made eyes at him all through the opera.

The interval came and only Bimbo rose to leave the box, going out, he said, to smoke a cigarette in the foyer. As he went, Kanakis offered him his cigarette case, sleek and golden, smooth to the fingers and the eye. Bimbo took several cigarettes. 'Thanks, Theophil. Are you coming?'

'No, I'll stay with the ladies.'

Resi turned to see Bimbo slip out of the box, but he was gone before she could decide to join him. Kanakis smiled at her intention but ignored it. 'Are you enjoying the opera, Miss Larsen?' he asked.

'Immensely, it's wonderful.' Her eyes shone.

'You have never been to a performance like this before? Am I right?'

'No, never. I've been told about them, but it's even lovelier than I imagined. What is going to happen next, do you know?'

'Oh, yes. I'm afraid it's very sad. Tatiana has fallen in love with Onegin and writes him a letter to tell him of her love, and he rejects her – tells her he is not a marrying man.'

'She should not have written to him!'

'Oh, I quite agree, it was foolish of her, but her feelings ran away with her. Then Onegin fights a duel with Lenski about another girl whom he also does not love – Olga, in fact – and kills him.'

'How dreadful!'

'Dreadful indeed, and so unnecessary – but that's the story.'

'What happens to Tatiana?'

'She marries someone else – a very brilliant marriage – so all ends well for her, and then Onegin is sorry he missed his chance.'

'I wonder whether she still loves him.'

'Oh, I scarcely think so.' Kanakis turned to Nina. 'That's the story in a nutshell, isn't it, Princess?'

'In a nutshell, as you say, Herr von Kanakis, very matter-of-fact the way you put it, an edition for schools.'

'For the non-sentimental young, Princess; romance begins at thirty, don't you agree? Besides, I didn't have time for elaboration. The lights are going out, and here comes Bimbo. Tchaikovsky will supply what I left out.'

Once more the audience sat in silence and the occupants of No. 4 box were quiet. Invisible currents of emotion re-sumed their flow, and the curtain opened on the letter scene. Nina concentrated on listening, but could not entirely sup-press an undercurrent of thought about the deliberately prosaic and unromantic way Kanakis had summarised the libretto for Resi's benefit. Had he wanted to disenchant her in advance, with the infectious pathos of its romance? Put her on her guard against Bimbo? How awkward of him, if he was seriously attracted to the girl, to invite the two of them together to drink in Tchaikovsky's impassioned harmonies. Romance begins at thirty, he had said. Begins? Nina doubted this was true – but it certainly depends. She turned her head in the darkness, as she felt rather than heard Kana-kis breathing deeply in rapt concentration – watching Resi, she thought. But he was not looking at Resi. He was looking at Bimbo.

# Nineteen

Another Thursday evening, and Theophil Kanakis was standing in the marble-paved hall of his little hidden pavilion. He had just welcomed two of the guests who came fairly regularly to his Thursday gatherings; they had gone through into the drawing room, leaving the door half-open for their host to follow. But Kanakis loitered, partly in anticipation of further arrivals, partly because he delighted in contemplating the hall itself when it was lit by candles in the old green and gold wall brackets. Then a figure appeared behind the plate-glass door and the bell rang. Kanakis opened the door himself to find Marie-Theres standing there, wrapped in a bulky raccoon coat, with a gauze scarf over her hair.

'Marie-Theres, you have surely not walked here all alone!'

'No, only this last bit through the courtyards. I had a taxi. Even so, it *was* very dark. But I did so want to come.

Georg came for Hanni, and of course they wanted to be alone. Aunt Fini fussed about my coming here, but I said I had promised, and Mizzi went down and got a taxi.' Marie-Theres chattered as Kanakis helped her out of her fur and she untied her scarf, while Hansi, a boy to whom Kanakis had given houseroom and a white jacket to act as manservant at his parties, went down on one knee to unfasten her snow boots.

'How sweet of you to have insisted. Though I'm afraid you are going to be terribly bored tonight. We have practically no young people. They've all gone to various dances. Someone ought to have taken you. There's only Bimbo here.'

*Only Bimbo!*

'My dear child, if I had known you were alone I would have sent my car for you. You should have telephoned. A girl ought not to go out by herself at night, even in a taxi.'

Resi turned round from fluffing out her hair in front of a tiny gold-framed looking glass. 'How kind you are, Mr Kanakis!'

*Only Bimbo!*

'Theophil,' he said gently. 'You promised the other evening to call me by my name. It means lover of God or beloved of God, whichever way you like to put it. A nice name, don't you think? Please call me by it. Come in now. I'll see what I can find for you. But there's no dancing tonight. Everyone is just talking and eating.'

Two more guests were arriving, the actress with the sleek black hair and the large gold circular earrings who had been there the first time Marie-Theres had come, and her inseparable companion, and Kanakis left Marie-Theres to go to her and kiss both her hands, exclaiming at the honour and pleasure she was conferring on him. Marie-Theres went into the long, softly-lit drawing room. Compared with the crowded 'first night' when she had come here, it seemed almost empty. The small number of guests were clustered round the buffet table which Kanakis had had moved in from the dining room. They were moving round with plates and glasses in their hands, giving far more attention to the ham, the *chaud-froid* of chicken and Russian salad, to the cakes and meringues and the wines, than to talking to each other; there seemed to be no affinities at work inclining anyone to withdraw into a more intimate *tête-à-tête*; no one was sitting in the shadowy corners or on the low couches where, once settled, one was more or less committed for the evening; a catalyst was missing and Kanakis himself seemed unable to supply it, for he drifted about without much purpose between the unoccupied chairs, and went up to first one and then another of his guests with no suggestion other than to offer more food or a different wine.

Then two things happened. Marie-Theres saw Bimbo emerge from the closed door at the far end of the room, and he was alone. She looked at him intently and she thought he had seen her, but he did not come in her direction. Instead he turned aside to speak to Hansi, the white-coated boy who was collecting the used plates on the buffet table. Then he came towards her with that inimitable walk of his which seemed to glide an inch above the ground. He came closer, he was alone, he was going to speak to her. She felt a flutter in her throat, she felt sure she had lost her voice. Here he was, dark eyes smiling between long lashes and a gleam of white teeth as his lips parted. She mirrored his smile, she mirrored him entirely. In that instant she lost consciousness of herself as a separate entity and felt every movement of his hands, his shoulders, the flicker of his eyelids as her own. He was not very tall, his eyes were on the same level as hers, and she could not look away.

'Let's sit down,' he said, and taking her elbow in his left hand he propelled her towards the sofa where she had sat on the first evening she came here. Just then two more people were greeted by Kanakis, and came with him towards the circle of chairs in front of the sofa. Bimbo had gone to the buffet table and was asking Hansi to serve a choice of dishes and wine to the newcomers, and this precipitated a general movement of the people standing around towards that circle of chairs. These were soon all occupied, so much so that some had to be drawn apart to allow spare ones to be inserted into the gaps. Marie-Theres saw her sofa being invaded and tried to spread her dress, putting her gloves and handbag on the seat next to her in the hope that Bimbo would return and sit down in the place he had left. The newcomers were Dr Helbling and his wife. Kanakis had met them a couple of weeks ago at a one-man show at one of the small private galleries that were opening up once more after the blight of the war years.

'A few friends every Thursday evening, Dr Helbling – a glass of wine and conversation, almost a lost art I'm afraid nowadays, but I'm finding that among congenial minds it comes to life again. I'd be so delighted if you would both drop in, and with anyone else whom you would care to bring with you.' Helbling had been polite but uninterested; however, it was not long before he heard from two or three others that these evenings were worth going to, and so they had come.

It happened that their coming on this particular evening – when the company was comparatively sparse and loosely-knit, but drawn together into an integrated circle round the table – provided the setting for a plan Bimbo had long been preparing in his mind. He came back and sat down next to Resi again, very close to her but not looking at her. His hands rested on his knees, he seemed deep in thought. 'If only I had something to say to him, now that he's here,' she thought, but all she could do was look at his hands, smooth, brown hands with long fingers, on one of them a ring set with a large dark blue stone that was carved in a peculiar way. She had never seen a man wear a ring with a stone in it. Should she ask him what it was? It would be something to say, but it might be the wrong thing. It might break the spell of this feeling she had never experienced before, as if all the nerve endings in her skin were alert to something unknown.

It was Bimbo who broke the spell. His eyelids fluttered, he whistled softly under his breath. 'Yes, yes, I think so,' he whispered, 'this is my opportunity, I can ask Helbling's opinion.' He jumped up and gave her a bland, angelic smile. 'Would you like to see some pictures,' he asked, 'some drawings I got from a friend of mine? I'll show them to you and to Dr Helbling since, by a stroke of luck, he is here this evening.' Bimbo went out into the hall and came back with a large folder under his arm. It took a few moments before he could attract Dr Helbling's attention. Eventually he asked:

'Well, Prince Grein, what is it you have there?'

'A few drawings, Herr Doktor, done by a friend of mine. He is anxious to get an expert opinion on them, on his draughtsmanship, I mean, and as I told him that I might sometime have the great good fortune to meet you here – without having to consult you, so to speak, officially at the gallery – I have brought them along. They are, as you will see, well, how shall I put it, a little bit out of the ordinary, rather special, shall I say.' And he made some play with un-tying the tapes of the folder, thus succeeding by his words and fingers in arousing the expectation he desired.

Helbling was sitting opposite on another sofa, with the woman with the sleek head and large earrings beside him. Bimbo gave the second sheet to his neighbour and the third to Marie-Theres, who only glanced at it superficially, while Helbling, who had been called upon to judge, took out his spectacle-case, placed the spectacles on his nose, and looked. Then he raised his bushy, brindled eyebrows in silence and took up the next sheet as Bimbo handed each one on. The drawings, done in charcoal and red chalk, were of a nude woman, with the emphasis neither on shape nor texture, but, quite blatantly, on provocation. The unusual combination of the two media, the black and the red, were employed to fo-cus the erotic intention on the position of the limbs and, on some of the sheets, on the distorting spasms of the face. The subject as depicted was not an individual person nor a stylised female shape, but a woman dehumanised by the stark grip of lust in its ambivalence of obsession and disgust.

No one holding a drawing said anything. There was complete silence round the table, as if nobody ventured to breathe lest by a sigh they should betray an emotion. And Kanakis's voice as he chatted to his neighbour – they were the only ones who had not yet seen any of the drawings – suddenly sounded very loud in the general hush.

'What's the matter?' he asked, looking round at the faces, which all seemed wooden with embarrassment. No one, however sophisticated, relished being caught in public in the role of 'voyeur', and no one ventured even by the flicker of an eyelid to condemn, or acknowledge, what they felt to be pornography, in case it might, after all, be 'art'. It was for Dr Helbling to decide. Most of the sheets had now been passed to him, and he had them stacked on his knees while also holding one in each hand and looking at these thoughtfully between narrowed eyelids. At last he spoke, quietly, in a flat voice.

'The draughtsmanship is not bad, if that is what you want my opinion about, Prince Grein,' he said, 'but it is not of such excellence as to make these sketches artistically valuable. There is an element of intended sensationalism in them which, in spite of a certain undoubted ability, stops them from being works of art and relegates them, to put it bluntly, to pornography – as undoubtedly you knew.' He put the two sheets he was still holding down on the sheaf on his knees and the whole sheaf on the table. 'Distasteful, to say the least, Prince Grein, distasteful,' and he flicked the fingers of one hand with the fingers of the other, by which gestures he seemed to shake off some contaminating dust or dirt. Then, taking off his glasses, he polished them with his handkerchief, as if they, too, had been besmirched by what he had been looking at.

Bimbo smiled, unperturbed. 'My friend will be disappointed by your verdict on his talent, but I find it strange that the subject should have shocked you.'

'It is not the subject which is shocking, Prince Lorenzo, and, by the way, I didn't say shocking, I said distasteful. If we have to speak of shock, which is a deep and powerful response to an artist's creation, and a truly legitimate one, we have far more horrifying representations by Hieronymus Bosch, by Goya, or nearer the idiom of our own time, by Alfred Kubin. But they, however much they differ from one another, are terrifying and astringent. This man gloats and nauseates.'

'But, Dr Helbling, aren't you introducing moral criteria into what should be a purely aesthetic evaluation of a work of art?' Bimbo asked with a smile of angelic innocence. 'Surely such considerations are out of place,' he added.

'It is not I who am introducing extraneous criteria, but your friend here,' said Helbling, gathering up the sheets and passing them across the table to Kanakis, who had reached out his hand for them. 'His intention was not artistic but simply sexual, and as such aesthetically uninteresting. I wonder what Herr von Kanakis thinks of them.' He shifted in his chair, turned to his neighbour, and resumed the conversation they had been having prior to the incident with the drawings, thus deliberately dismissing them as not worth further discussion.

But if the incident was closed for Dr Helbling – and indeed the desire to show the drawings to him had only been a pretext – they still had to produce their effect – if in fact they did produce any – on Kanakis and possibly on Marie-Theres. That was what Bimbo was waiting for, and the imp in him was all agog to see what it would be. A little pulse thrilled in his temples and, unconsciously, he squeezed Marie-Theres's hand; in response to this she closed her eyes for a moment in bliss. Meanwhile, Kanakis was quickly leafing through the sheaf of drawings without saying a word. Suddenly the woman sitting next to him, who was looking at them over his shoulder, started to laugh, a high-pitched, almost hysterical laugh out of her throat, which caused the other women to grimace in the way one does at the sound of a knife screeching on a plate. No one said anything, but they all, as if by common consent, reached for their glasses and drank or picked up a sandwich, and everybody's eyes, except Helbling's, converged on Marie-Theres. And Marie-Theres, who had opened her eyes again as if awakened by the concerted gaze directed at her, blushed. She blushed because of the way everyone was looking at her expectantly, expecting her to blush. It was this concerted stare that induced the blood to suffuse her cheeks, not the drawings Bimbo had shown her before he passed them over to Dr Helbling. It is doubtful whether they had made any particular impression on her at all. To her they were just ugly, but her eyes were not sufficiently schooled to comprehend what she saw. She had glanced at them with indifference, and if the blood now rushed to her face it was because she thought that everyone had noticed how Bimbo had held her hand and how she had responded to his caress.

Kanakis rose abruptly from the low divan on which he had been sitting, so abruptly that he knocked over some glasses on the table in front of him, spilling what was left of the wine in some of them and causing two to fall and splinter on the floor. He was very angry. His sudden movement had caused a minor accident, but his impulse was to sweep everything, glasses, plates, ashtrays, off the table, and only the utmost effort at self-control, set jaw and tightened muscles, prevented him from doing just that. But he succeeded in mastering himself. Everyone was getting up, chairs were being pushed back, the women clutched their dresses to save them from being stained, the men brought out their handkerchiefs to mop up the trickles of wine.

Kanakis said: 'Get a cloth or something, Bimbo. I expect Hansi will have gone to bed,' and Bimbo said, 'I'm going.' Then Kanakis, having regained his composure, said, 'I'm sorry, my friends, please sit down again. Don't let me break up the party. But Marie-Theres looks tired. I am going to take her home. I'll be back in quarter of an hour.' He went out into the hall and came in again with Marie-Theres's coat. 'Come, my dear, I am going to drive you myself.'

But everyone else seemed ready to leave as well.

'It's getting late.'

'Tomorrow is another day.'

218

'Sorry about those beautiful glasses.'

'Oh never mind them – since you seem ready to leave, Dr Helbling, I can give you and your wife a lift, we are going in your direction.'

Distances are short in Vienna. The Helblings chatted cheerfully in the back of the car for the few minutes it took to reach their house, while Marie-Theres sat silently next to Kanakis. He glanced at her anxiously from time to time, but she seemed unperturbed. Then he stood beside her, shining a torch while she searched for her key and fitted it into the lock of the front door. Before she went in he put his hand lightly on her arm. 'Marie-Theres . . .'

'Yes?'

He felt he ought to say something to her, make some kind of apology, but it was too late for that and there was no time for any lengthy explanation now, outside the door, in the dark street.

'Yes?' she said again, expectantly.

He was moved by the calm purity of her lifted profile, so like that of a Filippo Lippi Madonna. But all he said was the conventional, 'please remember me to your aunt and don't forget, next time, if your cousin is not coming with you, to ring up so that I can send the car. You really must not go out alone at night, even in a taxi.'

'Thank you so very much, Mr Kanakis, you are very kind. Good night.'

'Good night, Marie-Theres.'

Getting back into his car when the heavy door had closed behind her, the sense of the outrage Bimbo had committed surged up again in his mind and his anger was rekindled. How had he dared to bring those drawings to his house and to display them publicly to his guests – to exhibit them in his house, in his presence, before Marie-Theres? Of course his wish to have Dr Helbling's opinion had been nothing but a pretext. He had intended – and perpetrated – a calculated affront to him, Kanakis, and had hoped to create a scandal. In that he had very nearly succeeded. If Dr Helbling had not been so matter of fact, if Marie-Theres – strange child – had not been so self-possessed, it was only himself who had almost played into the boy's hands. Such intolerable impertinence! The boy was both a guttersnipe and a princeling who believed in his superiority, who thought he could allow himself any kind of insult. He remembered how Bimbo had been watching him, waiting for his reaction. The whole scene now unrolled itself in his mind like a replay in slow motion of a film sequence. He heard Helbling's 'distasteful', his neighbour's hysterical laugh, saw Marie-Theres blush. His hands gripped the steering wheel, he found himself racing much too fast along silent suburban streets far out from his own house. He slowed down and turned. At last he drew up in the little side street next to the wall of his small back garden. He let himself in through the narrow, half-hidden door. The house was in total darkness.

He went in through the kitchen and from there into the hall. Here he switched on the lights. The black and white marble floor gleamed. The delicate wrought-iron banisters curved gracefully up to the landing above. Then he went into the long drawing room. It was in the same soft half light in which he had left it. But there was no one there except Bimbo. He was collecting the glasses onto a tray, rearranging the cushions, picking up scraps that had fallen on the floor. He straightened up nonchalantly as Kanakis appeared in the doorway.

'Hullo, Theophil, you've been a long time. They all decided to leave, oh, about ten minutes ago. I thought I'd better wait for you, and meanwhile I've been tidying up. Hansi can do the rest in the morning – if it isn't morning already.'

Bimbo was just chattering for the sake of something to say because Kanakis was standing stock still and rigid, and he could see that his hands, which hung down at his sides, were so tightly clenched into fists that the knuckles shone white.

'Half-past one,' he went on, trying to divert Kanakis's attention to the white and gold Louis XV clock that stood on a console between two windows. In the evening silence it ticked away for half a minute. Then Kanakis came into the room, unclenching his fists but swinging his arms. He was going to slap the boy's face, and that was going to be the end of Bimbo as far as he was concerned. Bimbo saw what was coming and stood up to meet him. When Kanakis was within arm's length he looked up at him coyly from under his long lashes, with a smile on his half-open lips. And Kanakis did not strike. Instead he let his hands fall on the boy's shoulders, gripping them violently, and drew him close. Then he bent down and kissed him full on the mouth. It was all done very quickly. For a moment Bimbo accepted, then he twisted himself away and walked to the door. Quietly, he spoke. 'Don't forget the auction at the saleroom tomorrow morning. I've left the catalogue in the hall and marked the items that might interest you. I'll meet you in the vestibule. Good night.' He closed the door gently, turned out the lights in the hall and was gone. Kanakis heard the glass door, then the outer door click into place.

# Twenty

Professor Adler had finished his solitary supper: sliced cold sausage, potato salad, a pickled cucumber, brown bread and butter and a bottle of beer. Most evenings his landlady cooked him something hot and left it in the oven for him to come and fetch from her kitchen if he came home late. But Frau Ziegler had gone away to stay with her daughter for a few days and Adler was alone in the flat. Having rolled up his napkin and put it in its carved wooden ring, he sat by the open window looking out into the night. The flat was on the third and top floor of a large house that, before the war, had been the home of one family – kitchen and laundry room in the basement, drawing rooms and dining room down-stairs, bedrooms above them, and servants' quarters at the top. It had, like most of the other 'villas' in the 'Cottage' district, been converted into flats. These designations – villa and cottage – were examples of the unashamed misuse of foreign words dear to the hearts of the Viennese and applied to their own purposes because of the associations they conjured up in their minds. Thus the 'Cottage', because of the cosy rural picture it evoked, was the name given to a fairly extensive garden suburb, or rather to an area of intersecting roads lined with trees and consisting entirely of private houses of various styles surrounded by gardens, the so-called 'villas'. These houses were neither country houses nor town houses, but had something of the nature of both, for the garden suburb had long since become engulfed in the town, and the houses, or rather their owners, had been forced to turn their family homes into multiple habitations.

On the top floor of one of these once sumptuous villas, Professor Adler had at last been able to rent a couple of small rooms, sub-let to him by the widow of an army officer who, with the help of an intermittent cleaner, was supposed to keep them tidy for him. If her efforts were not always successful, it was not entirely due to the fact that she had not been brought up to 'do housework', as she was wont to reply to the Professor if he ever remonstrated with her about the dust on his chest of drawers or the fluff on his carpet. The rooms were small, having originally been maids' bedrooms, and though the Professor's personal possessions were meagre, he had already acquired stacks of books and reams of paper in files and folders, just as he had at the Institute. Worst of all were the loose leaves covered with his spindly writing, and since these were never to be touched or moved, there was really very little point in 'doing' the rooms, as so much of them must not, on any account, be 'done'.

But although the rooms were small and the climb up the narrow stairs – the back stairs, of course, leading to the onetime servants' quarters – steep and tiring, everything outside their windows was sheer delight. These windows were just above the treetops, so their luxuriant greenness could be enjoyed without their shutting out the light; instead they reflected and softened it so that it was never glaring. They feasted the ears as well as the eyes with their rustling leaves and the sounds of the birds nesting under their spreading branches, and in the spring the dawn chorus which woke Adler in his cubbyhole of a bedroom did much to wash away the many years spent among fumes and dust and traffic. Best of all was the air that came wafting straight down from the western hills, from the Vienna woods, and over the vineyards and gardens on their slopes, bearing the fragrance of lime, chestnut blossom and may but chiefly of that most nostalgic of Viennese scents, the ubiquitous lilac.

For it was May, and an evening in May, and the sunset had faded out of the sky, the stars were coming out, and every breath one drew was infused with scent. The Professor sat by his window and felt that he could neither work nor sleep. It does seem ridiculous to feel as I do, at my age, he thought. This year I shall be fifty, and here I am, sitting at my window on a night in May as I used to do as a boy, breathing the scent of lime and lilac and feeling myself languish in an overpowering and aimless desire, the desire of the young man for love. He remembered it all so well. Oh, the solitude of youth, the solitude of the elderly and disenchanted! He got up abruptly to break the spell, closed the window, felt for his keys in his pocket and, seizing his hat from a peg in the tiny hall, ran down the stairs and out of the house. It was only a hundred yards down the dark leafy avenue to the tram stop, and there was the tram clanging on its way, blue sparks bristling from the overhead wires. The Professor jumped onto the rear platform, paid for his ticket and lit a cigarette. It was just an ordinary evening.

He would go back to the Institute and have another look at some cultures he had begun in his own private corner of the laboratory. These last few days had been crowded with routine jobs, he had barely had time to glance at the array of tubes and slides which he kept in the glass-fronted cupboard for his own research. For some time he had had an idea at the back of his mind, this had never really come into focus, there was probably nothing in it anyway, but tonight, at his window, during that strangely heightened activity of his mind, there had come something like inspiration – was it a real insight or a delusion, was it worth pursuing or would it have to be abandoned? He was going to find out.

He left the tram at the stop nearest the Institute and turned into the side street. There were no shops here, most of the houses were dark, a few windows showed a dim light between half-drawn curtains. Walking along the pavement opposite the Institute, he looked up at the dark facade. There was a light on in one of the laboratory windows. It was the window at the end where he did his own private work. He felt a rush of blood to his head, a sudden pounding of his heart in his chest. Was it possible? Had Dr Krieger come back at night to try and discover what he was doing? He would have had to force open the glass-fronted cabinet. But he probably had a second set of keys. What instinct had prompted him, to return at ten o'clock on that particular night to discover what was going on? Or had this happened before? He tried to remember whether he had ever noticed anything being disturbed.

All this ran through his mind as he let himself into the building by a side door. The front door was locked and the staircase in darkness; he switched on the light which would give him two minutes to reach the landing before it automatically went out again. The door to the laboratory was also locked – from the inside it seemed. His hand shook so much that he had to press the light switch again before he discovered that his key would not go in. He knocked on the door, then, in his impatience, hit it with his fist. He heard steps coming towards him and the door was opened cautiously. A figure in a white coat stood there. It was not Dr Krieger, it was Fräulein Grein. She stood stock still as she recognised him, and opened the door wider while uttering something between a gasp and a laugh.

'Herr Professor! What a fright you gave me! I thought it might be a burglar and I should be hit over the head.'

'Fräulein Grein! Whatever are you doing here at this time of night? And how did you get in?'

'I didn't get in, I stayed. One can always get out. There are keys on the inside. And it isn't really late, is it? Only about ten o'clock. In fact, I was just going.'

'But what were you doing?'

'To tell you the truth, Herr Professor, I was copying your notes. I have a folder of them here, in longhand. With a little patience I have managed, in time, to decipher your handwriting. Although I notice that even you yourself cannot always remember what you have put down in a hurry. I hope you will forgive me.'

'Forgive you! I am most grateful. But why, why do you do this work, and in the evening?'

'I find it very interesting. But now I will say good night.'

Nina Grein took off her white overall and collected the few odds and ends of her belongings – a small plastic box into which she folded the crumpled wax paper which had wrapped the buttered roll and slice of ham she had brought for her supper – and went to rinse her hands at the sink. 'I'll leave the light, as I expect you want to do some work yourself, and I won't lock up. You have your own keys, of course.' She turned to go, walking carefully between the overflowing tables, the light at her back.

'Fräulein Grein.'

She turned again, the light now shining full on her face. He looked at her. He had seen her every day for months, but now he was seeing her for the first time. She was smiling, the smile was in her eyes more than on her lips, she had beautiful eyes like living topazes, alight with an inner fire which imparted to her whole face a spiritual illumination that was almost breathtaking. So he looked at her – for seconds, for timeless seconds.

'Was there something you wanted to say, Herr Professor?'

'Yes. How are you going to get home?'

'I shall walk. I always do. It's a beautiful night and I haven't very far to go. I like walking at night, there are street lamps now and there's nothing to be afraid of. This isn't the Russian zone.'

'May I come with you? I, too, like walking at night.'

They locked up and went downstairs together, then out into the silent street. A street lamp threw their shadows in front of them, then there was darkness, until another light shone in their faces and threw their shadows behind them. They did not look at each other, but kept their eyes on the uneven pavement. Without touching, their bodies moved together and their footfalls on the paving stones beat the same rhythm. In the surrounding silence each of them, both used to the emptiness and solitude of the night, realised that they were no longer alone; when they came to the corner where the side street joined the main thoroughfare, and the arc lights diffused a pale all-over visibility, they stood for a moment looking at each other, and hesitantly, they smiled.

They continued on their way, down the broad street in the direction of the Inner City. As they passed by the gardens laid out in front of the Votive Church, that rather artificial neo-gothic building erected in thanksgiving for the escape of the old emperor from an attempt on his life, the heavy scent of lilac from the bushes in the gardens wafted across to them on the night air. They crossed the Ringstrasse into the Inner City. It was Nina who walked purposefully, Adler accompanied her unquestioningly, although he wondered where she lived.

They first went along a broad street and then a narrow one flanked by imposing old buildings, and here, in front of one of them, she stopped and, opening her bag, began searching for her key. All the time the two of them had been silent. While Nina was feeling in her bag, Adler looked up at the great front door and the large escutcheon above it, shadowy in the faint light of the stars. He had never seen it before, but in a flash the coincidence fused into recognition: The Palais Grein-Lauterbach. Fräulein Grein had found her key and was about to insert it in the lock.

'I have managed to get a little coffee – would you like . . .' she said, but could not finish the sentence, spoken slowly and with diffidence, for an elderly man came running towards them from the opposite direction. He was waving his arm, his hand held a key.

'*Küss die Hand*, Princess, I'll open up, I'll open up. Please forgive me. I just went round to the coffee house, they told me there were some American cigarettes.' He had opened the door, pulled a packet out of his pocket and turned to Adler. 'Perhaps the gentleman would like a few, to take home with him, with your permission Princess, *Küss die*

*Hand.*' Adler made a negative gesture, Nina went through the door, the porter was about to follow.

'Where can I see you?' he called to her.

'Tomorrow, early morning, the Heldenplatz,' she answered, and the porter closed the door.

# Twenty-one

Heldenplatz, the Square of the Heroes, early morning – the words stayed in Adler's mind all night. He had caught the final tram car out to the 'Cottage': the so-called 'blue one' because it showed a blue light at the rear of the last carriage as a warning to would-be passengers that it was the last to run that evening. Sleep had lain very lightly on his eyes that night, instead of a blanketing oblivion, an almost diaphanous veil through which he could still see the luminous eyes of 'Fräulein' Grein, Princess Nina Grein, and hear her voice: tomorrow, early morning, Heldenplatz.

He was there at six. He did not expect her to come so early, though for him it had been a long way and for her it would be a very short walk. But he wanted to look at the place where they would meet. Not that he hadn't seen it before many times in his pre-exile days, and he must have passed that way on his reminiscing rambles since his return. Nor had he ever gone there deliberately: it held no early memories for him. And yet it was a lovely square, one of the largest and most tranquil in the heart of a noisy city. On his left was the grey facade of the old Imperial Palace with its double row of windows, on the right the railings of tall iron bars topped with gilded arrowheads separating it from the thoroughfare beyond. Opposite, but at a distance, lay the wide semi-circular wingspan of the 'new' Palace, designed to show off majesty in its most sumptuous attire. But the majesty of the old Emperor had refused to inhabit it and the young Emperor, ascending the throne in wartime and abdicating almost immediately afterwards, had never had a chance to live there. And so for many years it had remained something of an artificial construction that had never come to life, a stage backdrop whose florid pomposity older people were prepared to overlook because they didn't take it quite seriously.

The Square of the Heroes: the two over-lifesize equestrian statues on high pedestals are what give it its name, two great military commanders on rearing horses with flowing manes and tails in the Baroque style, one carrying Prince Eugene of Savoy and the other the Archduke Charles, brother of the first Emperor Francis who, in one victorious battle, had stemmed for a while Napoleon's advance on Vienna. They seemed to have sprung from the glowing pages of school history books, visible embodiments of *Dei Gesta per Austriacos* which are such a necessary ingredient of national consciousness. And yet, with all their panache, there is so little boastfulness in this square. What first meets the eye and impresses the mind are the broad avenues of chestnut trees lining it on three sides, chestnut trees that bear a profusion of red candles in the spring. They give the square its peaceful, almost countrified look; they are conducive to slow perambulation and quiet contemplation. It is so spread out and open to the sky that roofs and church spires can only be seen in the far distance, leaving room for clouds to pile up overhead on stormy days and for the winds to sweep in from the limitless plains in the east. So the Square of the Heroes is not very heroic, in spite of the dashing figures of the two great soldiers that were intended to dominate it; instead of which they blend with the predominantly horizontal line of the treetops and the clouds drifting to the far horizon.

It was wonderfully quiet here in the early morning light and the air was sweet. Adler walked for a while, then sat down on a bench looking towards the Ballhaus, the Foreign Office, from which direction Nina would come. Nina Grein: she had been an assistant to him for the past year, she had been so helpful but so discreet, so retiring, so unassuming, that he had scarcely noticed her. Just a girl in a white coat. Just a cleaner, Dr Krieger had called her. But she had been copying his notes, in longhand, in a folder. He had seen the folder in a drawer but had not bothered to look inside it. A cleaner could never have deciphered those scrawls, made sense of the chemical formulae, the Greek terms he had been using. Why had he been so blind, why had he not seen through the disguise? 'Kiss your hand, Princess' the porter of the Palais Grein-Lauterbach had said. Would he had not said it at that moment – she had been about to ask him to come in. Never mind – she was coming to meet him now – not a laboratory assistant, not a 'cleaner', but in every sense a princess. The revealing transformation had occurred – now everything was quite different.

She came, and he kissed her hand. She was not embarrassed by his gesture. It was obvious to them both that he must do so, since he now knew who she was. Then they walked side by side under the chestnut trees, up and down, slowly and without touching. She asked him about himself, about his exile, his life over there and his return. For the first time the seal was broken and he was able to talk to someone who really wanted to know – about Melanie, his Americanised daughters, their early struggles, his wife's success, and his own lack of it – his inability to acclimatise, his increasing loneliness. He praised his family, he blamed only himself, and the more self-deprecatingly he spoke, the greater the feeling of comfort and relief that welled up in him in response to the disbelief he sensed in his companion. She did not sentimentalise or console, in fact she spoke very little, but in the presence of her listening, much that had been twisted and cramped within him began to untangle and relax.

When, after an hour, they parted to make their separate ways to the Institute, Adler had unburdened himself of only a fraction of what he had wanted to say, and Nina had told him nothing of her own life, much as he wanted to know about her and what had brought her to accept the menial job she was performing. It would not be wise for them to speak privately to each other at the Institute, even after hours, so they agreed to meet again in the early mornings when the square would always be deserted. Mothers and nursemaids with their prams and toddlers would not invade it until much later, and the stream of men with briefcases and of typists taking a short cut into the city would not start until after they left. Of course they were not entirely alone. One or two isolated figures also walked along the leaf-sheltered avenues, enjoying the freshness of the morning before going to their shops or offices. On one or two mornings during the latter part of the week Adler noticed, out of the corner of his eye, a priest reading his breviary on the other side of the square. That was nothing unusual, and so engrossed were they in conversation that he made no comment. Nina had not even seen him.

It was not many days later when, one evening, Father Jahoda knocked on her door. The Palais Grein-Lauterbach was at that time entirely occupied by various government offices, or rather not entirely since a few rooms in what had been the attics had been given back to the heirs of its former owners. Lorenzo Grein refused to inhabit them as being too inaccessible and uncomfortable, but Nina lived her frugal, undemanding life there, climbing the five flights of stairs past the sumptuous apartments of her childhood. Father Jahoda had climbed them tonight and was slightly out of breath.

# Twenty-two

Nina went to the door and opened it. 'Come in, Father, come in. How very kind of you – climbing all those stairs.' Father Jahoda was out of breath: after six o'clock, when the offices shut, the lift didn't work any more and in any case it would have stopped short of the attic floor. Father Jahoda came in and looked round. The low-ceilinged room was in semi-darkness as the deep-set windows overlooked the court-yard; although outside the spring evening still lingered with a tender caressing light. Coming in from the street the room seemed even darker to Father Jahoda as he glanced to the right and left of the door looking for a light switch.

'I'm so glad you have come, your Reverence,' Nina said, 'I want to talk to you. Please sit down. If you don't mind I won't turn on the light – not just yet.' Father Jahoda crossed the room and pulled an armchair round so that it faced away from the window. His eyes soon adapted to the gloaming. He wanted to see as much as he could of Nina's face but she was sitting down opposite him, her head bent forward, resting her chin on her hand and looking at the floor.

'Do you know,' he said, 'that I have been here twice before at this hour, when I expected you would have been back from the Institute, but fortunately Habietinek told me that you were out, or I might have climbed the stairs for nothing.' She murmured something about being sorry. 'And now you say you want to speak to me. But you know where you can find me, my child, where I am always ready to listen to you, to counsel you – in the confessional. Yet for more than a month now you have not come. Neither have you come, in consequence, to the Altar to receive the Holy Sacrament, not having prepared yourself, by an act of contrition, to receive the Body of Our Lord. Oh, I know you have been to St Michael's several times in the early mornings and have knelt at the Altar of the Virgin. Perhaps you didn't know I was there, although you could have found out if you had asked. Private prayer is a good and beautiful thing, my child, but without spiritual guidance it loses much of its value – it can even lead to aberration. I also know that you have not just been in the church in the early mornings. The gardens close by are not always entirely deserted at that hour.'

Nina lifted her head. 'Oh, Father, you have been spying on me!'

'No, Princess, mere chance, and then my own inevitable conclusions from that one instance. You are in trouble, my child, and you are very dear to me. As you would not come to me, I have come to you. You say, now, you want to talk to me. Why didn't you come to confession?'

'I cannot come to confession, Father, because I do not repent, and I do not intend to repent. I should be deceiving you if I accused myself of sin, for myself I cannot deceive. In my heart I admit no sin. If you saw me kneel at the Virgin's altar, it was not in distress or in contrition that I prayed to the Mother of Divine Love, but in gratitude and in joy. If I told you this in the confessional you would impose a penance on me which I could not perform, nor would I ask for an absolution which you could not give and which I am not prepared to receive. Oh, Father, I do not want to speak to you as a priest but as a friend. Since childhood you have been a friend to me and more than a friend, both father and mother to me, tender and kind. Will you be a friend to me now? I have no one else.'

'These are wild words, my child, words which it grieves me to have heard from you, especially from you, of all my spiritual children. But I am your friend, as I always have been and always shall be. You may speak to me as to a friend.'

'Thank you, Father. But why do you say "you, especially *you*, amongst all others"? What is there so special about me? I'm just a woman like all other women!' Her voice quavered. She was taken aback by the passion that had risen in her throat in making this unspectacular assertion and she tried with all her strength to control it.

Father Jahoda said very evenly without a trace of surprise or reproach: 'What you mean is that you are in love with Professor Adler.'

'I love him.'

'Of course, it was inevitable. But you must remember that many weeks ago, very soon after he joined the Institute, and also several times since, I warned you about the dangers of seeing too much of a married man.'

'I know you did. You advised me to resign from my job. I thought it was a preposterous idea. Just as it was getting interesting.'

'*Because* it was getting interesting. Do you remember what I said?'

'Yes, you said that continued proximity between a man and a woman, however neutral their attitude to each other, however disinterested their intentions, would inevitably breed undesirable emotions. I was very much upset when you said that. I felt that you were trying to detect impurity where none existed. I felt you were insulting a man who just did not happen to share our faith, because he was a Jew. I was determined to continue to work for him, to prove you wrong.'

'You were very sure of yourself.'

'I didn't think of myself at all. I thought only of the work. It had been such dull routine drudgery throughout the years. But *he* made it interesting. When I helped him, he explained things. He was also doing some research of his own which was very interesting. And he made notes about it in English. I transcribed them for him. No one else knows any English at the Institute except me. We never spoke a word about anything but the work, and that was all there was between us, all the time – until . . .'

'Yes, my child, until. Such a very old, threadbare device of the Eternal Tempter, known to those whose business it is to study him during all the centuries of Our Lord. But you, with all your intelligence, and in spite of my warnings, were taken in!'

'Taken in? No Father, I knew my own feelings, I had to admit them to myself, I admit them to you, but I can assure you I never showed them. But he, he did nothing, not by a word, not by a gesture, not even by a glance to attract me. Why should he? How could he? It never crossed his mind. I think he was scarcely aware of my presence. I had nothing to fear from the Tempter, I was perfectly safe. I have never attracted any man.'

'You were very sure of your own virtue.'

'No Father, I have never thought myself virtuous,' her voice dropped to an almost inaudible whisper, 'only ugly.'

Father Jahoda made a slight movement with his right hand, his smooth white hand, which he unclasped from his left and stretched forward as if intending to touch her. Somewhere beneath his armour of discipline, in the core of his common humanity, a nerve of compassion had suddenly quivered. But he controlled his gesture halfway and re-clasped his hands.

'You were in even greater danger than I anticipated.'

'Why?'

'Because you set yourself apart. You compared yourself, brooded over your appearance, I suppose, in your looking glass and rebelled against what you saw.'

Nina shuddered. How could Father Jahoda possibly guess

241

at those secret, entirely private and solitary moments when, emerging from her bath, she did force herself to contemplate her body, her compact, four-square body, the width of her shoulders equalling the width of her hips, her drooping breasts with the downward-pointing, dark brown nipples, her short thighs and hard, rounded calves. A healthy body, she would try to console herself, a strong, sturdy one without a flaw or disfigurement, but such a disheartening one. The lacklustre, faintly yellowish colour of her flesh disgusted her, though her skin was smooth and sleek to the touch when she stroked herself with the palms of her hands – but no one would find out how smooth and sleek it was, for none would want to touch.

'If I did look in the glass, I had no reason to accuse myself of vanity. That at least was not a sin that burdened my conscience. And a woman does not need a looking glass in this town to tell her she is ill-favoured. She can read it in the eyes and feel it in the behaviour of every man she meets and may even be told so to her face.'

'You have not accused yourself of vanity, but you should realise that you have been lacking in humility. You are not beautiful, my child, but not all women can be beautiful. Neither are you what you yourself have so drastically called "ugly", and certainly not disfigured. Yet there are many such in the world and even they must bear with themselves. As it happens, I observed when I last saw you what almost amounts to a transfiguration in your whole appearance, a light in your eyes, an alertness in your movements, the source of which I have not found it difficult to surmise. Your Professor has responded to your emotions and you now believe he shares them. That, apart from the fact that you have been keeping aloof from me, is the main reason why I am here this evening.'

'So you have come to tell me to give up my love! I cannot, I will not do so.'

'I do not want to hear about what you call "your love". Don't you understand, Princess? I am warning you, as I have warned you before, but this time with all the urgency in my power and with all the authority of your spiritual father, against a sinful association with a married man, against adultery and, if you were contemplating a form of marriage, against bigamy.'

'He has told me that his wife will refuse to divorce him.'

'Even if she did, theirs was a sacramental marriage. Divorce would not put them asunder. Do you understand now what you are doing?'

'You are very hard on me, Father. I was not seeking the discipline of my confessor, I had hoped for the sympathy of a friend. Oh, you promised to be a friend!'

'Don't make absurd distinctions, my child. I should be a false friend indeed if I pretended to condone what it is my duty, for the sake of your soul, to condemn.'

'So you have no pity. You have known me from child-hood, you know the life I have led – work, austerity, self-denial – and you know my brother's life – all pleasure and self-indulgence. Yet I am sure you never speak to him as you have just spoken to me. To him you are all gentleness; for me you have only iron.'

243

'Your brother has nothing to do with this and I cannot discuss with you what I say to him. That is solely between him and me. But I will point out to you that you have misunderstood. I am divulging no secrets if I admit what you know as well as I do, that your brother had weaknesses inherent in the nature of a young man, and that he sometimes succumbs to the temptations to which, by this nature, he is exposed. I cannot tell you how I see fit to deal with his lapses. But your problem is different and far more serious. You are setting yourself up to *judge* what is right and what is wrong. Your sin is the sin of the fallen, the sin of rebellion and of pride. You assert that what you are doing is right and that you are justified in so doing. You tell me that you refuse to repent and do not desire absolution.'

'As yet, Father, I have done nothing.'

'What you are thinking, then, of doing? Where, my poor child, is the tenuous dividing line between the thought and the deed if both spring from the same self-opinionated heart? You could not be convicted in a court of law for what you had thought of doing if you had not done it. But before God? Only if you humble yourself in your heart and pray for grace and help to resist your thoughts when next you kneel at the altar of Our Lady – then indeed you may pray in thankfulness that your thoughts have not culminated in action. And now, Princess, I will leave you. Don't think I don't know I have caused you pain. It is necessary pain. Pray, my child, and God bless you.'

After Father Jahoda had gone, Nina sat rigidly in her chair, clutching the armrests and staring at the faintly-lit window, for the room was now quite dark. Then tears began to run, like hot raindrops, out of her open, unblinking eyes. Silently, unmovingly, without distortion of feature or gesture of body, she wept. But she was quite sure. She did not repent.

# Twenty-three

Professor Adler had not been near the Western Station since that grey day in March – what a long time ago it seemed – when he arrived there at the bare platform, in a waste of emptiness and desolation, ruined stonework and improvised wooden constructions. During his wanderings through the city and out into the suburbs and surroundings he had avoided this district and the approaches to the station. The first shock he received there had gone too deep, his first disillusionment had not healed, and that initial and almost irresistible impulse to escape, to run away from the disappointments of which this place had given him a bitter foretaste, would, he felt, be revived if he returned there. And in spite of everything he had been determined to stay.

Now, as he entered the new building, the sun was shining. The great entrance hall was high and full of light. Its shell was finished, though the various offices, kiosks and furnishings of a modern railway station were still under construction, but it was already functioning well despite some improvisations. It was Saturday and a bright spring morning: crowds of people thronged through the hall towards the fresh concrete platforms, men and boys in grey loden or leather shorts, girls in country-style dresses, older women in tight-fitting jackets, all leaving the city on excursions to visit the family in country towns and villages or returning home to the provinces after a stay in the capital on private or official business. Cheerfulness reigned, purpose and vitality propelled the people who jostled their way good-humouredly through the barriers. Hesitating, diffident, looking cautiously right and left, Adler felt himself surrendering to the light-hearted mood, felt a sense of belonging, and realised he was smiling.

He had every reason for doing so, for there, coming into the hall and looking a little bewildered herself, was the Princess Nina, Fräulein Grein to him no longer, dressed in grey loden with green lapels and carrying, actually carrying, not only a handbag for a day excursion, but a small case suitable for a longer journey. For a moment Adler watched her before she saw him; he enjoyed knowing that she was looking for him, that in a minute they would be together and together would go through the gate and get onto the train. There! She was coming towards him. He went to meet her, to take her case, while she only pretended to protest: 'It is so light, no trouble to carry – Herr Professor. Have I kept you waiting? I hope I'm not late?' Just words, to cover up embarrassment.

'We're in plenty of time for the train. I've got the tickets.'

'Really? I was just going to get mine.'

'No, no you must allow me,' and turning sideways to have them punched he said, 'please call me Kuno – Nina.' And so they went through the barrier and got into the train a little out of breath, as if they were both barely twenty instead of fifty and thirty-four.

They could only get seats in the middle, facing each other, for the train was very full and all four corners, those by the window and those next to the corridor, were already occupied. Adler had taken second-class tickets; it had not occurred to him to do otherwise for, since his return, he had got used to cutting his personal requirements to the simplest acceptable standard. For a moment, as they entered the compartment and he saw how hemmed in they were going to be, he had qualms – but then he saw how Nina had pushed her way in with a smile and an 'allow me' as a matter of course, and realised that she who called herself Fräulein Grein would not have expected to travel first-class. So they sat opposite each other with their elbows close to their sides and both were really rather glad that, being so situated, they could only exchange glances and a few non-committal remarks fit for all the other travellers to hear, while inwardly marvelling that they were actually going away together.

Conversation between the two groups with whom they were sharing the compartment, a family of four and a young couple, soon became lively. They were telling each other where they were going, unwrapping sandwiches and fruit, and Nina and Adler were soon being asked to help themselves out of a bag of cherries. Adler declined rather stiffly, but Nina graciously accepted three or four to be companionable. When the smell of garlic sausage became overpowering, her request that a window be opened was cheerfully complied with, and when the draught made the paper wrappings flutter and caused a greasy one to fly across the compartment into someone's face, this gave rise to a great deal of laughter.

Then, all at once, their destination was called out, and they clambered down the steep steps onto the platform of the little wayside station. The air was clear and heavy with sweetness, the sun was shining and the day was theirs. A little post office bus took them on side roads to a small country town, scarcely more than a village, and deposited them in the market square. Old houses washed in pink and yellow, some with white stucco mouldings over the door and windows, enclosed it on three sides, cobblestones paved it, a curtain of trees on the fourth side afforded a view of a fast-flowing river and wooded hills beyond. They left Nina's suitcase and Adler's briefcase at the Golden Ox, whose painted sign crowned the low doorway of the only inn. They would come back in an hour for their midday meal, and meanwhile stroll through the few streets to stretch their legs, leaving the long walk and the sightseeing they intended to do for the afternoon.

They were both great walkers and immediately after their meal of boiled beef and dumplings they crossed the bridge over the clear-running stream and set out on the footpath that climbed the hill and unrolled across the green and gleaming landscape. The steady rhythm of their steps united them in an understanding deeper than words could convey. So they walked in silence on the hard-trodden earth, between grassy verges thick with wild flowers, clover and buttercups, little wild scabious and scarlet pimpernel and dozens of others, glancing right and left over the gently billowing fields of barley or rye. The path led to a crest of dark woodland, the earth grew softer and damper underfoot, the air was cooler and scented with resin and mushrooms. Adler, who had been walking behind Nina while the path was narrow, moved to be next to her. She stopped and turned to him, drawing a deep breath. There was love in her eyes. He saw it and embraced her. 'My beloved, my dearest.' The sun, filtering down between the branches, dappled them, throwing a crazy pattern of light and shade onto Nina's upturned face, picking out the silvery strands in Adler's close thatch of black hair as he bent to kiss her. There was such silence in the forest that the tiny hum of an insect whirring its wings in a shaft of light was clearly discernible, and the murmur of exchanged endearments was more felt than heard.

The wood was a large one and spread itself out. Soon the path began to rise and to weave in long loops up the steep incline: the effort of the climb relieved them of the need to speak. But at the summit – the wide landscape spread out below them, the river winding like a silver ribbon in the valley, and the little town with its market square and its onion-shaped belfry half-encircled in one of its bends – they embraced again in a surge of joy. A tall plain wooden cross was planted on the highest point, unadorned except for a wreath of half-faded flowers at its foot, and two steps below that was a wooden bench, grey and grooved from the rain and sun. There they sat very close to each other and looked out on the landscape.

Although they had met at work almost daily for more than a year they knew practically nothing about each other. Their personalities were defined by the image they showed to the world, by the exercise of the functions they fulfilled. He was a repatriated émigré, too old for the secondary role he had to content himself to play, ill at ease with the younger staff and definitely antagonistic to the Director, whom she also loathed. But he seemed determined to suppress his animosity, though it cost him a great effort, as his only alternative, if it came to an open clash, would be to resign. She would have liked to know what prevented him from doing so. In fact she had, from the first, greatly desired to penetrate the mask, to discover what lay behind the furrowed brow, the deep-set eyes, the full but compressed lips under the black moustache. When he arrived she had been fascinated by him. His presence in the laboratory, though he rarely spoke to her and then only with the polite detachment of a technical relationship, had introduced a personal interest into her workaday world. As she looked at him now, sitting on the rustic bench beside her, looking sideways furtively when he seemed absorbed in the lovely landscape below, seeing him in an open-necked shirt under a worn tweed jacket, she could hardly believe he was the same man as the one she only knew in a dark suit or white coat. And she was actually touching him, leaning against the side of the 'Professor' or the 'émigré', labels that could now be discarded. There was so much for him to tell her about himself, so much she must try and understand, and learn about herself, through knowing him – things she had thought she would never know.

He was not looking at her, he was looking into the distance; and the light and shade and sinuous lines of this God-created, man-cultivated, man-cared-for country melted with the love from his eyes into his heart. Without turning he put his arm round Nina's shoulders and drew her closer. She was not a laboratory assistant, she was not even a girl with a stocky figure – she was a woman of infinite tenderness, of perfect comfort and fulfilment, she was his heart-come-home, the incarnation of love.

The room they slept in at the Golden Ox was large, clean and very bare. The sun shone in through the slatted shutters, and the milk cans and vegetable carts clattering over the cobblestones woke them early the next morning. The bed – brand new, the landlord's wife had assured them – was more in the nature of a tabletop, and the overstuffed eiderdown slithered right and left and almost to the floor at the slightest movement underneath it.

The bright sunshine and the hard bed induced them to get up early. Washing arrangements were primitive, consisting of an earthenware jug of cold water and a basin on top of the chest of drawers. But the landlord told them that if the tourist trade picked up he had plans for installing running water and building a bathroom: he was definitely going to be up to date soon.

Adler scrambled into his clothes first and went down to the kitchen in search of hot water and a looking glass before which to shave, leaving Nina alone to dress at her leisure. She was in a state of euphoria that she could not understand, for the experience she had been through had been disturbing and not exactly pleasant. Kuno had been very nervous, and had begged her, with gentle caresses, to forgive him – she didn't really know what for; but he seemed to want reassurance, which she gave him in the only way she could, by saying again and again that she loved him. But now, as she dressed, she felt carried on a wave of elation, of release from a condition which, at her age, she had felt to be humiliating and even ridiculous. 'I always knew I had no vocation for virginity,' she told herself ironically, 'and yet I disliked lighthearted relationships: fastidious – and far from beautiful – what a burden these qualities have been!' No wonder she had wings on her feet now that the burden had fallen away.

They had not done any sightseeing the previous afternoon. Now they were eager to discover the art and architecture of the district. Nina knew the country well, Adler did not, but first of all she would attend Mass in a little church she wanted him to visit – an enchanting church she called it, however surprising this epithet sounded when applied to a church. But how to get there? Although only a few miles distant, it was too far to reach on foot in time for the service. But with the assistance of the landlord they managed to borrow a couple of bicycles; these partly solved their problem, although only partly since the many slopes meant there was a lot of dismounting and pushing to do; it made them think that on future excursions they would each acquire a light motorcycle or motorised bicycle to carry them painlessly up the steepest hills.

They managed to reach their destination just as the service was beginning, and while Nina knelt and rose and genuflected in the ritual she knew so well, Adler sat in a remote corner of the church in quiet contemplation. The church was indeed an enchantment, with a unique gracefulness which they would discover in detail when Mass was over. If Mary and Her Child have many times been depicted in a bower of roses, this church *was* Her bower: of delicate proportions, flooded with light, and decorated on walls and capitals and arches with garlands of tiny roses and blue ribbons and two curved and sculpted balconies facing each other across the Altar like opera boxes.

When the officiating priest had retired to the vestry, Nina rose from her knees and came towards Adler, her face alight with joy. She put her arm through his and together they walked round the church. 'I particularly wanted to come here today because I am so happy,' she said. 'Now we'll go out and look at the churchyard. It's as lovely as the church itself.' It certainly was today, with daffodils, peonies and early roses growing amongst the long, untended grass nearly smothering the grey stone crosses and slabs of the graves. As they bent to decipher the inscriptions, they noticed that there were many children among them, two, four, five year olds and babies of as many months. It must, over the years, have been a favourite place to bring the little ones to their premature rest, as if the bereaved and sorrowing mothers found some consolation in laying them close to this smiling, flower-bedecked church in which, as they had seen, even the Stations of the Cross had been depicted in sorrow rather than in agony.

Adler found it very strange, utterly beyond all his life's experience, neither his thoughts nor his emotions being attuned to understanding it. Yet he could not dismiss what he saw as a simply aesthetic phenomenon, something just seen, taken note of and passed over. He knew it had been more than that. It was as if a door had opened in his mind, not widely, not through the pressure of a strong gust of wind, but just a little way, to let a slight and gentle current of air, a mere draught, pass through the crack. He only knew that there *was* a door because it had opened. He had not known there was one before.

It was barely midday. 'Shall we do some more sightseeing?' Nina asked. 'We could find a place to eat, and then go and see the monastery's library; you know, the church is one of the most elaborate Baroque buildings in the country – quite different from the one we saw this morning.' She said this without any thought of introducing Adler to a religious experience, or, for that matter, seeking one for herself. She had been to hear Mass in the morning and had thus performed her devotions for the day, as was her practice every Sunday; he, of course, not being a Catholic, had been able, meanwhile, to enjoy a unique and delightful church interior, and had certainly not been bored during the service; so she had hoped, and so he had assured her. Now they were going to look at one of the most grandiose examples of Baroque architecture, one that she knew well but would be new to him. It might seem strange that this should be so, for though, as a native of his country, he was familiar with the style as an intrinsic element of his surroundings, he had not once purposely entered one of its Baroque churches. He had not been interested in architecture, and still less would he have thought of seeking a religious experience. Brought up in the shadow of the great Gothic cathedral of St Stephen, born a Jew and grown up an agnostic, he would have said, if he had given it any thought at all, that Gothic was the natural style for a church. Nor did he expect any experience other than curiosity, and perhaps aesthetic enjoyment, in entering this one.

Now he saw wealth and splendour beyond imagination: gold-garlanded marble columns, sculptured ornaments gleaming with gold, flights of rosy cupids in fleecy clouds ascending into azure skies, statues and paintings in many colours, while diamond-clear windows, so angled as to be themselves invisible, threw daylight onto the blaze of gold on the High Altar. Adler was overwhelmed. There was nothing he could say – nothing he could think. To accept or to reject seemed equally impossible. Had he been alone, he might have turned back to the door by which he had come in and gone away. But there, in the centre of the aisle, was the small, humble figure of Nina, looking up and around with a look of such beatific concentration on her face that he stood riveted to his place. Then she came and took his hand and with a sweeping gesture of her other hand, encompassing all they saw, said, in Latin: 'To the greater glory of God.'

Afterwards they sat drinking wine in the little, low, panelled guest room attached to the monastery's cellars, where visitors could sample the vintages stored below. They talked, but more to themselves than to each other, commenting on the art of Baroque, on the role of the Church, and the involvement of one with the other; they talked about history, the Counter-Reformation, the reaction against the reaction of Protestantism; it was a dialogue, but not a discussion, for what each one said was not an answer to what the other was saying or thinking, though it would not have been said if the other had not been present. They were both trying to put into words problems of the mind which they wanted to clarify, if they could, but which they might have ignored if they had continued their life alone.

They both spoke from very different experiences and backgrounds and, as it happened, with an oblique reference in their minds to conversations they had had, not so very long ago, with very different people. Adler the agnostic, the liberal thinker, who had never given a serious thought to 'Faith', was remembering his encounter with Dr Krieger, who had taunted him with harbouring preconceived dogmas about right and wrong, about being infected with a Christian ethic which warped his judgment as a man of science. Dr Krieger was loathsome, but perhaps, in this, he was right: he, Adler, did accept values which could be called Christian.

Meanwhile, Nina was remembering another conversation she had had and was trying to balance – though was not at present able to reconcile – the certitude of her faith with the admonishments of her Father Confessor. She had not gone to confession, for she was not contrite and did not accept his strictures. But she knew that, more devoutly than ever, she was obeying the first and great commandment of her Faith: to love God with all her heart, with all her mind, with all her soul and with all her strength, and she did so love Him. And so, although Kuno Adler had not given a thought to God, let alone to loving Him, since, as a small boy, he had been taught to repeat in Hebrew these very same opening words of the 'Hear oh Israel', so did he.

When, after many years of togetherness, they came to reflect on how all this had begun, they told each other that it was on a late afternoon in May, in that humble inn, drinking wine and eating rough country bread with it, that had consecrated their lives into an indissoluble union.

# Twenty-four

Prince Lorenzo Grein, Bimbo to his friends, was not *nice*. He was not nice in the sense of what Marie-Theres called 'nice', not nice as Budd was nice when she talked about him to Hanni on the shore of the lake – dear Budd, who wrote to her every week and whose letters lay, most of them unopened, though she did read one now and again, at the back of her drawer. Being nice meant to be pleasant company, to be at her service, to be undemanding and, above all, not to touch her, because she did not like being 'pawed'. And over here in Austria, Lucas Anreither was, though to a lesser degree, *nice*.

Lucas had, it is true, on one or two occasions, overstepped the strict limits she insisted on, especially on that disastrous afternoon on the Bichl Alm when he had tried to kiss her and been most decisively rebuffed. Yet from that incident, which would have seemed entirely trivial and ordinary to most girls, there sprang consequences both for Lucas and for Resi herself far beyond anything it would seem to have warranted. In Lucas it sowed the seed of a much deeper feeling than he had so far felt for Resi, turning what had been a light-hearted summer flirtation into a deeper and ever more passionate love. To Resi it had given an inkling of what love, erotic love, really was, of how one accepted, if one did accept, a kiss and how, if accepted, one returned it. Lucas, however, had resumed being nice, and if Resi's gratitude for his presence and companionship during her first difficult weeks in Vienna earned him the recompense of several illuminating smiles, how could he not cherish the belief that he was making progress in gaining a little of her affection?

So Budd was nice and Lucas was nice, but Lorenzo Grein was not nice, and never, from the start, qualified for that description. He was alternately, and sometimes simultaneously, enchanting and infuriating, exciting but not nice. It was not just that he was good-looking. Of the various young men Resi had met in the nineteen years of her life, several of them had been good-looking. Budd was definitely an attractive American boy, her cousin Franz Lensveldt was handsome, and Hanni's fiancé, Georg von Corvinus, had regular features and a tall elegant figure – yet Resi called them all 'ordinary' and at best 'nice'. Bimbo Grein was small for a man, when she looked at him she did not have to look up; her eyes were almost on a level with his. She did not know whether she thought him handsome, she only knew that once she had seen him she could not look away. When he was in the room, no one else was there, there was only him. She herself lost the consciousness of being herself, she was lost in her awareness of him.

He was not pleasant to be with. In fact he was not really *with* her at all. On the few occasions when they were in the same company, at Kanakis's house, or at small gatherings at someone's flat for sausages and beer and a little dancing to a gramophone, he had not sought her out and they had very rarely danced together; even then there was something impersonal in the way he held her, and there was none of that special look in his eyes which she used to find in the eyes of other men who looked at her admiringly. Did he, then, not admire her? Was she not beautiful? She was so used to being beautiful – all men thought her so, and women too, and she only had to look in her looking glass to be sure of it herself. And then she thought of the phrase her cousin Franz had once used, almost inadvertently and in fear of giving offence, 'Winter Sunshine,' he had said. 'It suits you, I hope you don't mind.'

Bimbo, on the other hand, was always sarcastic towards her. He tried to mimic her American accent, which she had inevitably carried over into her German speech. He said she was a half-princess, because her mother was a princess, but he was sure it was lucky for her that she bore her father's name because a princess's name would be so awkward in America. She had the spirit to answer that she understood his sister called herself Fräulein Grein at the Institute where she worked, and Bimbo said, yes, indeed, so she did. And besides, Resi said, Americans loved titles and she had often been asked whether it was true that her mother was a princess. And do *you* love titles like a true American? Bimbo asked. Would you like to have one? You could marry one and get one that way, he added laughing. I am not proposing marriage, you know, only making a general suggestion. Poor Resi was deeply embarrassed. She coloured: I never supposed you were, she said. Well, Bimbo said, not so much to her as to a few people standing around, we must find a title for Miss Larsen, one she can wear in America like a peasant-style dress such as her compatriots love buying over here and which are so flattering. This kind of sarcastic talk was what Resi encountered whenever Bimbo spoke to her, nevertheless she always tried to be near him, it was so much better than him remaining engrossed by that dark-haired girl Hertha to whom he always paid so much attention. For when Resi did succeed in making him look at her, and even if he then spoke mockingly, there was something in his smile, a smile in his eyes, which belied his words and betrayed his admiration. It was such a novel experience for Resi not to be sought but to seek. She often tried to imagine what it would feel like if Bimbo kissed her, and how she would put her arms round his neck and cling to him if he did. And once or twice when they were dancing she felt that it was going to happen, but then there came that mocking twinkle in his eyes and when the music stopped he would bow to her in mock formality and turn away.

So the winter wore on and Resi went to her lectures, taking less and less interest in them and also becoming more and more discouraging to Lucas when he met her as she came out of the lecture room. And it was useless for him to take her to a gathering of students who discussed politics or talked shop about the legal or logical problems that had occurred in the course of their studies: she was too obviously not intellectual enough to want, or to be able, to join in the talk, and too beautiful in her American clothes not to be disturbing to the other girls. After one or two attempts in this direction Lucas realised that it was he who would have to make contact with the set in which Resi moved, the 'bourgeoisie' for whom he felt nothing but contempt; contempt with a touch of envy perhaps, but that was never to be admitted to.

A substantial step in this direction was achieved when Lucas received an invitation to the Ball the American High Commissioner's wife was giving at the end of this very muted and still depressed Carnival Season. There had been signs and rumours that the Four Power occupation of Austria might be coming to an end. The Russians were near to agreeing to the signing of a State Treaty and then the bulk of the allied personnel, both military and civilian, would be withdrawn. The Austrians would be on their own – neutral of course, uncommitted to either side, though no one doubted that they were Westerners, in culture and mind.

So it seemed desirable that American young people, and British and French too, who had been spending a lot of their time in Vienna and around the country during the occupation, should be given a chance to make friends with the indigenous society in order to be invited back to the festivities which were bound to be revived when the country began to recover its spirits and its prosperity. So there should be a

Ball in the splendid staterooms of the noble palace in the Inner City – still designated as the International Zone – which the American High Commission had taken over from its owners for the duration. All the young people who had attended the lectures in which Resi had so reluctantly taken part would, of course, be going to the Ball, and Lucas, who had struck up an acquaintance with one or two of them, had not found it difficult to be taken along. A young American military attaché had volunteered to take on the organisation, and had recruited Prince Grein to make himself responsible for the Austrian contingent. And what would be more fitting than that he should have as his partner that pretty American girl who was half Austrian herself, to open the Ball?

And thus it was arranged. Resi felt, when she received the invitation, that this was going to be the greatest day, or rather night, of her life. She was going to spend a whole evening with Bimbo as her partner. She must have a new dress and, she thought, it must be a white and gold one. Three years ago, on her sixteenth birthday, when she had gone with Budd to a college dance in Eden Rise, she had tried to make one for herself from a pattern in a fashion magazine. It had not been a success. The dress had been meant to look glamorous, made of a length of white and gold brocade, but it only looked cheap, and she herself, who had wanted to look stately and regal, like the princess she really was, had simply felt awkward when it wrapped itself round her legs. When they got to the party she found the other girls dancing wildly in blue jeans. Budd had been so kind and understanding, though she had felt he was embarrassed, and she soon said she felt ill, as indeed she did, and asked him to take her home. There she had cried herself to sleep.

This time it would be different. And in fact it was. The dress, an ivory silk which her dollar allowance had enabled her to buy and have made up, very simply, by the expert little dressmaker to whom her cousin Hanni had introduced her, flowed softly over her hips and her long slender legs, held over her breasts by two narrow gold ribbons on her shoulders. A gold and ivory belt clasped her slender waist. She felt *herself* inside her dress. This is how she was meant to be. Never before had she been so conscious of her body.

When she came up the wide blue-carpeted stairs flanked by bronze candelabra and entered the gold and white ballroom, she felt that this was where she belonged, a dream come true, a fairy tale in which she herself was the princess. And there, at the far end of the room, detaching himself from the group of young men awaiting their partners and coming towards her, was the fairy tale prince himself. Bimbo was wearing tails and a white tie, as were almost all the Austrian contingent. They were at home in this palace where their fathers and probably their grandfathers had danced before them, and it was *their* evening dress they were wearing, exhumed out of ancestral chests and refurbished expertly for the occasion. Not many of the Allied contingent could match them, for they were new arrivals to whom traditional evening dress did not come naturally. Those that wore uniform looked best, in spite of the drabness of the cloth; but the civilians seemed more like an incursion of tourists on a sightseeing expedition, whereas they were, of course, the actual hosts of the party and those that belonged here as of right were their guests.

Bimbo came towards Resi and took her hand. 'You look really lovely this evening,' he said, this time without a trace of irony. It was the first direct compliment he had paid her and there was something in his voice and in his smile that responded to her feelings towards him. It was love, love, love. They opened the Ball to the strains of the Emperor Waltz. Resi had practised the steps assiduously and there was no hesitation or discordant movement when Bimbo held her closer than ever before as they circled fast anti-clockwise round the stately room. It was a professional performance, so beautifully executed that other couples moved out of their way to watch, and there were numerous whispers. What a handsome pair, who are they? It is young Prince Grein, but who is the girl? She's new. I've never see her before.

No sooner had the music stopped than there was a crowd of young men around Resi clamouring for the next dance. Before she had time to see who it was, there was an arm round her waist, a hand grasping hers, and she was launched into the swirl of dancers scarcely knowing what language her partner was talking, German or English, both equally incomprehensible through the throb of the music. Again and again other partners cut in; she scarcely looked them in the face except for a fleeting glimpse to ascertain they were not Bimbo. No, they were not. Her eyes despairingly searched the crowd for him. Where was he? Why had he deserted her? Then she saw him, dancing, laughing with the dark-haired girl she had seen him with so often. Her throat contracted in a grip of pain.

The music stopped and the musicians got up from their seats leaving their instruments on their abandoned chairs. A pair of folding doors were opened at the side of the ballroom leading into the dining room, where a buffet was set out on a long table. The young man with whom Resi had just been dancing offered to find her a chair and a drink. He found her a seat at a small table against the wall and went on his errand, pushing his way through the crowd surging towards the refreshments. 'My name is Hans Collalbo,' he said, 'please excuse this informal introduction.' But before he came back with a glass of wine in each hand – Resi longed for a long cool drink of lemonade – happiness returned to her sadly wilting spirits: Bimbo appeared with the much desired frosted tall glass. He was smiling and his voice still did not have the ironically cutting edge to it which she dreaded so much. No, he was gentle, he was actually penitent.

'Forgive me for abandoning you, I saw you were enjoying yourself, surrounded by so many "courtiers", the queen of the Ball. No room for your humble partner.' A slight note of mockery surfaced once more in his voice as he went on to say, 'I will do my duty now and get you some food. What would you like – old-fashioned or American?' For here, too, in this stately dining room of stucco and gilt, there was an incursion, among the traditional ham and chicken, of corned beef, hot dogs and Coca-Cola.

Meanwhile, Hans Collalbo had returned, and hard on

his heels, embarrassed but determined, Lucas Anreither. The two men stood looking at each other and at Resi. Uncertain of what she ought to do, she felt she had to introduce them to each other, or rather explain Lucas to Collalbo: 'A friend of my cousin Hanni Lensveldt, he comes to Wald, I met him there last summer.'

At that moment Bimbo came back, to hear Resi's last mumbled words. 'Of course,' he said, putting down the plates full of cold meat and salad on the little table – 'Anreither – I know all about you,' and he held out his hand to Lucas. '*Servus*,' he said, using that informal familiar greeting, 'sit down, come and join us. You, Hans, will you go and find Hertha? She must be around somewhere.' Lucas sat down – he could hardly do otherwise – and helped himself from the tray Bimbo offered him. He didn't know whether he felt disconcerted or flattered by the friendliness showered on him by Prince Grein. Was there, perhaps, a hint of paternalism, of condescension in all these smiles? Was he being treated as his grandfather had been treated by old Prince Altmannsdorf, whose head forester he had been?

Lucas hated himself for allowing even the shadow of such a thought to enter his mind. Such feudal subservience belonged to the distant past: young Grein, with his empty title and equally empty pocket, was not his superior. No, but he was his rival, his rival for the favours of Resi, and he only had to look at her to see the expression of her eyes, which he had so often seen staring so vacantly at him, now fixed in what seemed to him silent adoration on Bimbo. It made him feel pity for her, for he was sure Bimbo would not marry her, he

would marry money, and he saw no answering devotion to
Resi's adoring glances in the laughing eyes of the young man.
My turn will come, he thought, my turn will come all the
more certainly when disappointment sets in.

His turn came, at least on the surface, sooner than he
expected. Collalbo returned with Hertha in his wake. 'Now,
I think,' Bimbo said when they had finished eating, 'we have
had enough of this duty-inspired official party. We have
done what was expected of us and we may go. It really is
rather boring. We will go and inspect this new cabaret
which has just opened, Heaven and Hell, it sounds promising. You, my dear Resi, will want to dance a little longer, I
leave you in safe hands. Herr Anreither will look after you
and take you home. So, good night, my beautiful partner.'
And he rose to go. But Resi rose likewise.

'No,' she said, 'no, no. This evening I am with you. I am
coming with you, we are staying together – to the end – my
partner,' she added after a slight pause with a tremor in her
voice. She had put her arm through Bimbo's and was holding
him fast. It was not possible for him to shake her off without
blatant discourtesy. 'Very well,' he said, 'if that is what you
want. So you, Hans, come along with Hertha,' and inclining
his head towards Lucas, who had also risen from his chair,
'Sorry, Anreither, you see how it is. It is not my decision. Auf
Wiedersehen.' And the four of them left the ballroom.

Resi drank a good deal more wine in Heaven and Hell.
There was semi-darkness and much laughter, which she did
not understand, at the comic songs. She danced again with
Bimbo, very close in the confined space, and when they were

not dancing she held his hand. She would not let him go. She would not give him up to Hertha, tonight he was *her* partner and she would stay with him to the end. She went with him to his flat, and when he took her home in the grey dawn of morning it seemed as if she were walking in her sleep.

# Twenty-five

Kanakis himself opened the door to his visitor. 'Come in, my dear boy, come in.' Bimbo came in, went straight to the chair opposite Kanakis's desk and sat down, knees apart, letting his hands hang down between his knees.

'Theophil!'

Kanakis went round the table and sat in his desk chair opposite Bimbo. He put his left hand in his jacket pocket and drew out a string of large topaz-coloured beads, letting the cold smooth globules slip one by one between his fingers. It was not a rosary and he attached no number or meaning to any individual bead, but their sliding motion through his hands helped to give him calm and countenance. He had learned the habit from his father, who himself may have picked it up from an oriental friend. Kanakis said nothing.

'Theophil!'

'Yes, my sweet, that is indeed my name.'

'Theophil, I have come to ask you – I mean, I am forced to ask you, because I need, I desperately need – your help.'

Kanakis still said nothing. He half-closed his eyes and without anything that could be called a smile, an expression as of bliss surfaced upon his face.

Bimbo gave an involuntary shudder.

'Why are you looking at me like that?'

'Like what? My dear boy, I am just looking at you. I always enjoy looking at you and at the moment I'm enjoying it quite particularly. I've never seen you quite like this before. This is a new Bimbo, a different Bimbo. I must take it all in, impress it on my mind, so that I shall always be able to remember it. Your eyes are cast down. I can see your lovely long lashes. And your mouth, your mouth has not got its usual rather insolent curl at the corners, but has a slight, ever so slight droop, not enough to disfigure, just enough to be appealing. Also your shoulders –'

'Oh, for God's sake, Theophil, stop it! Stop dissecting me! I can't bear it! I need help, help only you can give me. Money! A lot of money. Not for any silly investment which you have always refused, and I don't blame you, nor to pay off debts. I don't run up debts. I need money to save my life from ruin, for saving it from being wrecked. And I need it at once. You won't be pouring it down the drain. I shall be able to pay it back, and I will. You know one day I shall make a rich marriage, probably one day soon. You won't lose anything. Only I can't afford to wreck my chances now. I'll explain.'

'You don't have to. I know what's in the offing. Next winter, when the Opera is reopened with a great Ball, a group of American heiresses will be arriving in the care of two highly respectable, blue-rinsed, exquisitely-groomed elderly matrons, and you and several of your friends will be on the entertainment committee, to dance with them, to escort them, to give them what is called "a good time". All your friends are good-looking, titled young men. But what more dazzling looks, what more alluring title than yours, my sweet prince? You'll only have to make your choice. The fattest dowry will be yours for the asking. Let's only hope that it's not the fattest girl who's attached to it. But you won't mind, will you?'

'Never mind about that now, Theophil. It will be time to think about that when the occasion arises – if it does. And if it does, it would not be the first time that a fortune and a title have been married. It's a very usual occurrence and nothing to be ashamed of.'

'Nothing at all, my dear boy, nothing at all.' Kanakis continued to let the beads slip through his fingers. His expression was now positively beatific.

'Then stop looking at me like that and let me explain why . . .'

'Why you need my help. No, don't move. That look of exasperation is delightful. Your complexion is all aglow. Are you by any chance blushing? Are you embarrassed? Yes, I'll help you, but you must allow me my little modicum of pleasure too.' Bimbo's jaw tightened as he clamped his teeth together.

'Of course . . .'

'Oh, Bimbo, no! What are you insinuating? What do you take me for? As if I would ever take advantage of a friend in need! You should be ashamed of yourself, Bimbo. I am an artist, you should know that. I am just delighting in the contemplation of you under these particular circumstances. So now let me see what I can do for you. You have got yourself into a mess with a girl. That's it, isn't it?'

'That's it.'

'How very careless of you.'

'Yes, it was. Such a thing has never happened to me before. I have always been careful. And I ought to have been doubly so in this case, but it was all so unexpected, so unforeseeable for me, so . . . how shall I put it, so out of character. So now I am threatened with a most terrible scandal which would wreck all my prospects, all my life.'

'I suppose you are referring to Marie-Theres.'

'Yes. I can't marry her, I simply can't. I've told her so.'

'Because she has no money? Was that the reason you gave her? You didn't tell her you didn't love her?'

'No, I simply said that in my circumstances, with my name, I had to marry money. I was perfectly honest with her. I didn't say I didn't love her. I did not want to hurt her more than necessary.'

'Very noble of you. So perhaps she thinks you do love her, and that the money question is secondary and can be got over in some way. It must be inconceivable to Resi, who has been suffocated with love, or rather with desire, ever since she can remember, because of her beauty – she is too young to know the difference – it must be inconceivable to her that, once she was in love for the first time, that love was not reciprocated.'

'Then she is a fool. Anyway, I'm not in love with her. I never said I was, and if I were, being in love doesn't always have to lead to marriage. She thinks it does. I've had a hard time disillusioning her.'

'Do you think she allowed herself to get pregnant in order to force your hand?'

'No, I don't. She is too inexperienced. Besides, she isn't that kind of girl. She isn't a schemer. And as I told you, it happened so unexpectedly, even for me who ought to have known better, but also for her.'

'For her, because she is desperately in love with you, poor child. Of course she is, you are a fascinating creature, my Bimbo. At least you are not blaming her for what happened. That is a comfort to me. You do have some sense of values. I have a great respect for Marie-Theres. So what are you going to do?'

'What can I do, Theophil, what must I do? I can't marry her and I simply can't have a scandal. It would wreck my chances with any of those American girls you spoke of, whom my friends and I are going to escort next winter. It's not as if Resi were just some insignificant local girl – that wouldn't matter – but she herself is an American and her mother is an Altmannsdorf. In short, she is one of our set. It's quite impossible.'

'So what is the solution?'

'There are only two, and they both need a great deal of money. Either we must get rid of it, which is a criminal

offence, and a competent doctor would need a lot of financial persuasion; or Resi would have to disappear for a few
months, go and stay in the mountains, with a family, have
the baby and leave it with them. That I could arrange more
easily, but it would cost even more, and be an even greater
risk for me. For she couldn't do it without her aunts finding
out, and they could still ruin me by forcing me into marriage.'

'What does Marie-Theres say about it? After all, it's her
problem even more than yours.'

'She can't make up her mind. She first says one thing and
then another. She refuses to see a doctor who would do away
with it, either because she's frightened or because she says it
would be murder. And still less will she have it quietly, going
away for a while, because she too doesn't want her aunts to
know. At least I'm safe there; she won't tell them. She cries
and says, "I'm so ashamed, so ashamed – and why can't you
marry me, even if you don't love me, and we can divorce
later" – but of course I can't divorce. I'm a Catholic.'

'Poor Bimbo, what a quandary you're in. Neither of your
two solutions will work. So the only solution is: she must
marry. She must have a husband.'

'Oh, Theophil, could you, can you, find her one? I'd be
endlessly grateful, I promise, I really will be.'

'I don't much care for gratitude. It taints affection and
poisons love.'

'But you could manage it – with money? If you give her
a dowry, between us we could persuade someone to marry
her, quickly – that young farmer's boy, for instance, Anrei-

ther, who goes mooning after her all the time – he would marry her if she had money.'

'I wouldn't let him. I don't need to buy her a husband. I am going to marry her myself.'

'You, Theophil, marry Resi?'

'That is what I intend to do. Don't think this is a decision taken on the spur of the moment. I have had it in mind for quite some time, watching this situation develop, wondering whether it would come to a climax. It has. I may say I have done something to provide a favourable climate for it. I have taken the two of you out together, helped to detach you from that girl Hertha you have been going about with, and I can tell you that it was I who insisted to the Ball committee that Resi should be your partner for the opening waltz. Yes, you may well look astonished: how easy you were to manipulate, both of you! But I am delighted it has come to this. Resi is lovely. By the way, I don't like the name Resi. To me she always has been, and always will be, Marie-Theres.

'Do you remember the little Meissen shepherdess you had in your hands when we first met in Castello's shop? I simply adored that little figurine. I have it still, and some others which are almost priceless. Now I shall acquire one which is absolutely unique: a live one. And wait until I have a hand in dressing her. What an ornament she will be in my life. So far she has just been able to cover herself, poor child, apart from that white and gold ball dress. But when she is my wife I shall be able to dress her. All the couturiers of Paris, Florence and Rome will envy me. They will never have had such a mannequin. But she will not be a mannequin, she will be my own – my wife, Bimbo, my wife! People will talk. They will say: Theophil Kanakis has married a young and beautiful wife, not of questionable origin, not of uncertain reputation, but the daughter of an American scientist and of an Austrian princess. It will clothe me with the highest respectability. And to crown it all there will even be a child!'

Bimbo lifted his head and gazed at Kanakis in speechless amazement.

'My child,' he murmured.

'Yes, your child. A son or a daughter? I don't mind. In any case, it will surely be lovely, being yours and Marie-Theres's. It will look like her, of course, and I shall be accounted lucky not to have passed on any of my heavy features to my offspring, as your father did to your poor sister; such an admirable girl, but so ill-favoured, while you laid claim to all your mother's looks.'

At last Bimbo shifted on his chair, shrugged his shoulders, and rose. His problem was solved, but for some reason he could not quite explain to himself he did not feel very comfortable. Of course the relief was immense, and he certainly was not squeamish. He prided himself on being a man of the world, free of prejudices and inhibitions, but now, somehow, he felt degraded, selling his child to Kanakis, as he had sold him porcelain or furniture. And he had been manipulated into this, like a puppet. It was an outrage. 'May I ask,' he said in a voice that scarcely rose above a whisper, 'whether you have already proposed?'

'No,' said Kanakis, 'but I spent a most enjoyable morning yesterday choosing a ring. Would you like to see it? A really beautiful cabochon ruby, like a drop of blood.' He paused on the comparison.

'Yes,' said Bimbo, 'I didn't realise until it was too late. She will like the ring.'

'I hope she will. You see, I don't expect to be refused, thanks to you.'

# Twenty-six

Kanakis was not refused. He called on Marie-Theres's Aunt Fini, the Baroness Simovic, and asked her permission to see her niece alone. Resi was summoned to the drawing room and the old lady retired discreetly to another room, speculating on what this unexpected visit might mean, as did Resi herself. She looked at Kanakis, when he came forward and took her hand, with the bewildered and slightly harassed expression in her blue eyes she had had ever since she realised the predicament she was in. Kanakis immediately saw her trouble and he did not wish to prolong it.

'Will you sit down, my dear, while we talk,' he said, drawing two chairs close to each other, and while she hesitated a moment sat down in one of them himself.

'I am coming straight to the point,' he said, again taking her hand. 'I have come to ask you to marry me.'

'To marry you, Mr Kanakis? You want to marry me?'

She stared at him, and there was a long silence. Then a sob rose in her throat and she burst into tears. He waited a few minutes and then offered her a handkerchief.

'Don't cry, my dearest,' he said, 'just listen to what I have to say. I am very fond of you, Marie-Theres, in fact I can truly say that I love you. I love you dearly. I think, I hope, you have felt that ever since I have known you, ever since you came to my house with your cousin that winter evening, and all through the months since then. Whenever I saw you, whenever we were together, a wave of tenderness for you rose in my heart. Did you not sense that, Marie-Theres?'

'You were always so kind to me, Mr Kanakis,' she whispered between her sobs, which were gradually abating.

'Don't call me Mr Kanakis. Call me Theophil. It is a nice name, don't you think? You probably wonder why I never told you of my love for you? Well, dearest, you are so young, and I, in comparison, am so old, nearing forty, almost old enough to be your father, and there were many, I am sure, nearer your own age, who pestered you with their love. I say "pestered" because, if I understand you, you disliked it rather than enjoyed it, as so many girls would have done. All except me – and I didn't "pester" you.'

'No.'

'I would have looked a fool, wouldn't I, if I had tried to press my attentions on you, for all the love I felt for you?'

'You have always been so kind, Mr Kanakis.'

'Theophil.'

'Theophil.'

'You have regarded me, as a sort of kind uncle, haven't you? But now I am asking you very seriously, and with all my heart, to allow me to be a father to your child.'

She was startled, and jerked herself upright in her chair.

'So you know?'

'Yes, I know. The boy told me. I will say nothing against him to hurt you. You were, perhaps you still are, in love with him. I will only say that he is irresponsible, and in difficult circumstances himself. He may have misunderstood you, and you may have misunderstood him yourself. But we need not go into all that. All I am asking you now is: please marry me, Marie-Theres – marry me, but don't be frightened. Don't be afraid of me, I shall not ask anything of you as your husband that you are not willing to give. I know this is very unexpected, very sudden. But it has to be sudden, doesn't it? Time passes, I hope that in time you will become fond of me – I think you are, in a way, fond of me already, and I don't want this incident to cast a shadow over your whole life, your life, Marie-Theres, which is all in front of you. I can give you a marvellous life, a great life, a wide life, full of beautiful things.

'I am not saying this in order to bribe you, my dear. I respect you too much to believe that my wealth would influence your decision. You know that I am very rich. It is not an attribute that I take special pride in. It happens to be so. But I will not say that it doesn't make a difference. Of course it does. A large fortune, a very large fortune enables one to do things one could not do without it. It enables one to look at the world, to look at life in a way a person of moderate or

slender means could not look at it. You may not quite understand that at present because such a situation has not come
your way. But I can assure you that it makes many things
easy which in ordinary circumstances would be difficult.
Let me suggest, for instance, a circumstance which will con-
front us almost immediately if you do me the honour – if you
confer the great happiness upon me – of accepting my proposal. We shall have to inform your aunts of our engagement and enlist their assistance in obtaining your parents'
consent. Now your aunts, being women of the world, will
look more favourably on my suit because of my fortune than
they would without it.

'In fact, you know,' and here Kanakis interrupted himself
with a little laugh, inviting Resi to join him in making a joke,
'in fact, if I were not so rich, they would probably not think
of me as a suitable match for you at all. And if they do, as I'm
sure they will, it will be *because* of my fortune, which will
override the disadvantage of my years. They cannot object
to my family. Both the Baroness Simovic and the Countess
Lensveldt will know who my father was, and my grandfather. They may not have known them personally, but they
will soon discover that one of my uncles was an Ambassador
and another a Privy Counsellor of His Majesty the Emperor,
so they will be able to reassure your mother and father on
that account. Of course I know nothing much of what your
father's attitude will be, but there, my dear, I must rely on
you yourself to persuade him that you are doing the right
thing.'

Kanakis kept up this flow of talk, quietly and evenly,

while holding Resi's hand, making no move to embrace her and not inviting any response beyond the silence which he encountered. He was not sure whether she was listening to what he was saying, but he saw that she was hearing his voice; that it was soothing her, and a weight was being lifted from her shoulders. She only had to acquiesce. So she looked up at Kanakis and with tears still brimming in her eyes, she smiled.

Her fiancé put his fingers in his waistcoat pocket and brought out a small leather case. It contained a smooth gold ring with a large cabochon ruby of the deepest, purest red, set off on both sides by a diamond embedded in the gold. He lifted her left hand and slipped the ring on her fourth finger. It was a little too loose.

'I knew your fingers were slender, but even so I misjudged them. We shall have to get the ring made tighter, so that you don't lose it. Now let us speak to your aunt.'

Resi went to her aunt's bedroom and asked her to come back to the drawing room. In doing so she held out her left hand for her aunt to see the ring, at the sight of which she gave a little gasp. She came into the room in which Kanakis was standing up, looked from him to Resi and then, still speechless, saw that Kanakis wished to take her hand. He bent over it ceremoniously and kissed it.

'May I ask for your blessing, Baroness?' he asked, and Resi, who had at last regained her composure, said, 'Yes, dear Aunt Fini, it is true, Mr Kanakis has asked me to marry him. We are engaged.'

Then Kanakis said: 'Marie-Theres has done me the honour of accepting me. But you understand that we must keep this private until we obtain her parents' consent. And that is where we hope to enlist your help and your most valuable influence.'

The Baroness then sat down and motioned him to do the same. He went on to speak to her in his smooth, persuasive voice, much as he had a short while before to Resi herself, speaking of his family background in the first place and then about his wealth, with a little more detail and emphasis than he had used before. The Baroness interrupted him from time to time with short ejaculations such as 'I am so surprised', 'I never thought you were seriously interested in the child', 'I could never have imagined' and, finally, 'I must talk it over with my sister Francisca.'

'Yes, please do that, Baroness, and write, as soon as possible, to your other sister, Marie-Theres's mother, and your brother-in-law. And now I will take my leave and let my dearest one tell you that she is perhaps not as surprised as you are, since she has known of my devotion to her ever since we first met.'

When he had gone, the Baroness sat and looked at her niece in bewilderment, then with approbation. She did not ask her whether she loved Kanakis. Resi would not have had the courage to say that she did. All she managed to say was that he was kind and good and that she liked him.

'You are a very lucky girl,' her aunt said, again and again. 'It is a marvellous match for you: he is very, very rich. What a fortune has fallen into your lap. Well, of course, you are very pretty and men go crazy about a pretty face, but somehow I should have thought that for a man like Kanakis that would not be enough. However, you are being very sensible, you seem to have a head on your shoulders, and that is more than I gave you credit for. And you are very, very lucky. So now I'll write to your Aunt Franzi and we'll see what she says and how we should tell your parents. Perhaps you would like to go to Wald and tell Franzi yourself?'

'Oh, no, no,' Resi said very quickly and almost with alarm. She didn't mind her Aunt Fini talking and speculating about her, but she felt that in the presence of her Aunt Franzi she might break down and blurt out everything that had happened. And Uncle Poldo would have to know, and she would be back in that agonising situation from which Kanakis had just saved her, and she would be so ashamed, so dreadfully ashamed. No, no, nothing must happen now to upset her marriage. Kanakis was really very nice, and he loved her, while Bimbo, oh, Bimbo, Hanni had warned her and Nina had warned her, but she had thought she could do what others did, and she had betrayed herself. Aunt Franzi, of all people, must not know.

'Well, then, I will write to your aunt and to your mother, but I think the first thing you must do is write to your mother yourself. Oh dear, there are so many things that will have to be done. Your mother will want to come over, or perhaps you had better go home, and Mr Kanakis too, after all he is an American, isn't he? Although he was born Austrian. He will probably want to get married in America, won't he? That is a pity for me, for then I shall miss the wedding. I should be so sorry to miss it, I'd enjoy it, there are not many things for me to enjoy these days, and, dear child, you will look lovely as a bride. I'd like to see you –'

The Baroness rambled on and didn't notice that Resi had, very quietly, gone out. She went to her room and there, at last, gave vent to the pressure of so many mixed emotions in a long silent fit of crying. She wept for her lost innocence, though that was not what she thought about. What she did think about was her Aunt Franzi, the only person in her life in whom she felt complete trust and confidence. She thought of the tall, stately figure, the smiling eyes, the upswept hair, fair and interwoven with a few strands of white giving it a silvery sheen in the gold, the wide mouth showing those lovely strong teeth, and she heard the deep voice, so lovingly scolding: 'Resi, you lazybones, come bestir yourself.' Ah, if only she could go to her! But no, that was impossible, quite impossible – better let her garrulous, busybody aunt, her fussy Aunt Fini, deal with it all, and above all she must not betray herself. Let Kanakis and Aunt Fini manage. All she must do was to keep a hold of herself and never, never again – cry.

Resi sat down and wrote to her parents, and so did the Baroness Simovic, and the most incongruous pair of letters they turned out to be. The letter from the bride-to-be, the young newly-engaged girl, was a stiff statement of fact – her great good fortune in becoming engaged to an extremely rich man who was devoted to her and who promised to make her very happy. Then, as if realising that something more was needed, she added that he was good-looking, kind and gentle, and as he was a bit older than herself she felt she could lean on him and feel safe and protected. There was not a word of love. All the enthusiasm and exhilaration expected in the announcement of a prospective marriage was in the aunt's letter. She simply overflowed with joy at her niece's good fortune. She extolled the virtues of the suitor, explained his family background, which lent so much dignity to his person, and stressed the advantage of Resi marrying a man of an established position in life. He was capable, she concluded, of turning any girl's head. The two letters were put, at the aunt's suggestion, in the same envelope, to save postage.

The Countess Lensveldt read her sister's enthusiastic letter with some surprise, but not with dismay: in fact, after thinking it over for a while by herself, she felt a sense of relief. When she had told her husband of Resi's engagement to Theophil Kanakis and they had discussed the news with each other, Count Lensveldt's approval confirmed her confidence that this was indeed a good thing for Resi. While Resi was living in Vienna she felt rather anxious about her. She was inexperienced and vulnerable, she was beautiful, she would be meeting many young men of all kinds in those classes at the University she was attending, and God knows with whom she might fall in love.

Count Lensveldt said it was a good thing she had not accepted Lucas Anreither, he really could not have faced his sister-in-law if he had allowed her daughter to marry the grandson of the family gamekeeper. He knew his wife disagreed on that point, and indeed she did. She had thought it would be good for Resi to settle with such a reputable, steady young man whom she had known from boyhood and who would protect her from unforeseeable adventures. Hanni had told her that Resi was seeing a lot of Bimbo Grein. Now that was a boy who would definitely not do her any good! He was far too attractive and certainly wouldn't marry her. But Theophil Kanakis was in a different category altogether. Actually, he wasn't in any category at all. Older men with large fortunes were rare and did not lightly make offers of marriage to young girls, however attractive.

But her main reason for surprise was that Resi had been sensible enough to accept him. Of course she had, said the Count, think of the pretty clothes and jewels and the big cars he will have offered her. She has grown up in America, she knows what all those things are worth. Count Lensveldt also knew the name of Kanakis, as the Princesses Altmannsdorf, who had lived as girls in a very restricted circle of aristocratic society, did not know it. He had met members of the wealthy Greek community of Vienna, he had actually met the late Ambassador of that name who, he said, must have been a great-uncle or some other relation of the present Theophil. At any rate, he was quite as prepared to approve the match as was his sister-in-law Simovic, and so he would tell his other sister-in-law, Resi's mother, should she want his opinion.

Kanakis's forecast of Resi's family's approval proved correct, and he hoped they would not delay in paving the way for him to make a formal application to her parents for their consent. It was clear that the marriage had to take place as soon as possible, and since both he and Marie-Theres were

American citizens, he wanted the ceremony to be at the American High Commission in Vienna which, until the conclusion of a Peace Treaty, was the equivalent of an Embassy and by international usage American soil, and in the presence of the High Commissioner himself. He counted on this prestigious arrangement for being an important, in fact the decisive, argument he would put forward to Professor Larsen for his consent (essential because Resi was under-age) for having the wedding in Vienna instead of in America. He would say that he hoped Professor and Mrs Larsen would themselves come over for the occasion. He would be able to elaborate the advantage of their doing so by pointing out that all Mrs Larsen's family would be able to attend, that he himself had no relations in America, but that he had two distant cousins still living in Austria, that he had a town house in Vienna and a house in the country where he would be very happy to welcome his parents-in-law and Marie-Theres's brother and sister as his guests.

All this he explained circumstantially to Resi, who smiled at him and allowed him to take her hand and kiss it each time he came to see her, each time filling her aunt's drawing room and her own room with flowers. This was all very pleasant, and gradually, from day to day, a sense of happiness grew in Resi, she began to feel that everything was going well with her, doubts and anxieties were put to rest, she was floating again in that effortless dream world in which she had been so happy at Wald. She began to feel some true affection for Theophil Kanakis, who was giving her all this and demanding so little. He came every day and she began to look forward to his coming. She liked the deep sound of his voice, and when her aunt remarked on his manly presence, and on the excellence of his clothes and his authoritative manner, all of which impressed the old lady who had not seen the like of it in many a long year of widowhood, Resi also took notice and was herself impressed. That such a man should love her – her aunt said, looking as blissful as if it were she who was being loved – that such a man should love *me*, Resi thought over and over again; and she remembered that evening at the opera and the story of Tatiana who, rejected by Onegin, accepted the devotion of the General and was escorted into the ballroom to the admiration of all present, glittering in diamonds on the arm of her elderly husband.

# Twenty-seven

Bimbo had again come to see Kanakis. 'Theophil, I have a new candidate for your inner circle to propose to you, a very unusual one.'

'And who is he? Or should I say she?'

'No, it is a man. Father Ignatius Jahoda SJ.'

'One-time chaplain to the Princely House of Grein-Lauterbach?'

'And now in the Secretariat of the Cardinal Archbishop and a very important man indeed.'

'I shall be honoured to make his acquaintance.'

'He very much wants to make yours.'

'He is, I suppose, still your Father Confessor, and he is worried about your association with me?'

'Not worried, just interested. He is very much a man of the world, as are most members of his order.'

'A man of the world – but still with certain prejudices – or should I say principles. Concerning the Cities of the Plain, I presume.'

'He would say Commandments. Yes, I suppose that is at the back of his mind.'

'At the *back* of his mind? Hasn't he asked you any direct questions?'

'None that I could not answer truthfully. If he had, he would not be anxious to make your acquaintance. He will make himself very pleasant.'

'I'm sure he will, and so shall I – where shall we meet? I don't suggest you bring him to my house. My little weekly gatherings are coming to an end anyway, now that summer is approaching. We had better meet in town. And then I'll ask him to come and spend a few days at the Buchenhof, for the sake of his health, and the ease of getting to know each other better in the country. I'll ask him to come when my Marie-Theres and her aunt move out there. The Baroness Simovic is bound to find his company very much to her taste, and his being my guest will be another feather in my cap to qualify my being a desirable husband for her niece. Dear, beautiful Marie-Theres! I do hate to have to rely solely on money.'

'What a wonder you are, Theophil. I'll tell Father Jahoda. When will you take possession of Buchenhof?'

'I have already done so. I have rented the place for six months with the option of renewal. Dr Traümuller has surpassed himself – it is exactly what I wanted, nothing grand, a shooting box for you and your friends. Unlike my little pavilion in town, which had to be practically rebuilt, Buchenhof is fully furnished and the servants have all agreed to stay, gardeners and gamekeepers included. Of course I have doubled their wages. The owners won't like that when they come back and find out, but meanwhile they have gone abroad, pleased with the rent that has allowed them to do so. You must come with me next week and have a look round. And you can decide which of your friends will be best qualified to go out with a gun. The gamekeepers tell me there is a lot of game, both deer and woodcock.'

'I'm a good shot myself.'

'Well, all the better. That's something to look forward to when the season opens. You can ask Franz Lensveldt and Georg Corvinus. I shall be glad to be on good terms with the Lensveldts and to have all three Altmannsdorf sisters at my wedding when I marry Marie-Theres. The High Commissioner has agreed to perform the ceremony, as both Marie-Theres and I are Americans. We shall keep it an entirely American affair: no need to get entangled in any Austrian requirements. Extraterritorial, one might say, extraterritorial.'

All through that spring the pattern of Resi's daily life was unchanged. She still went to her lectures at the University, and she still met Lucas when he waylaid her as she came out of the lecture room. But she became more and more withdrawn, more and more aloof towards him, while he became more and more persistent. She would go for a short stroll, but refused to go to the coffee house. She was tired and she wanted to go home. He felt she wanted to get rid of him, but when he challenged her – 'what have I done to offend you? Why don't you like being with me any more?' – she would deny it and tell him to go on talking and to teach her more real history, as he called it, all about the inevitability of a future classless society and the withering away of the state.

Lucas, however, felt sure she was not listening, that she was thinking of something else while he was talking, or rather of somebody else, Bimbo Grein, of course, with whom she had gone off at the Ball. His heart burst with jealousy, but after a while he argued himself into a reluctant acceptance. Grein was not a serious rival, he was a playboy, he had certainly no intention of marrying her, she would soon discover that and there would be a rebound, and then he, Lucas, would have his chance. Resi had, indeed, discovered it, but the rebound was not in favour of Lucas; it was bewilderment and near despair until so unexpectedly, in so extraordinary a manner, Kanakis had come to the rescue.

Then Resi told him that she was going away, going to the country; she would not tell him where, only that she was going with her aunt and would probably not be seeing him for a long time. While he was trying to find out where she had gone, his mother told him, and she had heard it at the inn in Wald, where all the gossip concerning the Lensveldt family was bandied about, that it had come to her knowledge that Resi was engaged to be married. And to whom do you think? Well, you will never guess, to a Mr Kanakis, a man twice her age, a man mostly surrounded by a group of young men, the most conspicuous of whom was young Grein-Lauterbach, but a man of untold wealth. His parties in his house in Vienna were the talk of the town, and only recently he had bought, or rented, a Schloss in the Forest district of Lower Austria.

'My dear boy,' Frau Anreither told her son, 'that American girl you are so crazy about, your unworldly, innocent angel, is actually staying there now. She has been seen in the village wearing a magnificent ring of rubies and diamonds on her left hand. So you may be sure she *is* going to marry him, and that should be the end of your infatuation. I shall be most thankful. That girl was no use to you from the moment you met her. Your grandfather never approved of the old Prince's youngest daughter marrying that Danish man – if it was a proper marriage, he being a Protestant – and going off with him to America, and this girl their daughter. So what could you expect? She probably isn't even a Christian.' Lucas had been right when he told Resi his parents were 'Black', meaning strictly Catholic in their morals and their politics, his father a little more open-minded than his mother, to whom, however, his father obediently deferred.

Lucas was now faced with a desperate situation. He had been jealous of Bimbo Grein, but he had been able to persuade himself that he could bear it and live in the hope of winning Resi after all when she had become disillusioned. But this, this engagement to Kanakis, was intolerable. Not only, if she married him, would she be irretrievably lost to him but, even worse than that, her acceptance of Kanakis was a desecration of her whole person and being. She could not possibly love him, she was selling herself for his money. It was the most degrading of bargains. Thus Lucas, in his disgust and desperation, thought he could see through Kanakis's motives: he was buying himself a screen for his unorthodox tastes, he had chosen a girl who would know little or nothing of such things, and had dazzled her with promises of pleasures and luxury which would warp her mind and defile her character.

Lucas couldn't believe that Resi, the Resi he knew and adored, could have acted of her own free will. Her family must have talked her into it. He couldn't allow it to happen. He must rescue her. He must open her eyes to what she was letting herself be used for. He must tell her, crudely, brutally if necessary, even if afterwards, when he had made her see, she should then hate him for a while and not want to speak to him for a long time, but he would have saved her, he would have kept her integrity intact. It would be a very bitter satisfaction to him, but satisfaction it would be, and if he didn't do it, he would not be able to live with himself for the rest of his life.

But how would he be able to see her, to talk to her? To talk to her alone? She was a guest in a house to which he could not gain admittance, to which he would never be invited. Night after night he lay awake, planning and contriving like a conspirator. Should he write to her? Should he put his arguments on paper? That was impossible; he would only provoke a scandal, for Resi was bound to show the letter to her aunt, or even to Kanakis himself. He must take his chance of seeing her in the village near the Schloss or try to induce her to meet him somewhere they would not be seen.

He travelled to the neighbourhood, took a room at the village inn and explored the surroundings. It was going to be difficult, for the Schloss stood within a park which he could not enter in daylight without being seen by a gardener or servant and told he was trespassing on private property. But there was a home farm belonging to the house where, after a day or two, he was able to strike up an acquaintance with one of the dairymaids, and induce her to pass a note to her sister who worked as a housemaid in the Schloss and who would be willing to give the note secretly to Fräulein Larsen. A little courtship, a little money, and a romantic story of a mutual love affair, brought to a cruel and untimely end by family intrigues, persuaded the two girls to lend their assistance to a secret rendezvous. 'Resi,' Lucas wrote, 'dearest, dearest Resi, please, please let me see you just once more, even if it's only to say goodbye. I *must* see you, I must talk to you, because there is something very important I have to tell you, something you have to know. Please come to the little summerhouse at the corner of the rose garden when your aunt has retired for the evening. Your maid Leni will let you out and keep the door open for you. I shall not keep you long. I will wait for you all night if necessary, but come, come, come – take a match and burn this note.' Resi was puzzled, but she came. 'The poor young man,' the maid had whispered to her conspiratorially, 'he looked so unhappy, he is so much in love, it will be a sad meeting, but the Fräulein cannot be so unfeeling as to deny it to him. I am sure she will regret it all her life if she does not see him this one last time. The Fräulein is going to be such a great lady and will forget her poor lover, but he, poor young man, will remember her and this last goodbye for ever and ever.'

And so Resi went to see Lucas and to her destruction.

# Twenty-eight

It was a moonless night, only the stars flickered overhead, the garden was all shadows. Resi could hardly have found the path to the summer house had she not seen a pinpoint of light from the small torch Lucas held in his hand. But he saw her coming.

'Resi, Resi, thank God you have come! Oh Resi, I love you, I love you so much I must save you. I must open your eyes and make you see!' He put out his hand and tried to take hold of one of hers, to draw her close so that he could speak in whispers, but she resisted him. He was trembling with suppressed excitement, his voice hoarse, sounding un-natural as he tried to control its passion. 'Resi, Resi!' She stood away from him.

'What is the matter, Lucas? You should not have asked me to come out here tonight. What do you want to say? Be quick, I can't stay long. They might notice I am not in my room. I turned out the light.'

'Resi, my dearest, my beloved, I have come to save you, to save you!'

'To save me from what, Lucas? You know you should not speak to me like this, not any more. I am not your beloved, I never have been, and you know it. You must stop trying to see me. I don't know what you wanted to tell me, but I have come out only to tell you this: that we can't meet again, that you must leave me alone. I am going to marry Mr Kanakis. I am sure you knew that. So please go away now, I am going in.' And she turned to leave the summer house, but this time he had caught hold of her arm and held her tight.

'Resi, wait, you can't marry Kanakis. That is what I came to tell you, that is what I came to save you from! You don't know what you are doing. You can't marry a man like that!'

'What do you mean: a man like that? Of course he is much older than me, if that is what you mean, but he loves me, and he is good and kind and, and, I love him.'

'Oh Resi, that is not true. You don't love him, and he doesn't love you. He can't love you, he is only using you – as a screen. Tell me the truth: are they *making* you marry him, your aunts, I mean – are they *forcing* you to marry him, for his money?'

'No one is forcing me, or even trying to. Don't be stupid, Lucas. And what do you mean by my being used? Go away now, I am going back to the house.'

But he had caught hold of her arm again. 'Resi, I shall

have to tell you why he doesn't really love you. He only pretends to. He is a homosexual. Do you know what that is?'

'I have heard the word. I don't know what it means.'

'It means a man who does not love women, but loves other men, chiefly boys. He can't love you. He's in love with that young man, the prince whom he always has about him. If he wants you, it is only as a kind of decoration, a screen to hide his real passions. He is just using you, Resi. It's degrading, it's insulting. You can't, you must not allow yourself to be used in this way.'

'But Lucas, I don't know what you are talking about. What do you mean by "using" me? He loves me, I know he does, and he loves Bimbo too. Why shouldn't he? He is fond of Bimbo, they are very good friends, rather like a father and son. What has that got to do with me? I am going to marry Mr Kanakis and you must stop annoying me. You have been a nice friend but I don't love you and I never have. You know that. And now you must let me go.' Again she turned to leave, and again he caught hold of her arm. She was shivering in her thin dress in the damp night air, and he was trembling with passion. He saw that his words had made no impression on her because she did not understand them.

'Resi, listen, listen. I came to save you, and save you I *must*. I must make you understand, even if it shocks you.'

And he told her in crude, physical terms what homosexuality, what such a relationship, implied. 'Your Mr Kanakis is not fond of young Grein, as you say, he is his pleasure-boy – he probably pays him for it, as he is so rich and Grein has no money – and he is buying *you* to be his screen. That is how you are being *used*, Resi – for God's sake, open your eyes!'

Still she did not really understand, but the language he had used was so horrible that she was shocked and nauseated. She felt she would never be able to forget it when she saw Kanakis and Bimbo again.

She wrenched her arm free from his grasp and lifted both her hands to her ears. 'Enough, enough,' she whispered; she turned, swayed, and it was as if a cleft had opened in the ground at her feet. He though she was going to faint. Panic seized him – if she fainted, what should he do, out here in the garden, at night where he had no business to be? But she did not faint. Her inherent strength and stability, her integrity, saved him from such a predicament. She only uttered a low moan and ran, ran, unseeing, along the path back to the house, to the little side door which her maid had opened for her earlier in the evening, ran upstairs and along the stone corridor to her room. She was sufficiently in command of herself to close the door softly.

The night was very long. When she had reached her room, out of breath from running upstairs at top speed, Resi stood and looked round at her four walls with wide-open, aching eyes. Breaking away from Lucas, she had bolted for safety, blindly, like an animal under attack hoping to find refuge in its lair. Now she found she was in a cage, in a trap. There was no way out of her predicament. Her chest was bursting, her head was bursting, the walls were closing in on her, there was no way out, no room to move, no room even to breathe. If only she could cry. But she couldn't cry: her chest was so tight, her eyes burning dry. She went to the window. The night was black – no moon – a faint light from distant stars distinguished different intensities of blackness – solid shadows of trees, swaying against the more diaphanous darkness of air. But the window was not an opening, only another aspect of the wall of her prison. No way out through the window, no way out through the door. Nowhere to go, no one to turn to. She was caught, irrevocably caught.

She began to pace up and down, up and down. She looked at the dressing table, brush and comb, scissors and nail file, powder and lipstick, all the familiar things belonging to the routine of everyday life, meaningless, useless now. She would never need them again. She stared at her bed, so clean, so white, the sheet turned down, the pillow rounded and smooth; if only she could sink into it, accept its cool embrace – sleep. But she kept on pacing the room, afraid to stop, afraid to give herself pause, to allow herself to think. Up and down, backwards and forwards.

At last, in utter exhaustion, she began to pluck at her clothes, and still walking up and down she unfastened her dress, let it fall, wrenched her slip over her head, pulled off her underwear. A sob rose in her throat, but some power stronger than her own will forced it down. It forbade her to make a sound, it held her in a vice. She was naked. A breath of air wafted in from the window and she shivered. She seized her nightgown from the bed and put it on, still walking up and down. After a while, a merciful numbness overcame her and she fell onto the bed and closed her eyes. Sleep came, or rather half-sleep, for it did not bring oblivion, only distortion. But it broke the brittle rigidity of her defences, the self-imposed ban on consciousness, it relaxed the tension which had been warding off thought. When it left her after a spell of scarcely an hour she was wide awake, and the window was as dark as it had been, the blackness even blacker, the walls of the room as enclosing.

But now the torture of her predicament was explicit. It was in her head and articulate, and at the same time it was diffused in some indefinable manner inside her where it could not be located, a spiritual pain more excruciating than any physical pain she could imagine and which, she felt, however dreadful, would be a relief from this all-pervasive anguish. As she lay on her bed in the darkness, exhausted and afraid, her mind was terribly clear, as she saw, without any hope of escape or salvation, herself and her life in ruins, utterly, irretrievably destroyed. For she had committed the one great fatal sin, the one against herself, against her own integrity and moral being. She had committed self-betrayal. Others might pass such an action off with a shrug. There was no shrug for her, only shame and dishonour, and a self so despicable that she could never bear to live with it again. She did not think of the child in her body – she had never yet thought of it as a child – only that she had behaved like a common slut. And then she had allowed herself to be sold by the man who had so beguiled her (and who had never pretended to love her) to a man who wanted her as a social convenience and had got her because she was going cheap. So far nobody knew the real reason why she had agreed to marry Mr Kanakis. Her Aunt Fini thought it was because of his money. But her father and mother were coming over, and she would never be able to look into her father's eyes without telling him the truth. And her father would undoubtedly find out that horrible thing Lucas had been telling her; Lucas, of course, was insanely jealous, but even he could not have said a thing like that if it were not true.

She was wound around and around with coil upon coil of shame and disgrace. Disgrace, disgrace, and nothing would ever wash her clean again. Suddenly tears came, released by an upsurge of self-pity. How could she have known? How could she have understood? She was alone, alone, with no one to turn to, in a strange, complicated country where everything was different and people did not mean what they said. Nothing was plain and straightforward, everything was full of pitfalls, of hidden purposes and implied meanings she could not grasp. Resi turned her face into her pillow, and sobbed, sobbed with pity over her own sad fate, over her poor lost self, working herself up with every convulsion of her shoulders, with every spasm of her body, to a paroxysm of grief. Exhausted, she relaxed and lay in a stupor, she did not know for how long.

When consciousness returned and she opened her eyes, the window was no longer black but pallid, as the cold grey light of pre-dawn crept into the sky. Day was beginning. Life was going to continue. But for her life could not continue. That horror must come to an end. Full stop. The words formed themselves in her mind. Something had said them to her while she slept, something outside herself, beyond her control. 'Full stop': that was what it said. Tremendously powerful, intensely comforting. The trapdoor which held her was opening, the vice was removed. No more unanswerable questions, no more bewilderment, no more pain. The end of life would be the end of trouble. Full stop, and no more pain. If she were not there, no one would be able to torment her, to pull her this way and that for their own purposes. She would have slipped through their fingers, she would be nobody's plaything, she would, at last, belong only to her herself. As she lay, very still in the grey half-light, a feeling of exultation came over her, as if in response to that power that had spoken to her from somewhere beyond herself saying so clearly and decisively: 'Full stop.'

It would be quite simple. How fortunate that she had learnt how to handle a gun. The guns had all been cleaned the day before, they stood in a shining row in the rack in the gunroom, and the cartridges were in a drawer under the rack. She knew which gun was Bimbo's. She would use that one. Open the breech, cock it, all so smoothly, so silently, so well-oiled. She did not dwell on the last stage of the operation, the crucial one, but she knew, without putting it into words, what it would have to be. Place the butt on the floor, bend over the muzzle, pull the trigger with her bare toe. Don't think about it – *do it*. Do it quickly, don't hesitate, or it will be too late. It was getting lighter already. Very soon the men would be down for the early-morning stalking. She slipped out of bed and opened the door carefully. The corridor was almost dark, no sound or movement anywhere in the house. She ran on her bare feet on the polished floor to the head of the stairs and down to the gunroom.

It was Father Jahoda who found her. He was in the room only seconds after the shot had gone off. And within the next seconds, in which he bent over the stricken girl whose beautiful face was beautiful no longer, he had decided on his course of action. There must be no scandal, no sensation. His status was one of authority and he would use this authority to its limits and beyond its limits to prevent it. From then on his authoritarian personality dominated the situation and everyone involved in it. He telephoned for a doctor. And then, in spite of the early hour, he telephoned the Chief of Police in Vienna and got through to him. The Police Chief promised to send down a high-ranking officer at once, for this fatal occurrence must be kept out of the hands of the local gendarmerie, who would only create a confusion.

Then he set to work on Kanakis. He had been the first to appear downstairs after he had heard the detonation and that was fortunate as Father Jahoda said he wished to speak to him alone. He ordered the others, who had come rushing down in disarray, full of excitement, surmises and apprehension, to return to their rooms. Such was the daunting severity of his appearance, and the authority of his voice, that he was instantly obeyed. And obeyed also by Kanakis, after he had been informed, and who was so stunned by the terrible news imparted to him that he had no heart and no will to ask any questions, but acted like an automaton at the Jesuit's directions.

He must, Father Jahoda said, take advantage of the circumstance that he was an American citizen and well-acquainted with the American High Commissioner, that his house was situated in the American zone of occupation. He must get in touch as quickly as possible with the High Commissioner himself, so that he might send down a senior official to take charge, in conjunction with the Chief of the Vienna Police, of a tragic accident of which he, Father Jahoda, had been the sole witness. The victim of the accident had also been an American citizen. It was in everybody's interest, and especially in the interest of the American authorities, that there should be no scandal or sensation-mongering. No Austrian had been involved, it should not be allowed to create tension between the local and the occupation jurisdictions; the matter should be treated on a quasi-extraterritorial basis. And so it was agreed.

Then Father Jahoda made his deposition, later that morning, in front of all the inmates of the house, the police and the American representative. He spoke drily and dispassionately, suppressing with a gesture of his hand every attempt at interruption or questioning as irrelevant and not to the point.

Marie-Theres Larsen had shot herself. But the shot had been accidental. She had not committed suicide. It had not been suicide. Father Jahoda repeated this again and again. It was true that she had been handling a gun. Why and for what purpose was beside the point. She might possibly have thought of using it against herself, but the fact was that she had not done so. That the gun had gone off was his, Father

Jahoda's, fault. It was he himself, to his profound sorrow and distress, who had brought about the accident in that, by opening the door of the gunroom rather precipitately, he had startled her. Her toe, which had been on the trigger, had twitched. As the shot went off, she had called out loudly 'No!', which was incontrovertible proof that even if she had had some suicidal intention she would not have carried it out.

There was some restlessness among the audience and a murmur of 'Why? Why?' Father Jahoda looked at each one of them severely, but the Police Inspector took up the question. Why had the Reverend Father gone down to the gunroom hastily at such an early hour of the morning? Had he suspected anything out of the ordinary might happen? Anything at all, or anything relating to Fräulein Larsen in particular?

Father Jahoda felt that he had to answer that question. Yes, he had felt that Fräulein Larsen had been disturbed, or should he say, excited. She had been engaged to be married to Mr Kanakis here present, and he had felt, during the few days that he had spent at the Buchenhof in her company, that she had been rather tense, far from at ease. However, that was probably not unnatural in a young girl engaged to be married to a much older and very rich man. But she had her aunt with her, who must have been a support for her, and anyway it was not his business to inquire. She was not a Catholic; he could not expect her to unburden herself to a priest.

Then, last night, she had gone out late and come back a little later. He had heard her go into her room – their rooms were near each other on the same corridor. He had heard her pacing up and down, obviously in some distress of mind, and he had twice gone to her door to see whether she had at last gone to bed. When all was quiet he had retired as well, but he had made up his mind that, though she was not a Catholic, he would try and speak to her the next morning. It was then, in the early hours, when he had got up, as was his habit, to perform his devotions, that he had heard her running down the corridor, and as within several minutes she had not returned, he had put on his dressing gown and gone down in search of her. The door of the gunroom had been ajar. He had pushed it open and as he did so, that shot had gone off, accidentally.

He had been there, he had been in the room when it had happened and he, he alone, had been the sole witness. No one else was involved.

There was a profound silence, broken only, after a few seconds, by a sobbing sound. It came from Kanakis, who was bent double on his chair, his head almost between his knees. Father Jahoda went over to him and put his arms around his shoulders. Kanakis sat up, and his face was ravaged with loss. His grief was so real and so sincere, and the Father's concern for him so full of compassion, that the emotions of these two hard men, neither of them naturally given to sentiment, impregnated the atmosphere of the room and impressed itself on all present. It impressed itself quite particularly on the two officials, the Police Inspector and the American. Father Jahoda now turned to them both, and to the constable who had been taking down his, Jahoda's, statement. 'I'll initial this,' he said, 'and when the protocol is typed, I will sign it, and I hope both gentlemen will do the same. There will then be no need for any further formalities.' The two officials looked at each other for an instant and then nodded in agreement. The Police Inspector held out his hand. 'Thank you, Hochwürden.' And the American said, 'Thank you, Father.' Bending over Baroness Simovic, who was weeping silently into her handkerchief and was now holding Kanakis by the hand, Father Jahoda said, 'Please convey my profound condolences to the bereaved parents. I shall not see them. I shall go into retreat as soon as these formalities are concluded. But you can tell them that I shall pray for the repose of their child's soul.'

# Epilogue

Soon after the incident of Marie-Theres's tragic death, which by the joint intervention of the American High Commissioner and Father Jahoda was kept out of the sensational press, the State Treaty between Austria and the four Occupying Powers was signed. Austria was restored to sovereignty and to independence, her neutrality guaranteed. Reconstruction and renovation now began in earnest.

The Opera House was completed, unchanged on the outside but on the inside entirely rebuilt and made more modern and more beautiful. It was opened with a gala performance of *Fidelio* and later was the venue of the first great post-war Opera Ball, in the course of which the engagement was announced of Prince Lorenzo Grein-Lauterbach to Jo-Ann, only daughter of the owner of the largest meat-processing and meat-packing business in Chicago. In the big rambling castle of Lauterbach in Carinthia, the four Venetian glass chandeliers in the ballroom were carefully taken out of their protective burlap bags, cleaned, polished and restored to their dazzling pristine brilliance, while plumbers installed new bathrooms with gold-plated taps. These were of more concern to Jo-Ann than the chandeliers, in which Prince Lorenzo took greater interest.

A list of prospective wedding-guests, both Austrian and American, was being drawn up, but this did not include the bridegroom's sister, the Princess Nina, who had formed an undesirable connection. She had, in fact, herself declined to emerge from the inconspicuous private life she had been leading since the war, the only change being that she now called herself Frau Grein instead of Fräulein Grein.

If anyone had been interested in scanning the list of new graduates at the close of that University year, he would have found the name of Dr Lucas Anreither.

What happened to a certain little rococo pavilion hidden in the depths of the eighth suburban district is not reported. It was certainly sold, but whether it was acquired by the chairman of one of the big industrial organisations (who could afford it) as a home for his family, or, as is more likely, it was demolished in the course of the redevelopment being undertaken in various parts of the city, is uncertain. Anyway, as the young taxi driver stationed near the Opera said to his elderly colleague, who was still musing over the name of Kanakis, which for him evoked such nostalgic memories – who cares!

# Historical Note

*The Exiles Return* is set over the months from March 1954, when Kuno Adler takes the train for the final stage of his journey back to Vienna, to its culmination in spring 1955, just before Austria recovered its independence in the State Treaty of May 1955. Its background is a country still convalescing from the events of the previous seventeen years, the Anschluss, the Second World War, and the postwar hardships of Four Power Occupation and food shortages.

Austria had lost its independence in March 1938 when Hitler's troops marched into Austria and it became part of Germany – the 'Anschluss', or merger. Immediately after the defeat and collapse of the Austro-Hungarian Empire in 1918, and the creation of a small, unviable 'rump' Republic of Austria, many Austrians had felt drawn to union with the greater Germany. The politics of the country were bitterly, and often violently, divided between the Christian Social party (the Blacks) and the Social Democrats (the Reds), and unemployment was high. But support for Anschluss faded when confronted with a Germany led by Hitler.

For five years Hitler schemed to bring Austria under his influence. By January 1938 he was threatening to invade, and on 9th March the Austrian Chancellor, Schuschnigg, announced a plebiscite on Austrian independence, and called on Austrians to 'Say Yes to Austria'. This provoked Hitler to prepare for immediate invasion. On 11th March Schuschnigg called off the plebiscite, resigned, and at the same time ordered the Austrian army to offer no resistance.

On the morning of 12th March 1938 German troops marched into Austria, and Hitler followed them into the country of his birth that afternoon. That evening in Linz almost all the population turned out to greet him, 'the ecstatic crowds assembled in one provincial capital literally cheered their country into extinction' (Gordon Brook-Shepherd *The Austrians* 1997 paperback p. 327). The same evening in Vienna the *Daily Telegraph* journalist, G.E.R Gedye, saw 'a Brown flood . . . sweeping through the streets. It was an indescribable witches' sabbath – storm-troopers barely out of the school-room with cartridge-belts and carbines . . . men and women shrieking or crying hysterically the name of their leader . . . leaping, shouting and dancing in the light of the smoking torches, the air filled with a pandemonium of sound . . . until long after 3 a.m. the streets of Vienna were an inferno' (*Fallen Bastions* 1939 pp. 295–96). The Anschluss triggered a horrific period of indiscriminate and popular violence against Jews and Jewish property (cf. Edmund de Waal's *The Hare with Amber Eyes* Chapters 24–6). But as George Clare explained in *Last Waltz in Vienna* 1981 p. 191 'the paradox of Vienna's volcanic outburst of popular anti-Semitism was that it saved thousands of Jewish lives . . . (It) left no Jew in any doubt that he had to get out of the country as quickly as possible.' Well over half Austria's 185,000 Jews had left by the autumn of 1939. By the end of 1942 only 8,000 Jews remained at liberty in Austria, mostly in mixed marriages.

When Hitler first spoke in Vienna, in the Heldenplatz (the Square of the Heroes), 250,000 Viennese turned out to applaud him. A month later, in April 1938, a plebiscite on the Anschluss was held, and endorsed by 99.73% of those voting. Why was this? There was a mixture of helplessness after five years of harassment and international isolation, but also hope for a better economic future. And 'no other point of the Nazi programme found a more resounding echo in Austria than its anti-Semitism' (Clare ibid p.187). The Anschluss received the support both of the country's Catholic bishops and of at least one socialist leader.

Austrians fought in the Second World War, with a large number playing a prominent role in military and administrative positions in the Third Reich. But it suited the Allies to agree in 1943 that Austria was 'the first free country to fall victim to Hitlerite aggression' so that it should be reestablished as a 'free and independent state'. After Hitler's defeat it was occupied by the Four Powers, the US, UK, the Soviet Union and France, each with its Occupation zone, and with

Vienna shared between them. The government was a coalition between the People's Party (the Right) and the Social Democrats. The immediate post-war years were grim, with severe shortages of food and a flourishing black market – the Vienna of Carol Reed's *The Third Man* with Orson Welles.

A process of denazification took place, initially carried out by the Four Powers, but then delegated to the Austrian government. However, denazification petered out and attitudes to the Nazi era remained ambivalent: in August 1947 'those who thought Nazism was a good idea which had merely been badly executed actually exceeded (at 38.7 per cent) the 31.6 per cent who still thought it had been bad all along. By the spring of 1948 . . . opinion was equally divided . . .' (Gordon Shepherd ibid p.392).

At this time Austria was an unresolved frontier in the Cold War. The Soviet Eastern zone and the Western zone were divided by barriers. Many feared that Austria might suffer the fate of the rest of central Europe, in which Communist governments took control, most dramatically through the 1948 anti-Masaryk coup in Czechoslovakia. The Marshall Plan provided American food aid and financed investment in heavy industry. In 1950 the small Communist party unsuccessfully attempted to destabilise the country through the occupation of factories, offices and post offices.

But the situation changed rather suddenly in 1953, with the death of Stalin and the election of a new Austrian Chancellor, Julius Raab, committed to achieving independence. The new Soviet leadership, under Khruschev, decided that a neutral Austria on the Swiss model would suit Soviet interests, and in April 1955 this was negotiated and agreed. The State Treaty giving Austria independence was signed in Vienna in May 1955; the last Occupation troops left Austria in October; and the historic Vienna Opera reopened with a gala performance of *Fidelio* on 5th November 1955.

# About the Author

ELISABETH DE WAAL was born in Vienna in 1899.
She studied philosophy, law, and economics at
the University of Vienna, and completed her
doctorate in 1923. She also wrote poems (often
corresponding with Rilke), and was a Rocke-
feller Foundation Fellow at Columbia University.
She lived first in Paris, then Switzerland, and settled in England with her husband, Hendrik de
Waal, and her two sons. She wrote five unpub-
lished novels, two in German and three in English,
including *The Exiles Return* in the late 1950s. She
died in 1991.